I've travelled the world twice over,
Met the famous: saints and sinners,
Poets and artists, kings and queens,
Old stars and hopeful beginners,
I've been where no-one's been before,
Learned secrets from writers and cooks
All with one library ticket
To the wonderful world of books.

© JANICE JAMES.

THE COCKATOO CRIME

A small carefully chosen group of desperate men board and rob the luxury yacht *Cockatoo* in the Clyde. The crime is well prepared but even then bullets fly before they make their escape. The pursuit, in which death is an ever-present partner, leads Detective Inspector Bill Wilson from the shores of the Clyde to the snow-covered mountains, where the climax takes place in a giant Electricity Board post serving the Highland hydro scheme.

BILL KNOX, 1928-

THE COCKATOO CRIME

Complete and Unabridged

ULVERSCROFT
Leicester

First Large Print Edition
published November 1989

British Library CIP Data

Knox, Bill, *1928*–
The cockatoo crime.—Large print ed.—
Ulverscroft large print series: mystery
I. Title
823′.914[F]

ISBN 0-7089-2091-8

Published by
F. A. Thorpe (Publishing) Ltd.
Anstey, Leicestershire
Set by Rowland Phototypesetting Ltd.
Bury St. Edmunds, Suffolk
Printed and bound in Great Britain by
T. J. Press (Padstow) Ltd., Padstow, Cornwall

For
SUSAN

1

THE slightest of bumps and the flickering rush of snow-fringed runway marker lights, bright in the darkness of the Newfoundland night, were the only indications to her passengers that the giant Stratocruiser air liner had touched down on Gander runway. Expertly handled, the plane taxied along the tarmac to the reception block, engines dying away in high-pitched whine.

Seconds later, the stewardess had begun shepherding her passengers across the brief, freezing-cold gap of open space between the plane and the airport building, where, in the North Star restaurant, a meal awaited them. Mechanics and a refuelling tanker crew stood by, ready to go to work on the aircraft during its brief halt. In small, talkative groups the new arrivals, strangers to each other when the plane left New York a few hours before, poured into the centrally heated building, shivering from their brief encounter with the outside world.

One man, a tall, slim figure, hatless, his heavy brown overcoat flapping unbuttoned around him, had a puzzled frown on his tanned, moustached face as, rubbing a sudden coating of steam from his rimless glasses with a handkerchief, he tried at the same time to peer short-sightedly at his wrist-watch. Slowing, he turned to the couple strolling arm-in-arm behind him. "Is the clock an hour-and-a-half back, or forward here?" he asked. "I can't remember which way they told us it was."

"Forward," grinned Dwyatt Ronaldson. "Though I always lose all idea of time on these trips. Just go by my stomach—it's a sure guide, eh honey?" He smiled affectionately at the woman by his side, wrapped deep in a luxuriant sable coat.

"'Fraid so, darling," she agreed. "But before we have this breakfast, or whatever it is, remember you're on a diet."

Her husband shook his head in mock grief. "Thanks, thanks very much," said the stranger. "It seems stupid, I know. But I've a little personal fetish about having my watch right . . . just one of those things which make you Americans think all Englishmen are slightly crazy. Well . . ." he hesitated, "thanks again. I want to see what I can get in the way of magazines . . . there's a stall over there. Thanks again." Replacing his spectacles, he walked away.

"Nice guy," remarked Ronaldson. "Well, Julie, get out that diet sheet, and off we go." They walked through the lounge of the terminal building, Ronaldson, heavily built and chubby faced, in a light grey suit, neat grey fedora and tightly belted black topcoat, his wife slim, brunette, neat feet in bootees trimmed with white fur, a sturdy trio of diamonds sparkling on the ring beside the plain gold band on her left hand. Leaving their coats at the check room, they were quickly shown to a table by a soft-spoken Canadian girl who handed them the menu card then stood waiting for their order.

"Leave this to me, dear," teased his wife. "Something nice and light."

"Married less than a year, and she bosses me around as if it was ten," said the American, shaking his head. "How about

3

tomato juice and—say, could I have just a li'l steak?"

"Uh-uh," Julie shook her head. "Cereal, toast and coffee will do."

Writing the order on her pad, the waitress blushed then, hesitantly, asked, "You'll forgive me, but aren't you Julie Martin, the actress? I saw you a couple of years back when I was on vacation in Montreal . . . We aren't supposed to bother the customers, but, well, you're a kinda favourite of mine."

"Ex-actress," corrected Julie, running a hand over her dark, flowing hair. "Now strictly a married gal, honey. But thanks for the compliment, anyway. Now, let's get down to this menu. I'm hungry, and I've no figure worries at the moment."

The Ronaldsons were busy with "breakfast" when the stranger wandered into the restaurant, two magazines in his hand. He gave a little bow towards the couple, and went to move towards the next table.

"Get your books OK, Mac?" hailed the American. "Say, is that the *Yachtsman's Monthly* you've got there? You interested in boats?"

The stranger nodded. "Yes, though it's more or less academic," he explained.

"Dwyatt," interrupted Julie. "Don't leave the guy there like a stranded fish. Won't you join us, Mr . . . Mr . . ."

"Russell, Jonathan Russell," offered their new companion. "Delighted to meet you."

"Dwyatt Ronaldson . . . this is my wife, Julie," said the American, waving the stranger to the seat beside him. "Let's talk boats, mister."

"If your wife doesn't mind," beamed Jonathan Russell. "Waitress, will you bring me bacon and egg, tea and toast?"

"I gave up minding Dwy talking when I married him," sighed Julie. "Go right ahead . . . I'll eat. This plane isn't here all day you know—or is it night, Mr. Russell?"

"Just into day, Mrs. Ronaldson," said Russell. "I know that much now, thanks to your husband."

The two men were still "talking boats" when the loudspeakers announced their flight ready to depart. "Come and sit beside us," invited Ronaldson. "There's a

5

spare seat and we can keep this going for a while. Julie, how about it?"

"You keep right on talking, honey," advised his wife. "But don't overdo it, you'll make me seasick."

Settled aboard the plane, safety belt in position, Ronaldson went on, "Like I was telling you, I've got this big diesel yacht, the *Cockatoo*. She's a real honey, an ocean going 500 tonner. I bought her from an Englishman about three years ago. He couldn't afford to run her any more, your taxes had seen to that. She was built in the Clyde just before the war, and she's having an engine overhaul there right now. More important, I've got a twenty foot sailboat on her that clips along like a bird. But I had a big business deal coming off, and couldn't get away till now. We're going to London for a couple of weeks—business again, I'm afraid—then heading north. The *Cockatoo* is nearly ready right now, and she'll be sailing to her new moorings on the coast any day. We'll board her there.

"You see, my grandfather was the youngest son or something of the Ronaldson clan chief, and the last of the other line, an old boy in his eighties, died a few years ago. That makes me chief, believe it or not, and so Julie and I are killing three birds with one stone on this trip. We're having a trip to Scotland for a clan gathering—250 years ago this month we whaled the daylights out of a bunch of English redcoats, so it's a really special occasion—then we're going on to the Mediterranean for a month's cruise on the *Cockatoo*. And, of course, I'll get this work done in London."

He stopped as the plane's engines revved to a climax and she thundered down the runway. There was the slightest feeling of sway, and the Stratocruiser was airborne, climbing steadily. As the engine noise decreased and they unfastened the seat belts, the American went on, "I'm in the canning business. You know, Ron Readimeets. We sell more darned tins of Readimeets a year than there are tin openers."

"Bore, honey, bore—" warned his wife sleepily. "You have hardly let Mr. Russell get a word in. What line are you in, Mr. Russell, if this big lug doesn't mind my asking?"

"Imports and exports, Mrs. Ronaldson. You might say my agency has a finger in half a dozen pies in a small sort of way," said Russell with a disparaging gesture. "That's why I was over in New York, meeting some dealers and exploring markets. We need dollars in Britain these days, you know."

"I haven't been over for long enough, Mr. Russell. But from what I hear, your sort of business men have been doing all right. You certainly find plenty of British goods in the department stores back home," said Julie. "And say, they make the cutest sweaters. Cashmere knitwear, that's the way you call it."

"Sheer whistlebait, I call it," gurgled her husband. "Uh . . . you know what I mean, honey."

"I know," nodded Julie. "But just wait. You'll be some whistlebait yourself in kilts. He's going to have to get kilts, Mr. Russell. His clan's got the cutest plaid— oops, tartan—you can imagine."

Generalities, boats, more generalities, and back to boats again, the travellers continued their roaming conversation while the stewardess came round with

8

drinks and magazines, sweets and cigarettes and, finally, pillows and rugs. At last, all but a few dimmed lights extinguished, the passengers slept while the air liner droned on, clawing its quick way through the air, high above the Atlantic. Stabs of yellow, pulsing flame came from its engine exhausts, as regular as the tick of a jewelled watch.

It was, of course, raining when the air liner landed at London Airport. As its passengers trooped down the gangway stairs to the ground, at least one seemed all too sorry the trip was over. "It's been wonderful meeting you and your husband, Mrs. Ronaldson," said Jonathan Russell. "I hope you didn't mind us talking so much. That's just the way it happens between enthusiasts, I'm afraid."

"Think nothing of it," laughed the actress. "It couldn't have been with a nicer guy. Well, here we are in England again. Funny to think we're the foreigners here."

"Americans have honorary citizenship, especially when they come over with beautiful wives," complimented Russell. "I'll need to go now, I'm afraid. Though maybe you and I can get together again some time, Mr. Ronaldson . . ."

"Bet your life we do," agreed Ronaldson. "And the name's Dwyatt, I told you already. I'll be in London a couple of weeks on business. Give us a ring some day, and we'll have a meal together. We're staying at the Selwyn. It's quiet, and they have things like iced water and decent central heating . . . little America, I hear they call it at the Embassy."

The two men shook hands and, with a little bow to Julie, Russell moved into the customs room to find his luggage.

"You know, Dwy, if he took off those glasses he could knock a lot of the Hollywood glamour boys into a cocked hat," mused Julie as she watched him go. "No need to be jealous, though, honey. Mr. Readimeet will do me."

"Lay off, Julie," protested her husband. "Still, he is a nice guy. He's really keen on boats too. I was telling him about our sailboat aboard the *Cockatoo*. He knows quite a bit about them, from the way he talked."

A few minutes later, away from their

10

gaze, Mr. Russell was not particularly interested in boats. Safely through the Customs, he dumped the bundle of magazines from his coat pocket into a wastepaper basket and, leaving his briefcase and bag on the carpeted floor, entered one of the telephone booths which stood in a row beside the main lounge. He waited until the pennies had clicked home, then swiftly dialled a number and made an impatient, clicking noise with his tongue while the ringing tone began. He pressed the "A" button as soon as a man's voice replied.

"Harry? Russell here. I just got in."

Anxious, eager, the voice on the other end of the wire asked, "Did it go well?"

"Couldn't have been better. You can start going ahead with final arrangements. I'll leave our friends for about another ten days, then make the main effort. It should be a walk-over. These Yanks are all the same, so big and innocent it seems hardly possible. Phone me at the office tomorrow and let me know how things are. You'd better travel north the day after."

The other voice crackled agreement. Russell replaced the receiver, opened the booth door, and, picking up his luggage,

strode off, whistling something suspiciously like a sea shanty. He took a taxi
from the airport on the long trip to the
office block in Temple, close by the
Thames where, at the main door, the long
list of business occupants included the
legend "Russell Enterprises Ltd." Paying
off the taximan and briskly returning the
greeting of the commissionaire, Russell
went up the stairs two at a time to the first
floor, and, turning right, opened the fluted
glass door of Russell Enterprises. Three
typists were hard at work within, and an
elderly clerk rose from his desk beside a
glowing gas fire and came forward, a
pleased expression on his lined face.

"Welcome back, Mr. Russell . . . did
you have a good trip?"

"Fine, Lloyd, fine. Come on through."
Russell walked across towards the door
leading off the main office, a door with
"Jonathan Russell, managing director," on
it in bold black letters. Throwing his bag
and briefcase down on the big oak desk,
which was the room's main furnishing, he
asked, "How are things here?"

"Fairly quiet, I'm afraid, sir. There's
not much business at the moment. We've

had a little trouble about the last shipment of plastic kitchen fittings to Portugal. The makers weren't able to effect full delivery in time, and now our agents are demanding we rush the rest."

"Take care of it, then, Lloyd. Pour it on hot to the makers that if we don't get the stuff immediately, they've had the last order from us. Now I want to shove off to the flat. I'll get some rest, then do some paper work on the results of the trip."

"New business, sir? We could be doing with it."

"A little, a little," replied Russell. "But I've made some important contacts that may pay off in the near future."

"A worthwhile journey then?" queried the clerk.

"Very," smiled Russell. "And that's an understatement."

The restaurant was a hum of chatter, a bustle of waiters, with the softly toned lights and gay murals aiding the appetite and general atmosphere.

The Ronaldsons, settled at an alcove table, were busy with a tasty grill, an attentive waiter hovering near, when they saw the tall figure approaching. A look of pleasure flashed over the American's face. "Say, Julie, look who's coming over—Jonathan Russell!"

Russell, in a dark charcoal grey suit, white shirt and dark wine tie, returned the greeting. "I just dropped in for a meal," he explained. "As soon as I saw you, I had to come over."

"Grand, grand," boomed the American. "Julie and I were talking about you just the other night. You know, I've had a pretty hectic ten days of it, but I've been hoping to see you again."

"Boats, boats, boats," sighed his wife. "Sit down, friend . . . if you wait on Dwyatt remembering his manners you'll grow old and grey."

"Thanks." Russell took the chair whisked out by the waiter and sank down with a sigh. "I've had a pretty busy time myself since I saw you. But that finishes the day after tomorrow. I'm taking a holiday for a change. Just going to loaf about and do as little as possible. No rushing, no meetings, no letters."

"Good for you, Mr. Russell . . . heck, Jonathan. I'm finally getting this husband

14

of mine to do the same. The yacht's ready and waiting up in Scotland, and we're going off there tomorrow."

"How grand for you," said Russell. "So this will be your last night in London. Look, if you aren't doing anything special, how about spending it with me? We could take in a show, then go to a couple of clubs I know. How about it, Mrs. Ronaldson?"

"OK by me . . . if you call me Julie. Will we do it, Dwy?"

"Can't think of anything I'd rather, honey. Right now, though, Jonathan, you'd better get that lunch order organized. That waiter's still fluttering around."

Russell, smiling, ordered from the huge card before him.

They met for dinner at a little West End restaurant. Then the show . . . Russell took his guests to a new musical which, in its second week, was proving so popular that the possession of tickets for it was a major achievement. Julie, in an oyster pink brocade gown, a chunky pearl and emerald necklace at her throat, watched the performers with the highly critical air of the professional. Her verdict was favourable . . . and Dwyatt's equalled it when, after taking in a late-night cabaret and supper at a smoke-filled night-club, they went, not to another night-spot, but out in their host's Jaguar saloon on a midnight tour of some of the city's man-made scenic beauty.

"It's so quiet and clean," breathed Julie as Russell's Jaguar purred along the almost deserted streets. "It's the most unusual ending to a night out I've ever had, and one of the nicest."

"I'm only sorry we can't do it again," said Russell. "But you're off tomorrow. And I'm going away in a couple of days myself. I'm afraid we won't meet again—at least for some time."

"Where you heading for, Jonathan? Any plans?" asked Ronaldson in an unusually thoughtful tone.

"Not really. I'll probably take the car and head for Cornwall. It's nice down there in the early spring, and mild too."

"To heck with Cornwall. Come on up and join us on the *Cockatoo*." The American waved to silence the half-formed protest he thought he saw on Russell's lips. "Look, there's a couple of empty cabins aboard. We've got one or two local big-shots going to live aboard, and a few of our friends, people from back home, that sort of thing. But it's only a small party and say, think of what we could do with that sailboat!" He chuckled enthusiastically at the thought.

"That's a real idea," agreed his wife. "You come up and join us, Jonathan. We'd love having you."

"But . . . I'd love to, of course, and, well, it's too kind . . ." Russell left his sentence hanging.

"No buts. It's settled," declared the American.

"See you aboard the *Cockatoo* on—this is Tuesday, we'll expect you Saturday. Then you'll sample some Scots-American hospitality!"

"And Dwy in his kilt! You can't miss that," chimed in Julie. Laughing, profuse in his thanks, Russell capitulated. A little later, he dropped the Americans at their hotel and, refusing a last drink because he would have to be in at his office early that morning, turned the car in the direction of his flat.

Parking the Jaguar under a lamp and

17

locking it, he practically sprinted up the stairs to the flat and grabbed the telephone as soon as he had shut the house door behind him.

"I want a call to Glasgow," he told the operator. "The number is Clydeside 6843."

There was a little delay before a sleepy voice—Harry's voice—replied.

"Harry—we're in business! I go up to join the yacht at the week-end."

A delighted exclamation echoed over the wires.

"We're in, Harry. Your arrangements are all set? Good. Then get the boys together at the end of the week as we planned. I've done it, Harry! The rest is plain sailing."

He replaced the phone, and poured himself a large whisky, chuckled, and raised the glass. "To the *Cockatoo*," he toasted.

2

THE greyhound out of trap four at Harringay *should* have been a cert to win. On form, there was nothing to touch it. But it didn't—a poor-looking brindle crossed the line a good length ahead. And a disgruntled Con McBride tore up his tote slip and began to study the field for the next race.

A certain black brute of a dog, temperamental at times, but fast as the wind when it wanted, was to have been in his choice. But all thought of the dog left his mind when Jacko Bright appeared out of the crowd, gave him a brief nod, and slipped the envelope into his hand. Holding it close, McBride tore the flap open.

The message was a persuasive combination . . . £25 in fivers, a train ticket, and a slip of paper with the words "From Harry" scrawled on it. Eyebrows raised, McBride looked at Jacko for a long minute, then nodded.

"Got a car outside, mate," said the little

Londoner. "Let's go." He began to wriggle his way through the crowd, which was waiting patiently for the long pre-race inspection to be completed before the next batch of dogs burst loose on their seconds-long dash round the track. McBride followed him away from the floodlit track without protest. He'd been waiting on this summons for weeks now—though he hadn't known that Jacko would be the messenger. A good sign that, he thought, the sort of sign he had been needing in this strange deal. For all his lack of height Jacko was strictly big-time. His speciality was cars—especially other people's. He could outdrive almost any police squad man—and had often proved it. His natural Cockney accent could be deposed at a moment's notice by a cultured tone and air. Both were talents he had diligently acquired during his years as mechanic with a top-line motor racing team, and made him an exceedingly valuable member of any robbery gang. He was as expert in his own line as Con was at the gentle art of safe-blowing. They had "done time" at the Moor together, and if complete trust was not quite established in their relationship there was a definite respect for each other's skill.

Past the fringe of the crowd they went, Jacko short and neat, an indefinable middle age, McBride, tall, dark—Irish despite three generations removed from Dublin. As they walked through the greyhound track's exit gate, the safe-blower muttered, "What's it all about, Jacko? Who's running the show?"

"Tell you all I know in the car, chum. Just down the road a bit. Not one of the usual top men, this time, but whoever he is, he's no amateur."

"Car? Is it 'knocked'?"

"Nothing like that," grinned Jacko. "Part of the equipment, you might say." He fumbled in his pocket as they approached a black Ford Zephyr. "Locked it up. There's no knowing what characters you might find around here," he grinned facetiously, producing the key. Unlocking the door, he slid inside the car and swung open the passenger door. McBride climbed in, slamming the door behind him, and sank into the seat with a sigh.

"Give," he demanded.

"All I know is it's a really big job

somewhere near Glasgow. I was told you'd been sounded, and were ready."

"Sounded is right," complained McBride. "A fat character called Harry—wouldn't tell me his full name—came up to me in a pub and began talking. Then he turned up at my lodgings the next morning. Just asking questions, he was, and seeming to know the answers before he got them. He 'sweetened' me with a twenty, and said there was a safe to be knocked over. Promised me a possible five thousand quid as my cut. But he wouldn't tell more, just said I would be contacted. If it hadn't been for the cash I would have said he was crazy."

"You'll meet him again," nodded Jacko. "He lined me up too. But he isn't the boss. Don't ask me who is, for I just don't know. But we'll see him when we get to Scotland. Harry phoned me this morning at my flat. He left the money and the message with me about ten days ago—but he wouldn't tell me who it was for, until this morning. I've been looking for you ever since he phoned." And what a ruddy welcome, a non-stop moan, he felt like adding. But prudence, and a memory of his companion's unpredictable temper, stayed him.

"I'm driving up tomorrow," he went on. "The car keys were left with your stuff but it was just a few hours ago when he was on the blower that Harry told me they went with this Zephyr, lying out at a garage at Finchley.

"Anyway, I'm driving, and you've to go by train. There's a sleeper booked for Thomas Bertram on the 9.10 train from Euston to Glasgow tomorrow night. From there, you take another train to Gourock —that's on the Clyde, about an hour away, Harry says—and I'll meet you there. Don't ask me why we can't go up together in the car. That's the way the bloke footing the bill wants it."

"But what's the job," persisted McBride, rubbing a thumb pensively over the shadow of a beard blueing his chin. "With my record I'm set up for a preventive detention stretch next time—and fourteen years is a long time to spend making mailbags. I'm not tying in with just any damn fool plan. I like the money they're offering, and I took their cash all right, but I want to know more before I start to work, I can tell you." He lapsed into worried silence.

"Easy, Con," soothed the little driver. "All I know, like you, is that we're part of a plan to knock over a small fortune. My guess is it is in jewels. This is all lined up from the inside. The fat man is the character who disposes of the stuff, and he swears the whole operation is organized to the last detail."

"He told me a lot of money was being spent," agreed McBride. "And the cut's worth taking some risks for. But why all the ruddy cloak and dagger stuff? Do they think we're kids? I'm thirty-four, and haven't made a fool of myself so far. I tell you, Jacko, there's something I don't like about it all, and I'm not just being windy."

"Let's wait and see, Con," coaxed Jacko. "We can't lose by just listening, anyway, and things are pretty quiet down here just now as far as our lines are concerned."

There was still a frown on McBride's face. But, lighting a cigarette, he raised no more objections as Jacko twisted the ignition key to start the Zephyr's motor, explaining as he did, "I'll drop you a few streets away from your home. Just to be safe. Oh, and don't bother about kit for the job. It's all waiting up there . . . part of the service."

The sleeper train crawled into Glasgow just before the cold March dawn, but it was an hour later before the majority of its passengers, including a tired-eyed Con McBride, who had dozed fitfully most of the 400 miles north, left the comparative warmth of their berths. He ate an unhurried breakfast at the station hotel, bought a couple of newspapers to glance at his favourite comic strips, then headed for the station wash-room to shave and freshen up.

Feeling brighter, he bought a ticket to Gourock at the booking office, and killed time for the twenty minutes before the next train for the Clyde town was due to leave.

The train trundled down to Gourock at a leisurely pace, while McBride, feeling the tension of the coming meeting growing on him, smoked cigarette after cigarette. He took a last quick draw, then ground the stub of tobacco under his foot as the

Gourock station platform finally appeared ahead.

Lifting his small suitcase from the rack, he jumped from the train almost before it had stopped, and strode briskly through the barrier.

Jacko? He slowed as his eyes, sweeping the station concourse, failed to spot the little man. Maybe he was waiting outside . . . he hurried to the station exit. Even as he reached the street, the black Zephyr swept up and came to a smooth stop. Jacko was only seconds late.

The little Englishman was dressed in a natty sports suit, with a quiet tweed tie. He looked—as he was meant to—like a fairly prosperous business man having a day off work.

Giving a wave of greeting, McBride walked over. A gust of warmth came from the car as the door opened. Jacko, fond of his comfort, had the heater on full blast, music playing softly from the car radio. The Ford was in gear, and purring away from the station as soon as Con had climbed aboard.

"You made it," grinned Jacko. "Nice trip?"

"Ruddy awful," replied McBride. "But never mind that. What's going on?"

"You're going to get all your questions answered, I think, Con. The boss wants to see us all. Yes, I've met him. He arrived just about an hour ago." The centre of Gourock was being left behind as Jacko added, "We haven't far to go, two or three minutes at the most will do it."

"What's he like?" asked McBride. "Any more hint of what's going on?"

"Looks OK to me. As for the job, he says he's waiting on you. You're the last arrival . . . ah, here we are now." The car swept up to a small collection of bungalows on the outskirts of the town, and stopped outside a small white-walled house, parking immediately behind a grey Jaguar.

"Home sweet home." He pointed. "Rented for the occasion. The 'tenant' is someone you've met before."

They walked up the stone-flagged path, and the blue-painted door of the house opened at their approach. A man in his late fifties, balding, cigarette-ash covered waistcoat opened allowing his tie to flop freely over a decided paunch, crinkled his jowls in a friendly welcome.

"Come in, Con," invited Harry. "The party's complete. Sorry about the quizzing the last time we met . . . all part of the build-up, I'm afraid." He led the two men into the small sitting-room, where three others sat waiting. One rose to his feet— an ex-officer type, guessed Con, taking in the other's expensively cut suit, neatly trimmed moustache, and smoothly brushed dark hair. Deep blue eyes shone through rimless glasses as the stranger offered his hand. "Welcome, Mr. McBride," he said in a hearty tone. Con, a wary look on his face, mind registering the commanding personality before him, returned the handshake and accepted the seat he was waved to.

"Whisky all round, Harry," instructed the tall man. As Harry's bald head bent over a tray of glasses, the voice, tone brisk and business-like now, went on, "First, let's go through the introductions. Con, I've told the lads here about you, and they've already met Jacko. My name's Russell, Jonathan Russell. This is my show that you're joining . . ." he silenced the protest forming on the safe-blower's lips. "You'll join all right, Con. When you know what our target is, you won't hesitate. But be a good fellow and listen just now.

"Call me an er—company director. I am, in fact. Some of the companies don't last long, it is true, but you'd be amazed what I collect in fees.

"Over on the sofa, with an atrocious taste in ties, is Mr. McKellar, known to his acquaintances as Flick. Flick is our muscle man. His nickname comes from the way he uses his pet spring-knife. That little scar over his eye was caused by a friendly pass from someone's broken bottle."

Flick, a tough young fellow in his twenties, a thin, white-faced, wiry figure born and bred in the Gorbals of Glasgow, nodded a surly greeting then returned to contemplating his nicotine-stained fingernails.

Russell went on, "Dan Travers—he's the one beside Flick—is our sailor. A key man, Dan. Quite a hero during the war, I believe. He was a petty officer in motor gunboats. When he went back to fishing after the war he ran into all sorts of trouble with the Customs people—something to do with cigarettes from Southern Ireland."

McBride exchanged dutiful smiles with the seaman, a stocky, sturdy barrel of a man, sitting back relaxed, hands deep in trouser pockets.

The fat man came over with the filled glasses. Russell picked one from the tray. "Thanks, Harry. This, Con, is Harry Vogt. Harry's job really begins when ours finishes. He's an expert in the jewellery line . . . though his employers got annoyed when they found him helping himself to samples. Harry's worked for me before. It was his job to approach the rest of you. With his help, and that of some friends of mine, it was easy to draw up my short leet for this team."

He looked slowly round the room, "Each man has been selected for a definite role. Like you, Con, none of the others knows—except Harry—just exactly what it is all about. Have your drinks. Harry and I will get ready to show you."

Russell and Vogt moved over to the table, and began unfolding a map, which the latter had produced from a drawer of the sideboard. As the others, glasses in hand, gathered round, their leader explained, "This is a chart of the Firth of Clyde. We're here . . ." He pointed to Gourock, lying on the one side of the sea estuary. "The Firth's only two or three miles wide here. Almost directly across the water, on the other side . . ." his hand moved across the map ". . . is Dunoon, a fair-sized seaside resort, and just above it is a bay called the Holy Loch. How long, would you say, Dan, should it be to get across there in a good motor boat?"

"From here, about thirty minutes," grunted the sailor. "Depends on tide and the weather, of course."

"That's the way I've it figured. Now there's a big yacht lying in the Holy Loch just now. It's called the *Cockatoo*. Ever heard of it?"

Vogt smiled faintly as the other four shook their heads.

"Does the name of an American called Dwyatt Ronaldson mean anything then? Or perhaps Julie Martin?"

Jacko gasped. "Sure it does. Julie Martin . . . she's the star Broadway actress who has got a mint in jewels. But there isn't a hope of getting near them. I was lined up for the job with a ladder gang back in London when she was over here three years back. The country house where she was staying had a guard on it all the time, and a couple of the hungriest looking dogs I've ever seen were thumping about outside. We gave up. You'll never get near her."

"That's where you're wrong, Jacko," smiled Russell. "Julie Martin is married to Ronaldson, who happens to be a millionaire a few times over. Ronaldson also happens to be the hereditary chief of the Ronaldson clan, and this year's an important anniversary for them. So his yacht is lying over there, and he and his wife are aboard. It's a big luxury diesel ship of about 500 tons, and they are holding court on her in the loch."

"And his wife brings the jewels over with her to shatter the natives," commented Jacko.

"Right. I've got friends who tell me that Mrs. Julie has got something like £70,000 worth of jewels over with her. She had to do a lot of talking to her insurance company to get bringing them, and they were guarded all the way across to Britain.

"Now, high spot of the festivities is to be a big clan ball in Dunoon exactly five days from now. The police will be watching the dance of course, and there will probably be some insurance man as well, as Julie's bound to be decked out in her trinkets. But precautions aboard the yacht the night before the ball are a different matter entirely."

"We swim out, Flick beats up the crew, and this woman leaves the loot lying in a neat pile on her dressing-table, I suppose," said McBride in sardonic tones.

"Take your time, Con," warned Russell. "I appreciate your distrust, but I'm in no mood for sarcasm. I've spent a lot of money obtaining information and arranging everything for this job."

A scowl spreading across McBride's face mellowed Russell's choice of words . . . for the simple reason that of all the men present McBride was the most valuable and, at this late date, one impossible to replace.

But there was still a perceptible hardening of tone as he went on, "I'm asking for a fair hearing, Con, nothing more. If you don't like my plans and have any better ideas, I want to hear them. But remember there's £5,000 cash for you in this job. Hell, of course it has its risks, man—what really big robbery hasn't? I'll have half of the value of our haul as my share—but I'm paying all the bills, and you'll find that's no small sum.

"Now will you listen? Or would you rather Jacko ran you back to the station? There's a train leaving in about half an hour."

"I'll listen," the safe-blower grudgingly agreed.

The other man nodded. "That's better. Now, first of all, I'm one of about a dozen guests aboard the yacht *Cockatoo* at the moment. How and why doesn't matter, but it took a trip to the States to do it, plus a full two months cramming on yachting. Ronaldson and I are getting on famously aboard the boat. I plan to remain aboard as an innocent bystander after the coup— don't worry, I've no police record, and I've no intention of doing anything foolish. Getting aboard, as you'll gather, has cost some money.

34

"Some more of that expenses money has been well spent on information, detailed information of the ship's layout, crew duties, Ronaldson's habits aboard." He stooped, and from a briefcase lying beside the table drew out a bundle of papers. "It's all here. The jewels are always kept in the only safe on board, in a small lounge behind the captain's quarters on the bridge superstructure. The place is really Ronaldson's private den, and is locked when he isn't around. The lock on the door will prove easy enough, I imagine, it's quite a simple affair. We can be sure the jewels will be in the safe—the insurance company make it a firm condition of their cover that they are kept in it when not on the lady's person.

"Back to the safe, however. It's a Gall make, small, but quite strong. That's where you come in, Con. It will have to be blown . . . and we want to have as little noise as possible and to get it open first time. You're the expert. You'll have to use as little explosive as humanly possible so that no one, apart from maybe the captain, is wakened . . . or there is little chance of your getting clear away."

"How do I get aboard, and how about the crew? There's sure to be someone on guard at night."

"One man," nodded Russell. "Taking care of him is my job. I'll hit him hard enough to prevent him bothering anyone for a few hours. Then I drop a rope ladder over the side, and get back to my cabin. Dan Travers here will get you out to the yacht by boat. You'll sail from this side of the Firth, across the estuary, and arrive off the ship sometime about four in the morning. Flick and Jacko go with you. Flick's job is to take care of the captain, and stop anyone else interrupting you. Jacko's task is to deal with the two motor boats they carry aboard so that they can't come after you when you make your getaway."

It was Travers's turn to protest. "You can't just pick up a boat like you would steal a car. And the noise of a launch coming alongside might wake someone."

"I agree on both counts, but the expenses sheet has taken care of these problems. About three months ago a Mr. Johnston bought an old but fairly fast thirty foot launch. The launch is lying at a pier near here right now, ready for sea. Mr. Johnston exists all right. At the moment, however, he's in London and he'll stay there with friends, officially knowing nothing about what's going on and being well paid for keeping his nose clean. He'll be suitably shocked to hear his boat was stolen. Dan will drift up as near to the *Cockatoo* as he can with safety, then you'll go over in a little rubber dinghy— the inflatable kind the RAF use—and get aboard. The launch will come in and take you three straight off when the job's over. You'll head away from the yacht . . ." his finger moved rapidly across the map ". . . cut back up the Firth under cover of the dark, and abandon the boat on the beach at this point . . ." he tapped a headland on the map, several miles away from the anchorage. "Harry will be waiting there with the Zephyr. Jacko will take the wheel, and you'll head north, towards the Highlands. He'll drop Con, you Dan, and Flick, then head north-east towards Aberdeen, with Harry aboard. A Dutch cargo ship leaves from there at 11 a.m. There's nearly 200 miles of road to cover, but Jacko can make it in time—that's why he's here. The captain of the ship is being well paid to smuggle Harry and the loot aboard unseen, then to get him off again at Holland in the same way."

The jeweller, hands nestling on his paunch, took up the story, addressing an audience listening with an intensity which would have been the delight of any university lecturer.

"I've got plenty of contacts in the Hague. The world's jewellery trade centre is there. Inside a few days we'll have these jewels so changed around their owner wouldn't know them, sell the lot at the top price, and then I'll be on my way back. Give me a fortnight at the outside."

"Aye, but what about us, eh? What are we doin' while the cops are screamin' about, eh?" McKellar, the 'muscle' man, brow wrinkled in concentration which showed his scar in a new prominence, had spoken for the first time. "You'll be a' right, but what about the blokes you leave behind? Do we just keep runnin'?"

He lapsed into silence, and, as if embarrassed at his outburst, busied himself lighting a fresh cigarette from the stub which had been dangling from his lips.

"A fair question, again," agreed Russell. "I was going to tell you about that part of the scheme next. You, Con and the sailor will be dropped off at a little cottage I've rented in the wilds. There's literally no one within miles, and you can hole up there without fear. Jacko will join you there as soon as he can. It'll be as quiet as the grave, but there's plenty of liquor, food, radio and books laid on. No TV, I'm afraid," he smiled. "But you can always start a game of poker to pass the time . . . and play for high stakes!"

The planner was mentally congratulating himself on the way opposition was being overcome. But the next broadside was the heaviest yet.

"And you, Mr. Russell? What are you doing all the time we're lying low? What's to stop you sliding across to Holland to meet your friend Harry and carving the haul up between you?" McBride, lounging against the wall beside the table, empty glass in one hand, heard a faint hiss of indrawn breath and knew he had voiced the unspoken thoughts of at least one other present.

"I'll have to stay on the yacht, Con, at

least for a day or two until the first round of police inquiries is over. Later I'll join you . . . but I daren't rush away. It would focus attention on me immediately," said Russell. "How can you trust me? Just on my word, I'm afraid. But I won't welsh on you. Con, Larry Finch was a friend of yours?"

The safe-blower's eyes flickered in surprise. "Yes . . . until he got run over by a bus and killed about a year back."

"And his wife and children?"

McBride nodded. "See Maisie every now and then."

"Then you know that she got paid for the last job her husband did, knocking over the safe in that Hammersmith bank? Larry was working for me, Con. That was my last venture . . . and now you're taking Larry's place. In fact it was Larry who first told me about you, while he was still on my pay-roll. I'll double-cross anybody like a shot if it suits the book, anybody except the men working with me."

A new friendliness had crept into McBride's expression. "Then I'm with you," he declared. "There's only about a dozen people know what you've just told

me, Russell. That's proof enough for me."
After a second's pause, muttered agreement came from the others.

Russell's face brightened perceptibly.

"Then let's get down to cases," he beamed. "I've got plans of the yacht, timetables, everything lying here worked out in detail. We'll knock it over sweetly and smoothly—and this time next month we can all be soaking up the sun in Monte Carlo."

"Blackpool'll do me," leered Flick. "Just show me who ah've to do up, and when, and Bob's your ruddy uncle."

"Tell me about the safe first," demanded McBride. "Is it a combination lock, or a key type?"

"Key," replied Russell.

The safe-blower nodded in satisfaction. "Just as well. If you try to blow a combination lock you're in real trouble." He explained, with almost clinical thoroughness, "All that stuff about gentlemen crackers listening to tumblers click is strictly for the marines. The only way to burst a combination job is to lever the dial back with a jemmy and expose the spindle underneath. Then you've got to blow a charge of 'soup' to blast the spindle back —and you need another bang after that to shatter the lock. With the key type, you can go for the lock first time."

"You'll need to get it first time, Con," agreed Russell. "How quietly can it be done?"

"That's got me worried," confessed the expert. "If it was in a house, I could blast a can in one room and the people next door would only stir in their sleep. But a metal ship . . . I don't like it. It might be like hitting a gong with a sledge hammer. Wait a minute, though . . . how's this safe mounted? Do you know if it's sunk in the wall, or whatever they're called on a ship? And it's definitely a Gall make?"

"I've seen it," said Russell. "Ronaldson's had me in his den two or three times for a quiet drink. The safe's on a pedestal mounting, bolted to the deck. Why?"

"Can you get at the back of it?"

Russell thought for a moment before answering, "Ye-es, you could, I'd say. But the safe is pretty close to the wall."

"Then I've a better idea, or at least one that might work. Can you get your hands

42

on a pair of surgical plaster shears? You know, the contraptions they use in hospitals to take plaster casts off broken legs."

Puzzled, Russell nodded.

"Good. It's a while since I tried it last, but I've opened one or two lightweight safes that way. You bore a hole—just a small one—in the back of the box, then put the shears in, and rip. They'll take a fair thickness of metal, and there's not too much noise, though it takes a little longer than other methods. If the shears fail, of course I'll have to blow it. But the shears are worth a try."

"You'll get your shears," promised Russell. "And the only person really near you will be the captain, as I said. Flick will take care of him—quickly and quietly, Flick—if he wakes up too soon. Now let's get back to this timetable. I want every man here to know his part backwards. And I'm going to ask you to look at the plans of this yacht until you could find your way through it blindfolded."

The six gathered more closely round the table, chattering like schoolboys at the relaxation of the tension and suspense. Sure, there were risks . . . plenty of them.

But the dice seemed at least evenly balanced in their favour. And that was all they asked for the rosy profits with which they were already mentally conjuring.

No cramming class ever studied lessons as intently as the assorted group did the master-plan before them. And, as each stage was explained, they were ruthlessly cross-examined by Russell on their individual parts.

"There's one thing you haven't taken into account," observed Dan Travers at one halt in the flow of questions and answers. "The weather. What if the sea is too rough? This isn't the best time of the year for weather. What if a storm blows up?"

"That's part of the gamble," shrugged Russell. "The moon's on the wane, so there won't be too much light. If the sky is cloudy, or it's raining, so much the better."

"Last time I was on holiday in Dunoon it never stopped raining," grunted McKellar. "But here, I'm no a very good sailor. Who's goin' to paddle the wee rubber boat?"

"You and Jacko, I'm afraid," grinned

Russell. "If the sea is too rough we'll have to call it off, and try again another night. But we haven't too many chances. Remember, the ball is only five days away. To make the best of the circumstances, the job must be done the night before the party. And if we can't, well, there are only a few days left after that before the Ronaldsons sail for the Mediterranean."

It was nearly ten o'clock when Russell took his leave from the bungalow. Just as he left the house he stopped, pulled out his wallet, and extracted a folded newspaper clipping from one of its leather pockets. "Hand that round," he ordered. "There's a picture and description of the stuff we're after . . . it'll make you feel good just to look at them glitter."

With a wave he walked to the Jaguar, and, seconds after its sidelights had winked on, churned the starter motor. The engine fired, and the luxury car purred away in a burble of exhaust.

Con, who had watched the tall, slim figure, bulked by a heavy overcoat, get into the car and drive away, turned from the doorway to find Jacko at his elbow.

"What do you make of it, chum?" asked

the little driver. "Seems OK, doesn't it? He's a queer cuss, though."

"Seems fine, Jacko . . . I just hope he's got his facts right. But somehow I think he's the sort of bloke who leaves nothing to chance. Come on, let's see if we can get another drink out of Fat Harry inside. Then I'm for some shut-eye. That ruddy train journey last night nearly finished me!" He glanced at the clipping in Jacko's hand. "Let's see what this stuff looks like." A low whistle escaped his lips as he studied the article and the picture that went with it. "Get a load of those diamonds on that necklace . . . and the rings . . . and get a load of what's wearing them! I wouldn't mind grabbing her along with them!"

Jonathan Russell was feeling smugly confident as he drove towards Glasgow. He had told the Ronaldsons he would have to spend the day in the city on business, and had in fact booked a room in the Central Hotel for the night. He would drive down to Dunoon, and the *Cockatoo*, in the morning.

It had been a good idea of McBride's

this substitution of surgical shears for explosives. Though Russell had been quite prepared to blow the safe, regardless of noise, and, if need be, chance having to help fight a way off the boat with the jewels.

He felt the hard, yet comforting shape of the automatic in its shoulder holster next his shirt. Russell had never killed a man in civilian life . . . it had never really been necessary. He had killed a few in war, though, before he discovered that there was a much happier existence to be had disposing of Army stores, especially food and petrol, to the commodity starved populaces of the towns and cities being "liberated" by the invading Allies. If Flick McKellar, that brutal, rather unsavoury but very necessary little tough, got hold of a gun he would probably shoot for sheer delight, he mused. Flick was the type who would twist a broken bottle in anybody's face just to work off steam.

"But to a business man like myself," he thought, "violence is only justifiable when it shows a profit. Coshing this ship's watchman, now, that will be profitable. The captain may have to be dealt with.

But it should end there. Just for insurance, though, it might be handy to have another gun around. That little driver, Jacko, would be a good man for it . . . level headed enough, a professional."

Making a mental note to mention the matter to Harry when he telephoned the bungalow in the morning, Russell settled down to the task of driving the twenty-five miles back to Glasgow.

3

LIFE was pleasant aboard the motor yacht *Cockatoo*. Its 160 feet of graceful steel hull contained practically every modern aid to luxurious living that money and space could provide, from air-conditioned cabins with deep pile carpets to the comfortable lounge, finished in light green, with deep moquette chairs and settees, and its neighbouring viewing room, where there was both projection television and cinema equipment. In the galley, a short but discreet distance from the dining saloon where the big oak table was set for twelve, the two cooks and two stewards were busily engaged in preparing the evening meal. In addition to fresh supplies brought from the shore that day, they could draw on the cold storage rooms, crammed with a variety of rich foods. The wine-bin close by held a range of carefully selected vintages.

Freshening in his cabin before dinner, Jonathan Russell took a crisply ironed white shirt from its hanger in the walnut wardrobe and laid it on the deep red bedmat. Then he stripped off the grey woollen shirt he had been wearing. Plugging his electric razor into the wall socket, he began a slow, leisurely shave before the mirror, watching his dark stubble melt away before the whirring onslaught, and carefully manoeuvring the instrument round the edge of his neatly trimmed moustache.

The darkness which lay outside the cabin port-hole, where blue curtains set off the gleaming brass of the frame, was split only by the regular flashing beam of the Cloch lighthouse. Miles across the water, on the other side of the Firth, its beam was backed by a faint, distant frosting of house lights on the mainland behind.

As he switched off the razor, Russell felt the faint sway of the ship underfoot . . . and his spirits soared. That faint, just discernible motion, sign of a quiet sea, had only to hold for a few more hours for the first major gamble of his plan, the weather, to have succeeded in his favour.

Slipping on the clean shirt, he took a fresh tie from the wardrobe rail and flicked it into a quick, perfect knot, adjusting it neatly to the collar.

He hadn't always had clean white shirts. Schooldays had been all right, with his architect father happy and proud of his son's passion for neatness. But when, at University, his neatness had also included beautifully detailed copies of friends' signatures on cheques, culminating in the quick buying of a car with a "dud" bank order, father had paid up, hushed up—and given up. When the circumstances repeated themselves twelve months later, father paid up again—and then kicked his son out into the cold, cruel world with a final £100 and a warning about the consequences of coming back looking for more.

The next three years had been, he reflected, pretty grim. He had always managed to stay out of gaol—that neat attention to detail took care of that. But he was down to living in cheap rooming houses, with one frayed suit, a spare shirt, and his overcoat in pledge at the local pawnbroker's when, of all strange agencies, World War II came to his aid.

Called up, his University cadet corps experience brought him an easy commission. He did a spell in the Middle East, served for a brief time in the Western Desert, then to his great relief, found a nice quiet corner in a Canal Zone stores depot. He had already learned most of the ropes in "fiddling" surplus stores. But the new posting brought him into more lucrative operations. Before a suspicious but unavailing SIB probe resulted in his being transferred to Britain and a training unit, far removed from such valuable and transferable articles as petrol, tyres and radio spares, Russell had succeeded in losing sufficient stock to interested customers to build up a tidy little wad of money—a wad that would have been much larger but for his frequent spending sprees in Cairo.

When the invasion of Europe and the urgent need for replacement officers resulted in the previous suspicions being overlooked and, as a captain, he found himself once more handling a torrent of supplies of all kinds, Russell really went to town. The penniless waster was demobilised a solid citizen with a nice healthy bank balance.

He opened his export-import agency

. . . though not all the deals he made with his war-time friends in Europe were known to the Board of Trade. And one night he met Harry Vogt. Vogt had been an enthusiastic aide in Russell's war-time Egyptian enterprises. Now he was looking for help to carry out a small-scale jewel swindle. Russell took over, transformed the deal into a major fraud . . . and from that point on the import-export business became a mere cover for even less lawful activities ranging from robbery with or without violence as circumstances warranted to insurance frauds and black market deals.

The pattern, however, remained the same . . . neat, well-planned, skilfully carried out, then a long rest before the next operation, a rest during which Russell exercised to the full his liking for expensive living.

Tonight's job, however, was the biggest in all these years. Pressing his face against the cold glass of the port-hole, Russell gazed pensively out into the black night. Somewhere over there, across the water, Harry, Con McBride and the others would be waiting the last long hours before going into action.

Turning away from the port-hole, he was slipping on his jacket when the cabin intercom phone buzzed softly. He took the ivory receiver off its stand.

"Jonathan? This is Dwyatt here . . . fancy a drink in the den before dinner? I want to show you something rather special."

"Be right along," agreed Russell. The invitation, he reflected as he replaced the receiver, would give him a last look at the safe before it came under Con McBride's expert handling.

Leaving his cabin, he walked along the wide alleyway, waving a cheery greeting to the elderly man just about to enter the cabin near the companionway. Nicholas Malahne, an American theatrical producer, and life-long friend of Ronaldson's wife, was one of the eight other guests who, with Russell, the Ronaldsons and the yacht's captain, would make up the party round the dinner table.

Up the steps of the companionway Russell clattered to deck level. On an impulse he opened the screen door to his right and stepped into the open, shivering a little at the chill night air's bitter contrast to the steam heated interior. The *Cockatoo* lay quiet at anchor, a full quarter mile from the Dunoon shore. Dunoon and its long appendage of interlinked shore villages glittered with light, but the sky was dull and black with heavy clouds. There would be little or no moon that night.

He stepped back into the warmth, closed the door, and went up the next flight of the companionway. Now, apart from the bridge above, he was on the highest deck level on the yacht. He rapped at the door before him—faced, like all the other furnishings of the ship, in natural walnut. It opened instantly, and a sheepish-looking face peeped round the edge.

"You, Jonathan . . . good. Come on in, quick."

As soon as Russell was inside the door was closed.

"Put me out of my misery," begged the American. "How do I look?" Ronaldson was dressed in a hectic green tweed jacket and a kilt, the latter hanging apologetically above snow-white knees.

"It just came this afternoon," revealed the embarrassed clan chief. "It's the first time I've ever worn one of these darned things. Julie nearly went into hysterics when I put it on. I managed to sneak up here and ever since I've been trying to pluck up courage to get someone to see it. I didn't want a Scottie, in case there was something drastically wrong, and one of our own folks might just faint with shock. But you're English . . . you're neutral. What do you think?"

"Smart," agreed Russell. "But the sporran is supposed to be at the front." The leather adornment was slung to one side.

"Yeah, I know, but heck, it's more comfortable round where it is," protested the American. "Still, I'll sling it round properly before I leave. Nothing else?"

"Nothing that I know," commented his visitor. "But don't hold it against me if you're committing sacrilege."

Sighing, Ronaldson commented. "It's a helluva business bein' a clan chief, I can tell you. I'm being shoved around like a crazy man. Tomorrow now, we've got this big dance on in the evening . . . four hundred guests, about twenty of whom I know from Adam. And before that I've got to lead an open air sports gathering in the morning, hold court at a cocktail party in the afternoon, and generally act the Highland hero. Heck, I love keepin' up the old country traditions and tellin' the boys back home I'm a chief, even if half of them think it's somethin' to do with the Apaches. But it lands you in some spots.

"You know, when I went ashore today the cops were even asking me to look over their arrangements for tomorrow—car parking, traffic control, a special guard at the dance."

"At the dance?" queried Russell.

"Yeah, all on account of Julie's stuff. Here, have a whisky . . ." he poured a stiff drink into each of two tumblers and handed one over. "Julie's going to put on her battle honours tomorrow night, you know, diamonds and stuff. She's got quite a collection, looks like somethin' out of an Arabian oil sheik's harem when she's finished. And the local cops are worried stiff in case any smart boys try anything.

"The jewels are in that safe just beside you," he nodded to the small metal box on the heavy wooden pedestal, which, apart from a roll-top desk, was the only business-like article in the "den" where a scattering of arm-chairs, a cocktail cabinet bookcase and a card table were the only other furnishings. Russell turned towards the safe. Yes, he thought as he glanced over its lines, there was just enough room between it and the wall to allow the back to be reached by McBride.

"In there," he queried in innocent tones. "Are they secure enough like that?"

"As good as in a bank vault," said the American in confident tones. "There's a lot of water between us and the shore, and there's always someone around, even at night. Over 200,000 dollars worth of rocks are in that little safe—almost £70,000 in your money.

"Mind you, I gave Julie only some of it. The rest she collected on her own before we were married. That girl gave up a lot for me . . . her name in lights, a herd of boy friends.

"Anyway, like I was saying, the cops are worried. So are the insurance company.

The way they behave, anyone with anything worth money should bury it beside the gold in Fort Knox. Julie likes to use her jewels. I like to see her wearing 'em."

A deep booming note filled the air.

"Food," beamed Ronaldson. "You know, we could use that gong as a fog signal any time. Well, I guess I'll go down and see if Julie's recovered yet . . . at least I know that someone's seen me in this outfit without creasing himself."

They left the den, and headed towards the dining saloon.

It was a good meal, as were all the meals aboard the *Cockatoo*. But for once Russell felt little appetite, and had to make an effort to eat sufficient to stop his companions querying his lack of interest in the food.

Gay talk flowed round the table, their host's Highland dress and the coming day's programme providing almost the sole topics of conversation. The yacht's skipper, Captain Vinator, an American like most of his crew, sat next to Russell.

"I guess we'll need both the power boats tomorrow, Mr. Russell," he remarked.

Russell jerked back from his wandering thoughts. "You think so?" he asked, trying to pick up the thread of conversation.

"Yeah, there's bound to be a lot of coming and going. We've just been using the big launch so far, but I reckon we'll have the eighteen foot job lowered in the morning. If we're really jammed up, there's the motor lifeboat, but that's pretty stark. Busy day one way and another, I'd say. Well, I got some work to do, and there's still the routine inspection of the ship waiting, so I guess I'll just skip coffee."

The captain turned to his employer. "OK by you if I leave now, Mr. Ronaldson?"

"Sure, if you want to, Vinator," said Ronaldson. "Will we see you later?"

"Uh-uh." The captain shook his head. "By the time I get through it'll be pretty late. Probably I'll hit the sack. Well, good night, Mrs. Ronaldson . . . everybody . . ." He left the saloon as the stewards began to clear the table prior to bringing in the coffee.

After coffee, the party drifted into the lounge, and the two women guests, a lithe blonde American girl, Valerie Van Kirken, and Rhoda Ronaldson, a distant Scots relative, joined forces to try to get Julie to sing. But Julie, busily engaged in dispensing drinks from the small bar in one corner, stubbornly refused. Instead, she soon launched a canasta game which dragged its way on for three hours and finished with victory for her and her partner over Rhoda and Nicholas Malahne.

Russell, Ronaldson and the others hung around the bar for a time, talking, then drifted into the other room and passed the time watching television. Russell was more than glad when the party finally broke up and he was able to get away to the sanctuary of his cabin. He slid off his jacket and sprawled on top of the bed, mind racing. It was twenty minutes after midnight . . . less than four hours to go. He daren't try to snatch a real rest, in case he overslept. Check the plan . . . check it again, and again . . .

At one o'clock he rose from the bed, undressed, pulled on his pyjamas, then dragged flannels and a thick pullover on top of them and put on his socks. Pulling back the covers, he switched out the light and climbed into bed, to lie staring at the dark ceiling. Now and again he caught the faint sound of a steward's tread as the last tasks of the night were completed. Then that stopped. The yacht was at peace. In all its length, only one other man should be awake, the night patrolman. Russell glanced again at his watch's luminous dial . . . 2 a.m. The waves still lapped gently against the hull. 2.30 a.m . . . at three he rose, and, still in the darkness and moving as quietly as he could, unlocked the small suitcase which he had told the steward contained "private documents".

Feeling his way through its contents, he drew out a leather shoulder holster and strapped it in position, checking the automatic that went with it before sliding the weapon back into the soft leather. A short but heavy cosh came next . . . that went into his right-hand trouser pocket, while a torch and a broad roll of medical adhesive tape went into the other. Last of all came a pair of rubber-soled plimsolls, which he pulled on his feet, fumbling with the laces.

Two cigarettes later, at exactly 3.30 a.m., he gave his spectacles a last nervous polish, settled them back on his face, and slowly slid back the lock on the cabin door. The corridor outside was faintly lit by one small all-night globe. He crept along, feet settling noiselessly into the fitted carpeting, past the cabins where the others were peacefully sleeping. Russell stopped at the foot of the companionway steps. The night patrolman should be settled in the little deck-level shelter below and for'ard of the bridge. But his rounds were to no fixed schedule . . . he could be on the move at that moment, inspecting the yacht from bow to stern, a duty he carried out two or three times during his watch.

There was no sound from above. He tip-toed up the companionway, edged open the screen door at the top, and gazed out into the night. Only the faint creaking motion of the ship broke the silence as she "breathed" in tune to the lap of the waves against her sides. He stepped out, on to the starboard deck, and, after a moment's hesitation, began moving quietly forward, keeping close to the side. Fifteen paces brought him below the bridge. From his right-hand pocket he brought out the hard rubber truncheon, and, holding it close to his side, looked round the angle of the superstructure.

A light shone brightly from the glass windows of the little shelter nestling under the bridge. The door was on the port side, invisible from where the raider stood. Pursing his lips, Russell listened. Then, reasured by the continued quiet, he moved very slowly across the few intervening feet, until he stood just to the side of the lighted window, body pressed against the cold metal of the structure. He peeped in.

The patrolman, a young seaman, sat beside the radiator, a large torch by his side, a luridly-covered cowboy book in his hand. His head was bent as he read, and an opened Thermos flask stood on the deck beside his chair.

Russell ducked down, and, crouching to come beneath the level of the glass windows facing the bow, moved round to the other side of the little shelter. Now he was on the port side, past the windowed doorway, a blank expanse of metal at his side. The next step was to entice the man out of the shelter, into the darkness. The stalker could have burst in and taken the man by surprise. But the sailor might struggle or even have time to recognize him. Russell's plan was simple—the oldest and most effective in the world. He would send his torch rattling along the deck past the door, away from him, and rely on the seaman coming out to investigate.

But fate took a sudden hand. Before he could move there was a scrape of chair legs, the sound of a loud yawn, and the man inside could be heard humming to himself. Then, so suddenly it almost took Russell off guard, the shelter door swung outward and the unsuspecting sailor, muffling another yawn, stepped through, framed by the light streaming out of the doorway. The yawn ended in a gurgle as Russell smashed the cosh down in a vicious swing and followed it up with another savage blow even as the youngster was collapsing. His attacker grabbed the falling man in time to break to a low thud the sound of the unconscious body hitting the deck.

Moving quickly, Russell took out the roll of sticky tape and lashed the youngster's hands behind his back with a long length of the tough material, repeated the process at his feet, then slapped on two more lengths, one across his mouth, the other across his eyes. Only the man's nose and ears were still visible. The tape was several times speedier than cord—and much more effective.

Leaving his victim where he lay, he moved again to the ship's starboard side, searching for the Cloch lighthouse, marking the far shore of the estuary. He panicked for a moment as he gazed into unbroken blackness . . . then gave a muffled curse at his own foolishness as he realized that the tiny world of the ship, swinging on the bow anchor chain at the will of tide and current, had caused him to lose his bearings. Stepping over to the port side, Russell saw the lighthouse beam streaking across the water. Taking the torch from his pocket, he pointed the lens slightly to the left of the Cloch light, and three times flashed short-long-short—short-long-short—short-long-short—the letter R in morse.

He dug his finger-nails into the palms of his hands as he waited, peering seawards. Then it came . . . another faint answering flicker of light . . . the answer he needed, the answer that the launch and his men were waiting.

It had been a long day—and a far longer night—for the makeshift crew of the launch *Tina*. The five men had wakened about eight in the morning at the little bungalow where they had been waiting for the past four days. During those days they had followed Russell's orders and religiously rehearsed times without number their instructions for the raid. Russell had visited them twice more, once bringing the long nickelplated plaster shears, the second time a mysterious bundle which he passed to Harry. The fat man refused to discuss its contents . . . "All in good time," he stalled.

On each occasion Russell had closely questioned his chosen group on their individual roles. Con and Jacko had been professionally perfect in their parts. The sailor, still inclined to look on the black side of things, was also reasonably proficient.

The only real trouble had been with Flick. "Ach," he declared on the second visit. "Ah cannny mind all these wee footery things. But ah'll know what to do when the time comes. Ah'll stop anybody gettin' in our way."

"You'll stop ashore if you don't get this into your thick head," stormed Russell, showing black anger for the first time in their brief acquaintance. "Every move has been worked out, timed, perfected—I'm not having a thick-headed tough foul it up because he thinks he can strong-arm his way through any situation. If we can, we do this job and get away without having to knock anyone out of our way. Remember that. We're not looking for trouble . . . and your job is just to be ready in case it comes looking for us."

The blast wilted the little Glasgow man. But the expression on his face was not pleasant to see as Russell turned away. The Scot did not forgive easily . . . and in other circumstances his answer to such an outburst would have been a vicious one.

That morning, however, with their big

effort now only hours away, it was a quiet group who drank tea and munched coarse sandwiches in the house . . . a group who kept silent for most of the day. Only Jacko was his usual cheery self—and he received no encouragement for his invitation to "let's get the cards out to pass the time."

So he spent the afternoon listening to the radio, through Women's Hour and a light music programme, Mrs. Dale's Diary and a jazz band show. The latter was still in progress when Travers came over and suddenly spun the tuning dial.

"Hey, I'm listening to that," protested Jacko.

"Weather forecast," grunted the seaman. "You want to know what the ruddy sea's going to be like, don't you?"

They waited through the end of Children's Hour on the Home Service. Then came the forecast . . . so much mumbo jumbo to Jacko with its talk of anticyclones and centres of pressure. But Travers looked reasonably happy. "Not too bad," he declared, switching off the set as the news broadcast began.

"What'll it be like, Sailor?" asked Flick, sitting up and taking notice. "God, ah hope it isnae rough . . . ma guts won't take it if it is."

"Not too bad," repeated Sailor. "Next to no wind, slight sea . . . you won't be seasick. But I don't like this snow warning they mentioned. It'll help cut down the light—the cloud will make it as black as the Earl of Hell's waistcoat. But if the snow starts falling we could be in trouble. It would be difficult to find the *Cockatoo* in a snowstorm, and twice as difficult to get ashore at the right place afterwards."

"Cheerful Charlie," cracked Jacko. "I'll wear my goloshes, Daddy."

They moved a little after 2 a.m. Harry and Jacko carried two heavy bundles out to the boot of the black Ford Zephyr. Then all five got aboard and, Jacko at the wheel, the car set off as quietly as possible to avoid waking the people sleeping in the houses around the bungalow. It was only a short journey along the coast road to the little pier at which a cluster of small boats were lying, some beached on the shingle, others moored in the water.

Harry, moving surprisingly quickly for his bulk, scouted the area while the others waited in the car a short distance away, drawn off the road on the grass verge, all lights extinguished. He was back within ten minutes.

"All clear," he told them. "I thought it would be, but it was better to be sure. There's an old geezer who acts as a kind of caretaker . . . but he'll be at his cottage up the road a bit."

Russell's training showed in the smooth way the group left the car and prepared to leave, Flick and Sailor each taking one of the bundles from the boot. McBride had his tools with him in a cloth-wrapped roll, but as he prepared to go Harry called him over . . . "and you too, Jacko."

Then he produced a slim package from the front of the car and quickly stripped off its canvas cover. As he did, Jacko drew a lungful of smoke from his cigarette, the tip glowing brightly, the reddish light dancing on the dull metal shapes.

"What the hell?" asked McBride. "Guns?"

"Two, Con," agreed Harry. "Russell thought we'd better have them. Automatics—they're for you and Jacko."

"Include me out," growled McBride.

71

"I've never carried one in my life, and I'm not starting now. I blow safes . . . but that's the beginning and end."

"Jacko?"

"If Russell wants," shrugged the little man. "But I'm not particularly keen. People get hurt that way . . . and I don't want to see a judge put a black cap on for me."

"Fair enough," said Harry. "I'll keep the other gun. Oh—don't mention the automatics to Flick. The boss doesn't want him to even sniff one."

"Jacko can carry one if he wants," muttered McBride. "I'm not touching them."

They set off after the others. Even as they walked away Harry started the Ford's engine and set off on the long coastal drive to the meeting place at Loch Goil, a sea loch only a few miles across the water, but nearly sixty by road.

The thirty foot launch *Tina* lay moored near the end of the pier, and the four men, hampered by their burdens, swore under their breaths as they fumbled their way down the iron ladder set in the wood of the pier, then dropped on to the wooden deck. The mere feel of the launch under his feet brought an amazing change to Travers. The seaman bustled about, suddenly sure and confident, checking everything by the shielded light of a torch, while the others waited patiently in the open well of the boat, aft of the cockpit.

Finally, he was satisfied. "I'm going to start her up," he said hoarsely. "There'll be a bit of noise, but it can't be helped. Flick, when I give the word get up to the bow and cast off the rope there. Jacko, you do the same at the stern."

Stooping over the engine housing, he made sure the fuel tap was at the "petrol" position, then pressed the electric starter button.

The power unit burst to life with a roar that seemed thunderous to the men beside it. Quickly, however, it died away as Sailor switched the engine over to its main paraffin feed and, the engine warming, started the sea-water circulating through the engine jacket and on its muffling way down the exhaust pipe. The note was a steady burbling murmur as Travers signalled the two men to cast off. As they did, he put the engine into gear, the propeller bit into the water, and the launch moved off in a rapidly gathering white wake. She pitched a little as she left the shelter of the pier, then settled into a steady up-and-down sway as she swung away from the shore.

No navigation lights burned. Only Travers stood by the cockpit coaming. The other three had scrambled into the tiny low-roofed cabin, bumping their heads on the timbers in the process. They sat in darkness, the steady throb of the engine in their ears, as the boat plodded on, doing a steady eight knots across the estuary. Her helmsman kept a wary eye open for any shipping which might be coming up or down the main channel. Unlit as she was, the launch would be invisible to other craft, but it was a double-edged measure . . . a brush from one of the ships which moved in the Firth at night would smash the *Tina* like an eggshell.

In the little cabin, thick with cigarette smoke and the stink of stale bilgewater and damp wood, McKellar, the little Glasgow tough, was far from happy. "How much longer huv we got tae stay here?" he appealed to McBride.

"About forty minutes," McBride told him. "But heavens, man, this isn't rough. We're lucky."

"Lucky be—Here, ah'm away out beside Sailor. At least ah can breathe out there."

He stumbled across the decking, banged his head again on the low hatchway, swore, then struggled through. "Here, Sailor, are we no about there yet?"

Travers, one hand on the throttle, the other on the steering wheel, didn't answer for a moment. Then, as he tugged at the wheel, he growled, "Get your big feet out of the road, or it'll be all night. That's the steering wire you're standing on."

"How was ah to know?" Flick removed the offending foot. "Here, mind me staying here?"

"You can jump overboard for all I care," said Travers. "Stay if you want. Won't be long now, anyway."

A few minutes later he throttled back the engine, put the boat out of gear, and stood back as the launch, losing way, began to rock and swing with the current. "Quiet now," he warned his pale-faced companion, only a dark shape behind him.

"Sound carries a fair way across water." The seaman repeated his warning as another bump and a curse heralded McBride's emergence from the cabin, followed by Jacko.

"The *Cockatoo*'s lying about half a mile away," the seaman told them. "Look closely over there. You can just pick out her riding lights. We're in roughly the position agreed on, so all we've got to do is wait for Russell to give us the OK for his part."

"What's the time?" asked McBride. "Russell's due to signal about four if all goes well."

"Ten—no, nearer to fifteen minutes to go," said Jacko. "Hey, Sailor, aren't we drifting away from the yacht . . . or is it just my technicolor imagination?"

"We're drifting a bit," agreed Travers. "But I'll pull her back into position before she gets too far. Now we're here we can keep the engine throttled right back, so's you'd hardly know it was working."

The minutes crept by. "Strewth, it's cold," shivered Jacko. "I could have done with my red flannels on."

"That snow in the weather forecast isn't

far off," agreed Sailor. "I just hope it holds off till this is over. It could be ruddy awkward trying to find our way to Loch Goil in a snow . . . look . . . that light . . . there's the signal! He's done it!"

The others gazed out towards the *Cockatoo* while Sailor scrambled for his torch and flashed back towards the yacht. "In we go mates," he said. "Better get that rubber boat out."

He slipped the idling engine into gear and fed it a little more throttle. The launch lost its bobbing motion and began to creep quietly in towards the anchored vessel.

Beside him there was a bustle of activity as the three men dragged out one of the bundles, clumsily undid the fastenings and laid the whole on the deck. Jacko snapped a little lever at one side, a compressed air bottle hissed, and the loose rubber swelled and ballooned into shape, fully inflating within a few seconds. At almost the same instant, Travers cut the launch engine altogether.

"This is where you get out," he told them. "You blokes are dead lucky, anyhow. You shouldn't even get your feet wet . . . it can be pretty sopping in these things if there's any sort of a sea running."

Gingerly, they lowered the rubber boat over the side into the water, and Jacko slid into the little craft. He steadied the toy-like shape as McBride awkwardly clambered over and joined him . . . plunging one foot into the water in the process.

"Come on, Flick, jump to it," whispered the safe-blower hoarsely. "Haven't all ruddy night."

The Scot obeyed, then, as the little boat bumped beside the launch, took the two paddles handed down by Travers. "Where's Con's tool kit?" he whispered.

"I've got it," growled McBride. "You might have dropped it in the drink. Let's go . . . see you later, Sailor!"

"I'll come in fast and loud when you signal," warned Travers. "So be ready to get off that ruddy yacht as quick as you can move."

He untied the slim cord which had held the rubber boat to the launch. Jacko and Flick slid their paddles into the water and, slowly, not particularly skilfully, began to wobble towards the *Cockatoo*, now only a couple of hundred yards off. The launch drifted silently away. Despite the cold, sweat beads quickly formed on their foreheads.

"Hell," gasped Jacko as, his paddle coming out awkwardly, he sprayed the boat with water. "Just as well it isn't rough. If those waves were much bigger we'd have had to take the launch right in, no matter what Russell planned."

They took fifteen minutes to cover the short distance. Then, drifting under the shadow of the *Cockatoo*, so close they could almost touch the metal side of the yacht, they saw the torch flash again, only a few feet away. As they drifted down, McBride made out a shadowy figure on the yacht's deck and, beside it, one of the ship's rope ladders, leading down to the water. Pointing, he guided the rubber boat towards it.

Russell helped the last of the three men up the ladder, and, as the abandoned rubber boat swirled away, told them. "Everything's set. The patrolman's taken care of. This way . . . and keep quiet." They followed him along the deck to a door. "Through here and up the companionway," he directed. "Then the door you want is straight ahead, just as on the plan. Remember the captain, Flick. Jacko, the boats are just a few yards astern of here. I'm off now . . . luck. And I'll see you in a few days at the cottage."

He slipped away, back to his cabin.

4

SILENT and diamond-hard, the little drill ate into the metal, biting the backplate of the *Cockatoo*'s safe. Crouching at an awkward angle over the box McBride, a small lamp on the carpet-covered deck lighting his work, handled the instrument with consummate skill and expert delicacy. It was a reasonably strong safe . . . but like many of its kind the back was its weakest point, the main strength concentrated round the door and lock to repel more conventional attacks.

Spitting out a corkscrew-like thread of metal, the drill slid through the last fraction of the backplate with a sudden grating growl, the bit disappearing into the interior of the safe. Quickly McBride's long supple fingers worked it clear, then, reaching to the tool kit spread beside him, he picked up the long, heavy plaster shears, smooth and nickel-bright, with their immensely powerful lever arms and cruel serrated beak. Tenderly he slid one jaw of the beak into the drill hole, took an arm of the shears in each gloved hand, and pressed, muscles straining with the effort. The metal seemed to hesitate, then ripped back with a protesting moan.

"We'll wake the ruddy boat wi' that din," warned Flick in a loud whisper from his shadowy post beside the cabin door. "Can you no do it quieter?"

"Metal's too thick," replied McBride. "But the carpet will dull the noise. Just do your end of the job, and leave me to this."

Like a giant tin-opener, the shears took another gnawing bite at the metal, another, and another, cutting a jagged tear in the safe. The sound of each rip sent an involuntary shiver through the man on guard, but McBride continued his slow-steady progress, the rip lengthening into a curving arc, beginning to assume a circular shape.

And the cabin door banged open.

Outlined in the sudden, harsh light that flowed from the passage, Captain Vinator stood in the doorway, uniform coat over his pyjamas, a large revolver in one hand. He ordered, "Get your hands up . . . move now." The gun was pointing squarely at McBride. Slowly, seemingly reluctantly, McBride obeyed, the officer stepped forward . . . and crumpled like a pole-axed bullock as Flick, stepping from concealment behind the door, smashed him behind the ear with a short length of lead piping using every ounce of strength in his wiry body. The gun thudded on the carpet. The captain, slipping like a slow-motion mechanism, followed it seconds later to lie face down in a twisted heap.

Flick pounced on the revolver and, giving the unconscious man a casual kick in passing, peered out the door.

"All clear," he reported. "But for God's sake get a move on, Con."

Years of nerve-hardening experience showing in every deliberate move, McBride took up the shears again and recommenced his slow, steady snipping. At last the curving cut passed the three-quarter mark in its circular path and neared completion. One more bite at the metal, and the shears were laid aside in favour of a heavy jemmy. McBride forced the bar's wedge-shaped edge into the cut metal, and heaved. The plate yielded a little. Again . . . the large, saucer-shaped section began to fold outwards. Twice more . . . and McBride, swiftly now but every muscle under steel-like control, slid a gloved hand through the hole, the jagged metal edge scraping his bared wrist in the process. His questing fingers, searching blindly, touched a small hard box, seized it and brought it out. Only the slightest of quivers revealing his eager excitement, he flicked open the box's catch . . . and a chunky set of diamond clips and ear-rings sparkled rainbow-like in the lamplight. Into the safe again went his hand, found a larger box and dragged it out. Two other morocco leather boxes, a bundle of papers and three tiny ring cases were scooped out in quick succession by his questing hand. Satisfied, he shoved the various articles into his coat pocket, gathered up the tool kit, methodically fastened its straps with as little emotion as a plumber who had repaired a burst pipe, then rose from his knees, grunting at the twinge of cramped muscles.

"How about him?" he asked, nodding towards the man lying sprawled at the doorway.

"Away with the fairies for hours. All

finished? Then let's get the hell out o' this place." Flick, 'borrowed' gun in hand, led the way out of the cabin and down the nearby companionway. "Jacko'll have his nails chewed off to the elbows waiting on us," he chuckled to McBride.

"Waiting's often worse than the actual job," nodded McBride. "But button up the talk till we get clear. We're not off yet."

As Nicholas Malahne explained to the police in great and growing detail later, only the fact that he was suffering from a touch of indigestion and as a result was in a very light sleep resulted in him waking at such a fantastic hour. For the first few moments the American producer lay "as if wrapped up in a big woolly cloud" then, as he reluctantly became more conscious, realized his awareness of the faint, regular thudding noise above his head. He switched on the bed light, glanced at the clock on the little table—nearly half past four. What on earth was that sound overhead?

He lay for a couple of minutes, becoming more puzzled and annoyed than ever at the noise above. Then, "needing to rise anyway," still slightly peeved at his wakening, Malahne got up, pulled on his dressing-gown and opened the cabin door. Tightening the cord round his waist, he began to walk along the passage. "Then I heard these voices, and stopped—why I didn't go forward, I'll never know, but" —with a distinct shiver—"am I glad I didn't!"

The voices, low-pitched, came from somewhere above, and he heard the sound of feet coming down the nearby companionway . . . no, it was the companionway flight from the captain's quarters and the "den" leading down to the main deck above his head. A screen door creaked open, and quietly shut.

"I was just plain nosey," he admitted. "I always have been, and I guess I always will be." Malahne climbed the companionway steps and stood, hesitating, on the landing. "I was going to go back to my cabin, but then I thought maybe Dwyatt was up and about above, and that something might be wrong—and frankly, I felt I could use a drink." So he went up the next flight of steps. Straight ahead of him, the door of the den lay open. "I really got curious then," Malahne explained to the police long hours later. "I'd never seen that door lying open unless Dwyatt was inside." He went to knock on the opened door—and practically fell over the outstretched legs of the captain's unconscious form. Kneeling, he peered at the man, and gulped a shaky breath as the light from the passage showed a trickle of blood running from the officer's scalp down across his face.

"My stomach looped the loop for a moment, then I nipped down the stairs, straight to Dwyatt's cabin, and thumped on the door."

Ronaldson, sleepy-eyed, came to the door in a few moments. "What on earth's the matter, Nicholas?" he yawned, rubbing his face with one hand.

"Something serious—real trouble. The captain's lying up in your den with his head stove in. And I heard a couple of characters going out on deck."

Ronaldson turned pale and snapped suddenly awake. "Julie's jewels. It's a stick-up . . ." He disappeared into the cabin, and re-emerged with his dressing-gown over pyjamas and a small automatic in his hand. "Wake up some of the others," he commanded.

Malahne rapped on cabin doors while Ronaldson went back into his state-room and, answering his wife's anxious questions with a brief "Trouble, honey—but we'll handle it, don't worry . . ." began feverishly working the little intercom telephone by his bedside, stabbing one button after another on the little panel beside it.

"First officer? Ronaldson here . . . something's happened to the captain. There are prowlers aboard. Get up and rouse all the others near you. Then get on deck fast." He repeated the message to the chief steward and the bosun, emphasizing the need for caution until they were ready to strike. In a very few moments after he replaced the phone a score of men were awake aboard the yacht, tired, bewildered, but willing to help. Ronaldson, leading the passenger party, waved towards the companionway. "Let's go . . . and be careful. These guys are dangerous. Johnson, you stay and guard my wife and the other ladies, will you, pal? Hendricks, see what you can do for the captain." He set off, followed by Malahne and three others, one of them Jonathan Russell, who had been among the last to answer the knocking on the cabin doors. Russell had finally emerged with flannels pulled on over his pyjama trousers, still struggling into a jersey . . . the same outfit which he had hurriedly shed when he reached his cabin a short time before.

There was an even colder nip in the air than before when Flick and McBride reached the main deck, and it was a shivering Jacko who materialized by their side. "Got the stuff?" he asked eagerly.

"The lot," confirmed McBride. "Let's bring Sailor in right away. We had to crown the captain, and I don't want to stay a second longer than necessary."

"The boats aboard are fixed," twinkled Jacko. "Two of them anyway . . . the boss said I needn't bother with the other. If they try coming after us they won't get far. I cut the plug leads to the engines."

"Call that ruddy launch in," pleaded Flick. "Somebody might find that bloke I slugged."

"There's not much chance of that . . .

take it easy," calmed McBride, taking out his torch and flashing a long, steady beam out to sea, swinging it slowly backwards and forwards. In almost immediate response there was the faint sound of an engine from not far distant, a muffled burbling from the still invisible craft. McBride continued to wave the lamp, guiding the boat, and gave a sigh of relief as the vague shape of the *Tina* became visible, coming in smoothly towards them.

Then, at the height of their relief, they saw the sudden glow of light fan on to the sea from port-holes beneath them, sensed as much as heard a hum of voices—and saw other lights begin to flick on in various parts of the yacht.

"The whole ruddy ship's waking," snapped Jacko. "Give Sailor the hurry-up sign—quickly, Con, or we've had our lot."

The safe-cracker began to flick the lamp on and off rapidly, holding it steady—and instantly the engine of the approaching launch rose to a full-throated bellow and a phosphorescent wake began to dance round the launch as, answering their appeal, its coxswain banged the throttle full open. In it roared, phantom shape quickly firming in outline.

"Down the ladder now, Con," urged Jacko. "Stick by the drill . . . you've got the haul on you, you're most important of the three of us."

McBride didn't stop to argue. Encumbered by the boxes stuffed in his deep pockets, his tool kit hanging by its strap round one shoulder, he began to climb awkwardly down the rope ladder, which swayed at the impact of his shifting weight. The launch was still coming in fast, still on full throttle. Jacko had just put his feet on the top rungs of the ladder, following McBride when, almost simultaneously, two small groups of men boiled on to the deck from different doorways. As they spotted the activity at the ladder, they raised a shout, and came racing forward. An intelligently-minded radio operator, wakened in his bunk off the radio room seconds before, tripped a switch—and the ship's deck lighting blazed on, illuminating the whole scene in a harsh, artificial glare.

Down at sea level, where McBride hung waiting and helpless on the bottom rungs of the rope ladder, the launch engine bellowed to a new crescendo as Sailor jammed the gear lever into reverse. The propeller churned the water to foam and slowed the launch as if powerful brakes had been jammed on. Her helmsman swung the wheel over, to bring her beam beautifully in to rub, almost stationary, along the yacht's plating.

While Jacko began a mad downward scramble and McBride half-fell on to the swaying deck of the launch, up above them a frantic Flick fired the revolver he had taken from the yacht's captain, fired low into the nearest bunch of men. A seaman howled and fell, a bullet in his leg, and Flick swung the revolver's muzzle up to body level, shouting as he did, "Stay where you are . . . don't come closer." The men slowed in their stride, and the little Glasgow tough backed towards the ladder, still swinging the gun in a menacing arc. "Just comin' boys," he shouted over his shoulder.

Ronaldson, manoeuvring desperately beside his companions in an effort to get a clear line of fire, saw his chance, and squeezed the trigger of his automatic. The bullet hit Flick in the shoulder, almost knocking him off balance, burning a searing needle of pain through flesh and muscle . . . and as he staggered, the vengeful men lunged forward in a mass and were on top of him. Strong hands seized his gun arm as, kicking wildly and struggling impotently, he went down helpless before their numbers.

At the roar of triumph above, Jacko made a desperate backward leap off the ladder, plummeted down the several feet that remained, and, more by luck than judgement, smashed down on the roof of the launch cabin. Engine rising to brutal peak revs, the *Tina* bolted from the ship's side.

Ronaldson, fighting mad, ran to the *Cockatoo*'s rail and fired wildly after the fast-moving boat heading so desperately away. At last the gun clicked, the magazine clip exhausted. With a last howl of blasphemous rage, he spun round to Flick, surrounded by a rapidly growing group as more members of the crew came scrambling up on deck.

"Where's the radio man—get on your set and contact the coastguards," their owner ordered. "Jorgens, get the boats out . . . take the twenty-two footer after that goddam' launch. Send someone ashore in the other to warn the cops and bring a doc . . ."

Peter Hendricks, a young American Embassy official from London, the man who had been sent to look after the unconscious captain, reappeared on deck. Worried and anxious, he told them, "Vinator is still unconscious. He looks badly hurt. And, say Mr. Ronaldson, the back's cut right out of your safe, heck knows how but it looks like a sardine tin."

"Then they've got away with a fortune —all Julie's stuff," despaired Ronaldson, his fingers raking through his hair in a nervous mind-racking gesture, stunned reaction overtaking him. But at least one member of his crew still had ideas. From the bridge deck, the *Cockatoo*'s searchlight blinked on, and its brilliant eye swept across the waves to pin on the fast-retreating launch. The fresh sight of the boat broke the American's momentary trance.

"Get a move on with those boats," he howled. "Where's that goddam' night guard anyway . . . what was he doing all the time this was goin' on?"

"Just found him, sir," reported a steward. "Tied and gagged in the deck shelter. He's conscious. Says he was hammering with his feet on the deck, but couldn't do anything else."

"That's what I must have heard," gasped Malahne. "That's the noise that woke me up."

"What about those boats," shouted Ronaldson again.

"No use, sir," hailed a seaman from the after deck. "Someone's knocked out both engines. We'll swing the lifeboat out, though. It hasn't been touched."

"That tub . . . it won't get near them. Oh, hell, lower it anyway, and I'll send it ashore," ordered the owner. "The coast-guard will be warning the cops now, anyway, if the radio message is through."

He turned to the captive. Flick was a sorry looking sight, face a mixture of fear and defiance, blood seeping from his shoulder while he watched the sailor he had shot being helped below.

"Where are your pals heading for?" demanded Ronaldson.

"Get stuffed," snarled Flick. "You won't find them."

"Why don't we shove him in the lifeboat and take him ashore to the police," suggested Jonathan Russell, who had a firm hold of the prisoner's jacket. "They'll take him off your hands, and maybe squeeze some information out of him."

"Good idea," agreed the American. "At least we've got one of the rats."

"I'll go along with him," volunteered Russell. "I've got a gun, that'll ensure him behaving." During the general bustle of the next few minutes as the lifeboat was lowered, Flick found himself with only Russell by his side.

"Boss . . ." he muttered.

"Shut up," hissed Russell. "Play along just now." Then, in a louder voice as a seaman approached, "Your friends won't get far, you'll see . . ."

"Boat's ready, sir," saluted the sailor. "Want any help with this runt?"

"I'll watch him," thanked the Englishman. "Come on you . . . and no tricks." Gun ready, he marched the wounded man to the ladder, at the foot of which the motor lifeboat was waiting, two of the yacht's crew aboard. "Down the ladder," he barked, as Ronaldson watched approvingly.

"My arm's sore," whined Flick.

"Get down, or I'll throw you down."

The Scot made a painful, clawing one-handed descent and was pulled aboard the boat in none too gentle fashion. Russell clambered down after him, with a last shout to Ronaldson, "I'll be back as soon as I can get a doctor." He nodded to the crewmen and the lifeboat began to plod towards the nearest pier, lying almost a mile along the shore. One seaman was at the engine hatch in the middle of the boat, the other at the tiller at the stern. Russell and Flick sat side by side in the bow thwarts.

The noise of the engine was sufficient to drown their conversation from the others, and as the boat left the pool of light surrounding the yacht the darkness became a thick cloak.

"You'll need to get me out o' this, Mr. Russell," pleaded Flick in a desperate mumble. "If you don't, ah'll carry the can for the lot . . . you're not really going to hand me over to the cops, are you?"

"Did Con get the stuff?" parried Russell.

"Aye, he got it . . . but we had to thump the captain. He tried to jump us . . . but what are you going to do about me, that's what ah want to know. Don't think ah'm daft enough to let you pull such a ruddy trick as throw me to the polis."

"Get a grip of yourself, you fool. I'm thinking of a way."

"It's no' ma fault ah'm here," the Scot whined. "It's yours, that's why you'll need to help me—and ah'm no kiddin' about what'll happen if you don't."

"What the hell do you mean it's my fault?"

"That patrolman woke the others up. If you'd bashed him properly he'd have stayed out, and ah wouldn't have been caught and ended up wi' this bullet in my shoulder."

Russell sat silent for a moment, while the lifeboat headed nearer to the shore. The man by his side would crack under any strong police pressure, it was obvious, and that would spell disaster. He injected a friendlier note into his voice as he replied,

"There's only one way out, Flick. We'll have to grab this boat if you're to escape. That means changing all our plans, but we'll have to do it. The police are almost bound to be heading for the shore now, and once we step on that pier your chances are nil. Don't argue now—get to your feet and pretend to struggle with me. One of the men is bound to come up to help, and we'll overpower him. Then we can force the other to turn the boat and land us farther up the coast. On your feet . . . *now!*"

He half shoved Flick up off the seat, and at the same time cried out, "He's trying to get away . . . help me."

Flick, playing his part, seized Russell by the arms and started to wrestle, grunting with pain as a needle of agony jarred through his injured shoulder.

Seeing the two shadowy figures swaying perilously in the bows and hearing Russell's shout, the man at the engine scrambled forward to help, his mate staying at the tiller, watching anxiously. As the man approached, Russell, lips close to Flick's ear, muttered, "Let go my arm."

99

And as the seaman came near, just a vague figure in the dark, Jonathan Russell, his gun-hand freed, coldly and deliberately swung his pistol barrel in a short chopping stroke which took Flick hard behind the left ear. Then, with another loud shout, he half-pulled half-pushed Flick's collapsing body over the thwart and followed him into the sea. There was a tremendous splash as the two men hit the water. Even as it died, the sailor clattered back to the engine-hatch.

"Swing her hard to port, for God's sake," he called to his mate. "They're both overboard." The lifeboat had too much way on her to stop, their best plan was to come round and drift down towards the men, who were already astern.

Russell, chilled to the bone by his sudden immersion, trod water as the life-boat turned, howled for help . . . and firmly, remorselessly, held Flick's head under water. "Over here," he yelled as the lifeboat, handicapped by the darkness, came floundering round. As it neared, he let Flick slide from his grasp, the limp head disappearing below the water, a last few bubbles of air coming from the slack mouth, body turning slowly over. Russell took a few smooth breaststrokes away, then, as the boat came alongside, gave a fair imitation of a panicking man, thrashing the water, making it amazingly difficult for the two men trying to pull him aboard. Finally they dragged his dripping figure out of the sea, and he lay gasping on the planking, water streaming from his clothes.

"Where's the other fellow, sir?" pleaded one rescuer. "We can't see more than a few feet in this ruddy darkness."

"Out—there—somewhere out—there . . . couldn't hold him," he said, between deep sighing gulps of air.

The lifeboat circled round the spot, its crew peering at the water. But nothing could be seen except the short, white-crested waves. As they watched, a new difficulty began . . . snow, quiet, gentle, hardly discernible in its first few flakes, but growing within seconds both in size and quantity, until the air seemed filled with lazy drifting balls of cotton.

"That snow finishes it. Not a chance, Rube," said the man at the tiller, shaking his head. "Let's get the hell towards the shore. This snow's been hanging around all night in these clouds . . . and, boy, look how thick it's falling now."

Russell, now shivering violently in his wet, icy-cold clothes, found a white covering building up rapidly around him as the lifeboat swung back on course, heading towards the pier. As they neared it, two cars were drawing to a halt on the roadway beside it, headlights bright but blurred by the thickening snowfall.

"What'll it do to the roads?" he asked himself. "Will it be heavy enough to block them? Surely to God nothing else can go wrong . . . but if the roads are blocked, and the car can't get through?"

There was little acting in the shaky way he climbed out of the boat and up the pier ladder, to be helped on to the planked surface by a brawny, sympathetic police constable.

5

DAWN had just been a grey hint in the velvet dark sky when the police-car had left Glasgow on the road to Gourock harbour. But now, though clouds still dulled the day, a long stretch of the white-mantled Argyll hills was spread to view as the British Railways car ferry *Arran* busily churned its way across the Firth of Clyde to Dunoon. Their Sunbeam snugly tucked in the "park" 'tween decks, the two men gazed out through the lazy, slowing snowfall from their stance at the little ship's boat deck rail.

"Reminds me a little of back home, round about Saint John," mused Detective-Inspector Bill Wilson as he leaned against the snow-crusted rail. "It's colder over there at this time of the year. In fact," his eyes twinkled, "back in Canada the temperature falls so low that in the real winter the sea freezes over. We just run a railroad track across it and use trains instead of ships." He grinned encouragingly at the figure by his side. "Come on, Sergeant, cheer up . . ."

Rab Kearns, Detective-Sergeant, Glasgow CID, shivered inside his heavy overcoat, buried his chin deeper into his thick woollen scarf, and grunted his misery.

"I wasn't built for this sort of weather, sir," he complained. "Give me a nice warm fireside any winter's day and you can keep your open air. If I thought the Chief would wear it I'd apply for a transfer to Hawaii or somewhere like that . . ." He envied the other man's obvious enjoyment of the wintry scene around them. Detective-Inspector Wilson, thirty-four years of age, Headquarters "trouble squad", Glasgow CID, was a tall, slim Scots-Canadian who had inherited his blue eyes from his emigrant father and a strong beaked nose and high cheekbones from a distant Indian relative on his Canadian mother's tangled family tree.

A lightweight military-style raincoat, worn over a single-breasted tweed sports suit, and a light grey snap-brim soft hat set off the Canadian's lean appearance to advantage. Rab Kearns could picture him in a more picturesque costume, moving on snow-shoes across his native Canadian forest land—and shivered at the very thought.

Rab, small for a policeman and plump, forty-three years of age, with thinning grey hair, blue pin-stripe suit and homburg hat, looked more like an insurance clerk than a policeman who had spent several years learning his job the hard way, patrolling one of the toughest beats in Glasgow's Gallowgate. One day long past his Superintendent had discovered that Rab Kearns had a peculiar gift for remembering faces. He had been transferred to the CID—and soon the underworld had good reason to know his strange talent. For that reason, when Bill Wilson was first ordered to Dunoon in answer to a request for assistance from the local police, who were concerned about their coming watch on the Ronaldson Clan ball, he had almost automatically asked for Kearns as his aide.

Wilson had "bought" the assignment because some Headquarters executive decided that a Canadian would probably get on more smoothly with the American chief than a homegrown police officer. And Bill Wilson, in turn, had decided that if any man could spot the odd rogue among the crowds milling the resort during the clan gathering celebrations, that man was Rab Kearns.

"A different sort of job now, eh Rab?" said Wilson, brushing snow off his coat and retiring to the shelter of the companionway which led down towards the wide garage where their Sunbeam waited. "Robbery, attempted murder and a few other things, from what I could gather in that phone call that dragged me out of bed. I didn't think I'd be getting up till now . . . and here we are, just about at Dunoon.

"This car ferry service is a pretty wonderful thing, when you think of it. Going the long way round by road would have taken us another couple of hours or so . . . and I wouldn't fancy it in this snow."

"Don't they drive in the snow in Canada then, sir?" poked his sergeant, slightly cheered by the warmth rising up the companion way. He ducked the playfully aimed punch, and went on in a more

106

serious vein, "What'll be the drill when we land? Any idea, sir?"

"Not yet. The police down here should have a full list of the stuff taken—£70,000 worth, near enough—and there's an insurance company watch-dog down here who'll probably be in full mourning over the claim he's been landed with. Say, we'd better get to the car now, the ship should be at the pier in a few more minutes."

Even as they entered the Sunbeam they could hear the tinkle of the engine-room end of the ship's telegraph, then a slight bump as the *Arran* "kissed" the pier, followed by a quiet broken only by a hum as her diesel electrics ticked over.

At the far end of the car-space deck a gate slapped open. Kearns started the police-car and edged it forward, close behind a butcher's van and a small Ford saloon, the only other vehicles on that early-morning crossing. All three manoeuvred on to the lift platform, and seconds later the metal "deck" began its upward path. A ramp slid down, thumped against the pier, and one of the ferry crew waved the vehicles ashore. As the Sunbeam bumped across on to the heavy planks, a young policeman walked from the shelter of the pier waiting-room and peered in the passenger window of the car to ask, "Glasgow CID, sir?"

"Right," nodded Wilson.

In a soft Highland accent the policeman —little more than a lad, reflected Wilson —said, "Superintendent Melvin has sent me down to meet you. He will be waiting at the police-station. I'll show you the way if you're ready."

"Jump in," agreed Wilson, swinging the rear door open. "Tell Sergeant Kearns the road, will you?"

The constable guided their car the short distance from pier to police station, along silent streets. Tartan banners erected in anticipation of the day hung limp and snow-flecked from lamp-posts and across buildings, the still dozing resort's almost only indication of the celebrations due to begin in a few hours. Parking the Sunbeam, Wilson and Kearns followed their guide through the main office of the small, grey stone police station and waited as he tapped on a glass-panelled door. At an answering bark from within, he opened the door, announced, "The Glasgow detectives, sir," then stood back to allow Wilson and the sergeant to enter.

Detective-Superintendent Melvin, senior CID officer in the area, rose from the desk at which he was seated and came towards them, a pleased look on his wind-beaten face, a burly figure in a light brown Harris tweed suit and dark brown boots.

"Reinforcements," he growled, "and we can certainly use you." He shook hands with them, then, glancing round the room, ordered, "Lachie, two chairs from somewhere."

Constable MacLeod appeared within seconds with the chairs and hesitantly asked. "Would you like me to be getting some tea, sir?"

"Damn good idea, lad," boomed the superintendent. "We'll get you in the CID yet with that outlook on life."

As MacLeod retired and the two men shed their coats and sat down, Melvin rumbled on, "Ever think how far the police would get without cups of tea? Sheer ruddy anarchy would be let loose around most places if there was no 'char' to keep us going. But let's get down to business. You and the sergeant know why you are here?"

"Originally yes, Superintendent. Now, I'm a bit puzzled as to our role," admitted Bill Wilson. "I could see the reason when we were to help as watch-dogs, but now that the main attraction has gone . . ." He shrugged his shoulders.

"Now that the main attraction as you call it has gone we need you more than ever," emphasized the superintendent. "Right now I wish that ruddy Yank had parked his yacht off some other county—any other so-and-so county.

"Ah, here's the tea. Fine, Lachie, and Heavens, the man's got some toast too. You'll make some lassie a fine husband, if you don't watch out."

Constable MacLeod blushed crimson for the second time and made a flustered retreat from the room.

"Where was I," continued the superintendent. "Oh yes. I don't believe in the wooden-headed attitude you get in other parts that it's an admission of incompetence to ask for help. You know without me telling you it's just as bad down in England when it comes to the local men letting Scotland Yard get a sniff. But I'm interested in catching crooks, not defending our honour." He took a long gulp of tea, and went on, "I know quite a little bit about you and Sergeant Kearns. To start with, Inspector, you're Canadian, aren't you?"

Wilson nodded. "Came over with the Black Watch of Canada during the war," he explained. "I couldn't settle when I was demobbed back in New Brunswick, so I joined the RCMP, the Mounties. Then I thought I'd come back and see Scotland again, and, well, that was a good few years ago, and I'm still here."

"From what I gather, you've helped put away a lot of the top boys in the robbery rackets . . . and as for your sergeant," Melvin turned. "Who's Spider Newson?" he barked.

"Victor Newson, alias Spider. He's got a Criminal Record Office number, was born in Liverpool, and he's at present serving six years for razor assault. Five previous convictions, I think. Tall, blond, weak mouth."

"We've heard about you," nodded the Argyllshire man. "That's a pretty handy gift of memory you have. Anyway, back to the *Cockatoo* . . . that's the name of the yacht. All hell's broken loose. I was just checking these rough statements when you came in.

"Briefly, a smooth bunch of operators boarded the yacht last night, opened the safe, heaven knows how, and got away with a cool £68,000 of jewels. They coshed the night guard, who managed to give the warning later on. They also smashed the captain over the head . . . the poor devil's still unconscious . . . and slightly wounded a member of the crew in the leg as they got away."

"Got away, sir?" queried Wilson. "Any idea which direction?"

"Not the slightest. They jumped aboard this motor boat and took off into the snowstorm in it. Coastguard stations and Lord knows how many police are watching for the boat turning up, but the odds are they have already run it ashore somewhere, and are well on their way to a nice safe burrow."

"The phone message I got said that one was caught," reminded Wilson. "Is there no lead there, sir?"

"There might be—if we still had him. He was being brought ashore with a bullet in his shoulder when he struggled with his guard the pair fell in, and only the guard was pulled out of the drink. Either he swam ashore, or he'll appear floating on his face in about a week or so when the stomach gases work up enough—sorry, Sergeant, forgot about your eating."

"What do you want us to do then, sir?" asked Wilson. "We'll pitch in and help in any way you want."

"First, come out with me and see the owner at the yacht. Then just prowl around as you please. Frankly, nothing like this has happened around here for generations, and our technique may be rusty on some points. I'll assign one of my men to you, to help you find your way around. In fact, how about young MacLeod? Lachie's born and bred around here, can natter away in Gaelic if needs be, and he's a keen lad. I take it you don't mind a uniform man tagging along?"

"Not in the least," thanked Wilson. "I'll keep in close touch with you, of course. When do you want to go out to the yacht, sir?"

"Right now, I think. They'll all be up and about, even though it's only 7.30 a.m. From what I gather, the whole yacht's been at panic stations since the trouble began. I've been out already, of course, and some of my men are still at work aboard her.

"And there's still this clan gathering. What's going to happen to it is anybody's guess. If they postpone it, an awful lot of people are going to be disappointed. They've been wandering into Dunoon for days now . . . even though some of them are about as Highland as Paddy McGinty's goat."

The superintendent's Jaguar leading, Wilson's Sunbeam trailing it, they set off a few minutes later, the two cars churning through the slush-covered streets, windscreen wipers slapping fresh snow off their glass. In the Sunbeam, Constable MacLeod, beaming with delight at his assignment, sat erect in the rear seat.

Keen as mustard, grinned Wilson. And he marvelled at the willing way in which the superintendent in the car ahead had taken the Glasgow men into his fold. Some other county bosses, he reflected, would rather have committed *hara-kiri*.

"Nearly there now, sir," said the constable. "Chust round this bend in the road, and we'll be at the slipway. One of the yacht's boats will be waiting . . . there has been a fair bit of coming and going all these last few hours, and they've been operating a taxi service to the shore."

"When did the *Cockatoo* arrive here, son?" asked Wilson.

"About ten days back, sir. She has been lying moored out in the Firth ever since. Goodness, this snow coming on top of the robbery will fairly spoil the gathering."

"Interested in it?"

"Aye, in a way, sir. My mother's mother was a Ronaldson, you see, which gives me a kind of personal link."

Concentrating at the wheel, Kearns spoke with the inborn contempt of a Lowland Scot for his Highland cousins. "I never could fathom the way you Highlanders go crazy over this sort of family party. You'd think you were all still running about the heather with bare feet and claymores."

"Never mind the sergeant," grinned

Wilson. "He comes from Ayrshire—and he's never got over the fact that his great-great-grandmother had a pass made at her by Rabbie Burns."

The Jaguar slowed, and pulled into the pavement opposite a small concrete slipway, and the Sunbeam came in behind it. A neat crimson-painted launch was bobbing beside the slip, and the little party of police headed towards it. "This is one of the boats that the gang put out of action before they left," commented Superintendent Melvin. "Simple job—they just cut through the plug leads, easy enough to fix, but it took long enough to allow the boat they were in to get clear away."

Within a minute the launch was cast off and headed out across the water. Salt spray slushed the snow almost as quickly as the white crystals landed on the boat, and Wilson watched fascinated as fresh "suicide squads" of flakes drifted down to the wood even as their fellows melted.

"There's the *Cockatoo* now," pointed Melvin. "Nice piece of work, isn't she . . . must cost a tidy packet to run."

The slim shape of the *Cockatoo*, cream-coloured, with a vivid crimson funnel, raked bow and flowing superstructure, lay quietly at anchor, the Stars and Stripes fluttering from her stern, no one visible on her decks. But the approaching boat had been seen, and someone must have turned a pair of binoculars on the launch's occupants. As the detectives came up the last steps of the lowered gangway, Ronaldson appeared at its head to meet them. Nodding to the superintendent, he greeted Wilson with a rueful grin, then suggested. "Let's go to my 'den'. The doctor's just finishing his examination of my captain in the next cabin."

They followed him along passageways and up companion ladders, the cream and crimson colour scheme everywhere in evidence, until Ronaldson stopped, opened a door, and announced, "Here we are—the scene of the crime. Come and see the only safe in the world with a back made of butter." Inside the cabin, the first mate of the *Cockatoo* was talking to a sparsely built civilian, while a police sergeant waited patiently by the door. The ship's officer turned as Ronaldson entered.

"Doctor Grant wants to take the captain

ashore, sir," he said. "OK to get it organized?"

"Go right ahead," agreed Ronaldson. "How is he, Doc?"

Doctor Grant, a worried look on his face, chose his words slowly and carefully as he replied, "I've made the captain as comfortable as possible, and of course, I can't be sure of anything until we get some head X-rays taken. But he appears to have a serious multiple fracture of the skull and possible brain injury. Still unconscious, of course. I want to get him ashore and on to an ambulance, then pack him straight off to Glasgow. Our own resources aren't enough for this kind of injury, and he really needs to be seen as quickly as possible by a brain specialist. No police objections, I presume?"

"None whatever," said Melvin. "He hasn't said anything—even a rambling word or two?"

"Not a peep. And he may not regain consciousness for a week—maybe longer."

"Maybe not at all, Doc?" asked Wilson.

"Mphh . . . that, I'm afraid, can't be ruled out. You never can tell with head injuries. But he's got a reasonable pulse, a pretty strong physique . . . I'd be inclined to say he'll pull through, though he'll be on the danger list for a long time."

"Poor devil," muttered Ronaldson. "Heck, Superintendent, haven't you any word of where these rats have melted to? Surely that goddam boat can't just disappear?"

"There's no report so far, I'm afraid. But we'll find it soon enough, don't worry. They've got to come ashore somewhere. Remember, within a ten mile radius of here there are probably a hundred miles of coastline, between lochs and inlets. The land around is a map-maker's nightmare. Right now, however, Mr. Wilson and I would like to have another look around . . . finger-print men finished yet, Sergeant?"

"Just about, sir," nodded the uniform man. "They're asking the guests and crew to give their 'dabs' right now so that they can be crossed off. But I gather they think this boy wore gloves."

"Is this finger-print business really essential, Superintendent?" queried Ronaldson. "Heck, we all want to help, but it's pretty miserable when the ladies are being lined up in this way."

"Sorry, sir, but if we do find any prints, we want to know if they *should* be there. That's the only way we can isolate any 'foreign' prints . . . and your guests can always refuse to help. While we're at it, maybe Inspector Wilson's got some questions. As I told you, he's down from Glasgow, and he's co-operating in the case."

"Sure. You know, Inspector, from your accent I'd say you are darned near as far away from your home town as I am."

"I was born and bred in the Maritimes," agreed Wilson.

"Well, fire ahead," urged Ronaldson, offering cigarettes from a plain gold case. "English on the left side—Chesterfields on the right. Sorry I can't offer you Sweet Caporals, Inspector, but maybe we can rise to a slug of Canadian rye later on."

Wilson grinned, waited until he had accepted a light for his cigarette, let a trickle of smoke slide from his nostrils, then, cocking his head a little to one side, said, "OK . . . but I'm pretty sure you won't be happy at what I ask. Will you draw up a full list of guests aboard and just when you met them and why they are aboard? And I'd like you to detail the first mate to do the same for the crew."

"What in hell's name for?"

"From the reports the superintendent's shown me this smells of an inside job. Someone aboard must have helped this gang, and the watchman seems reasonably in the clear."

"That's plain crazy," protested Ronaldson. "Most of the crew have been with me since I took over the yacht, some were even aboard with the last owner. My guests . . . why, it's stoopid. I can vouch for every one of them, and I assure you, Inspector, I'm reckoned to have my full allocation of marbles."

"I told you you wouldn't be happy. But you want your wife's jewels back . . ."

"You bet your life he does," cut in a voice from the cabin doorway. Julie Ronaldson, in a tailored grey wool dress, a patterned silk scarf at her throat, her long dark hair pulled back and piled in curls on her head, stepped into the cabin. "Dwyatt and I will do all we can to help . . . won't we, honey? And if these gentlemen want the low-down on our friends, then they must have a pretty good reason for asking . . . even though I think they're wrong myself. Is there any word about the captain, Dwy?"

"Pretty bad, I'm afraid," said her husband. "The doc's taking him ashore and then to hospital. He's in pretty bad shape."

"And the little guy that got away from Jonathan? Found him yet?"

Superintendent Melvin shook his head.

"Thank God Jonathan's OK anyway," sighed Julie. "If he had been drowned over all this, I would never have forgiven myself after us dragging him up the way we did."

"Jonathan?" queried Bill Wilson. "One of your party, Mrs. Ronaldson, isn't he?"

"That's right," answered her husband. "He's a guy we met on the plane coming over. We hit it off together in a big way, and I invited him up for a break from business . . . he's got an import-export outfit in London." He went on, "Look, honey, these cops want to pad about for a spell. Let's leave them to it, huh? Oh, and say, Superintendent, we've got some breakfast coming up real soon. Could your boys use some food?"

"Aye, not a bad idea," agreed Melvin. "Just a wee snack though, don't put yourself out."

As the door closed, Melvin turned to Wilson. "I'll just be off myself. Lachie can stay with you. Oh . . . and if you want me, I'll be prowling about the deck shelter where the guard was attacked, and then I'm going for another word with him. You may be right about there being someone aboard linked up with this . . . and I'm just hoping it isn't one of this American's pals. They read like a VIP list." He wrinkled his nose at the thought, and marched off, followed by the uniform sergeant.

"So this is the safe," said Wilson, sliding off his coat and dumping it over a chair before moving over to the box in question. "Wow, take a look at the hole in the back. It's been ripped open like a sardine tin."

"Weakest point on a lot of them," agreed Sergeant Kearns. "I'd expect to find something better on a floating palace like this. That's a pretty old pattern."

"Wouldn't happen with the newest types," nodded Wilson.

"Ever seen anything like this before, Constable?" he asked MacLeod, who was waiting by the door of the cabin.

"No, sir . . . except for the time the Co-op grocery shop safe was blown open about six months ago. How did they do it, sir?"

"Damned if I know." Wilson stooped to peer closely at the mangled metal, which was still coated with grey finger-print powder from an earlier inspection. "Take a look at this, Rab. Isn't this a drill hole?"

"Aye," agreed his assistant. "That's how they started it, I'd say. But after that . . . it's pretty thick metal for anything in the normal line of cutters, and it hasn't been burned."

Wilson peered closer still. "Got a torch? There's a bit of shadow thrown here . . . ah, that's better." Lachie MacLeod had produced a small lamp from his overcoat pocket, and turned the beam on the metal back. "Lower a bit . . . that's it. See these ridged bite marks on the edges of the metal? That should help a bit." He prowled round the cabin for a moment or

124

two, then shook his head. "That's the lot, I'm afraid. Let's go and see how the super's getting on."

They located Melvin in the fo'c's'le, where the crew mess-room had been converted into a rough and ready hospital for its two patients, the night guard and the seaman who had been shot in the leg.

"This is Frank Boehmer, the seaman who was on guard last night," said Melvin. "He says he knows absolutely nothing. Everything was quiet, then he stepped outside the deck shelter and—wham!"

"Dat's right, bud," agreed Boehmer in a strong Bronx accent. "I'm just readin' my book and mindin' my business. Then I sets out to take a trip round the hulk— yacht I mean. And that's all I remember, till I wakes up trussed up like a Thanksgiving turkey. The only thing I kin do is smack the deck wid my feet."

"At least you woke someone up, and raised the alarm," consoled Wilson. "How's the head?"

"Like th' original lost week-end," groaned Boehmer. "If I ever get the ape that does this, I'll moider him."

Back on deck they went. The snow had

125

stopped, though grey clouds over to the north showed that other parts of the country were getting their share.

"Boehmer's in the clear, anyway," commented the superintendent. "He wouldn't have raised the ship the way he did if he had anything to do with it. Incidentally, the doctor's moving the captain ashore within the half-hour and has all the travel arrangements fixed. My men have drawn a blank as far as finger-prints are concerned, but from their interviews they've built up a hazy description of the fellow who jumped off the rope ladder and a pretty concrete picture of the man who was caught. I wonder where that one is," he sighed. "Floating somewhere out there, I suppose, giving the fish a fright. It would help a lot if we found him."

"Any chance of a word with this Mr. Russell who went into the drink with him?" queried Wilson.

"He's still aboard. They all are," said Melvin. "Oh-ho . . . this looks like breakfast," he added as a white-jacketed steward came towards them.

It was. Set out in a small day-cabin, a neat white tablecloth carried an array of

126

dishes. Melvin thanked the steward and asked him to pass on a message to Ronaldson, suggesting he bring Russell to meet them as soon as he was free. Then the superintendent made a bee-line for the nearest chair, the two Glasgow men following him. "Come on, Lachie," urged Melvin, seeing the constable hold back. "Pull in a chair and eat your fill. It's on the house . . . and you can tell your kids some day about having a meal at a millionaire's table."

"I'm no' married, sir," protested Lachie.

"What the blazes has that got to do with it—here, help yourself to some of these kidneys and bacon," suggested the superintendent, lifting the silver lid off a large dish and sniffing appreciatively.

Bill Wilson was trying hard to squeeze a last cup of black coffee—his third—from the almost dry pot when Ronaldson entered the cabin again, followed by a tall slim man in flannels and roll-neck sweater.

"Just finishing, Mr. Ronaldson, and many thanks," said Superintendent

Melvin, rising to his feet and wiping a linen napkin across his lips.

"Good. I've just been having some myself . . . only orange juice and coffee, diet drill stuff. This is the guy you asked about—Jonathan, meet the police, police, meet Jonathan Russell."

Outwardly calm, inwardly trying to guess the reason for the police wanting to see him, Russell gave a brief inclination of his head. Probably mere routine, he thought. Flick was out of the way. But the launch?

"What exactly do you want from me?" he asked in a quiet, pleasant tone. "If it's about the boat, I can't tell you very much, I'm afraid. The business was pretty grim" —he shook his head—"horrible, but it only lasted seconds. I can't help feeling sorry for that fellow, even though he tried to kill me."

"Tried to kill you, Mr. Russell? How do you make that out?" asked Wilson.

"When we went overboard," explained Russell patiently. "I'm sure he deliberately dragged me over when he realized he was falling . . . wanted to take me with him."

"How did it happen, anyway? Didn't

128

you volunteer for the job because you had a gun . . . incidentally, sorry to ask, but I suppose you do have a licence for it?"

"Of course I've a licence," answered Russell in indignant tones. "I carry the gun with me because I often have to take large sums of money around—business deals, you know, and not always in countries as er—normally well-ordered as England."

"Britain, Mr. Russell, Britain," murmured Melvin, good-naturedly. "Want to start a war describing this as England? Some Scots still regard England as a dirty name. Using it to describe Argyll! Why, you're as bad as the BBC. But we would just like to hear what happened in that wee boat—just for the record, you understand."

"I went over it pretty fully with the police who saw me earlier," frowned Russell, now sure that this was a routine inquiry. "Still," he rubbed a finger over his moustache, and went on, "This fellow was sitting beside me, complaining about the pain in his shoulder—where Dwyatt 'winged' him, you know, when these thieves were making their getaway—and frankly, I thought he really was feeling bad. I relaxed a little, just holding the gun loosely in my hand. Then next second he sprang at me, and tried to wrest the weapon from me. Obviously he wanted to try to get the gun, then force us to land him somewhere away from where the police would be waiting. Anyway, we struggled, and before either of the seamen could come to help he must have overbalanced. He gripped me, and"—he shrugged—"the rest you know."

"Can you describe the man at all, sir?"

"Medium build, dark hair," Russell shrugged again, in a way that Bill Wilson found instinctively antagonizing. "Nothing really outstanding, I'm afraid."

"The scar, Jonathan, the scar," interrupted Ronaldson. "Surely you remember that about him? High on his face, a nasty looking pucker of skin."

"Mm-yes," Russell agreed. "I'd forgotten about that. Frankly, I was too busy watching that he didn't move, to pay much attention to his actual appearance."

"We've tested the gun he used," revealed Melvin. "But unfortunately he was wearing gloves, like his friend." Then, changing the conversation, he asked, "Are you planning to go ahead with the Gathering, Mr. Ronaldson?"

"I'll need to," replied the American. "There isn't much of an option with all those folks waiting for me. The show begins in—let's see, it's 8.30 a.m. now— in exactly three hours. I've to lead a march of the clan round the local football ground, pipes, drums, kilts, the lot. At least the darned snow's nearly off—and you can take it from me this is going to be the world's fastest clan march—gallop twice round the pitch and then into the nearest hotel for a damn good drink to stop me from freezing!

"The only consolation, as far as I'm concerned, is that these guys in the launch will be having just as rough a time—if you haven't rounded them up by then, that is."

"We're doing our best, as I've told you," sighed the superintendent. "And I'll let you know the moment we do get word."

6

SNOW, deep, soft, drifting, made the lonely Highland glen an artist's delight, a Christmas card maker's dream—and a major disaster to Jacko Bright and Fat Harry. The latter cursed fluently, fiercely and ineffectually as, with sagging spirits, he gazed at the massive drift in which the nose of their Ford was buried.

"Knock it off, Harry," snapped Jacko. "That doesn't help. We're jinxed again, and we may as well face it. The road along there is covered by more than six feet of this stuff, judging by the way the telegraph poles are sticking out from it."

"Isn't there another road?" pleaded his companion.

"Not unless the map's started growing them. This is the third we've tried, and it's worse than the other two. You know how far we've come since we dumped the boys at the cottage? I'll tell you. Exactly eight miles. And do you know how long it's taken us? Damn nearly two hours. You've had that boat at Aberdeen. In fact, at this rate we'll be ruddy lucky to get back to the cottage—and that's what I intend doing as soon as we get this crate out of the snow."

"But the jewels . . ." protested Harry. "We've got to get them out today, or the whole time-table goes to pieces."

"It went to pieces the moment they caught Flick," sneered Jacko. "I just hope he isn't 'singing' his head off right now to the cops. Oh, he did his bit, all right, holding them back at the ladder. I wouldn't be here if he hadn't. But once Flick's caught, that's a different dish of fish. If he's 'grassed' the way I think he has, Russell's probably in a cell right now."

"You can trust Jonathan Russell at any rate," said Harry. "I'd stake my life on that."

"You may have to," countered Jacko. "If Flick hit anyone when he fired that shot we may be accessories to a murder charge right now."

"Then why go back to the cottage?"

"Because it's the only shelter we've got

around here," the little driver explained patiently. "And Flick didn't know where it was . . . none of us did except you and Russell. Come on, help me try to move the car."

They scraped and shovelled snow away from the car's nose and wheels with their hands until all sense of feeling seemed to vanish from their fingers, their feet numb, faces nipping in the rasping wind blowing through the glen. At last, hands red and raw, they stumbled back into the Ford and slammed the doors. Jacko, teeth chattering, fumbled to start the engine and slammed the heater control to maximum. For long, agonizing minutes they sat silent, holding their hands to the blast of hot air coming in under the dashboard, wincing as feeling gradually returned. Shivering violently, Harry produced a battered packet of cigarettes, and the two men lit the weeds and drew in the smoke in deep exhausted gulps.

"Well," sighed Jacko, "Let's get it over with."

Feeding the engine more accelerator, he slid the gear-lever into reverse and gently, slowly, let in the clutch until it was

engaging a shade, let it out a little more
. . . the car moved backwards an inch at
a time, one back wheel slipping for a
moment, then gripping the glassy surface
again. Gazing over his shoulder, one hand
on the wheel, all his skill concentrated in
balancing clutch and accelerator, Jacko
coaxed the Ford along. For half a mile
they crawled in reverse, following their
own tracks, through rock-fringed scenery
whose normal grim beauty was covered in
a white blanket. Only a few outcrops of
stone and the tips of stumpy gorse hinted
at its true nature. Twice the car's wheels
spun madly, twice its driver managed to
juggle with the delicate pressures required
to regain control.

Finally they reached a narrow road junction, marked by a stone dyke and the
wheel-treads of an earlier attempt they had
made to get clear of the glen. Thankfully,
Jacko swung the car round in it, and with
a feeling of relief headed the Ford forward,
back down the road towards the cottage—
the cottage from which they had crawled
away a long, long time ago.

The house lay to one side of a patch
of tall trees, a low-lying stone building,

smoke already drifting from its chimney. The Ford's engine noise travelled far in the quiet of the bare countryside, and long before it pulled up beside the little house their two companions were standing at the doorway, bewildered, worried by the unexpected return.

"Road's blocked," Jacko laconically reported. "Let me at that fire—and a nice stiff double rum for both of us, if you've any charity in your hearts."

"Blocked?" repeated Con McBride. "You can't get through?"

"Not unless you find Father Christmas's sledge and a couple of ruddy reindeer somewhere in the house," replied Jacko, shoving past him into the house. "No sense in going back the way we came either. The detour would add hours—if the road isn't blocked by now."

"What can we do then?" asked Sailor Travers. The seaman, nervously licking his lips, went on, "Can't we get in touch with Russell . . . can't we find out what's going on back at the *Cockatoo*?"

"Ask Harry," shrugged Jacko, crouching in front of the blazing hearth in the little living-room. McBride handed him a tumbler containing a good three fingers of rum, then, as he passed a similar dose to the other shivering traveller, demanded, "Come on, Harry, is there any way we can get in touch with Russell and let him know the spot we're in? Didn't you have any plan in mind? How was he to know that you got away from Aberdeen all right?"

"There was a plan," admitted Harry. "Just before I left for the boat, I was to hand an advertisement to Jacko . . ." he stopped as an unbelieving grin spread on McBride's face. "I mean it. It was a pre-arranged message, innocent enough, that would go in the small ads column of the *Daily Gazette*. Jacko was to have handed it in at the paper's Aberdeen office. It would have been in tomorrow's edition."

"And if you missed the boat?"

"Then there was another advertisement to go in."

"Even if we could get a message across in another advert, we couldn't get it to the newspaper. There's no phone around here," cut in Jacko. "While we're at it, where are the jewels, anyway?"

"My God—I left them out in the car,"

gasped the fat man, jumping out of the arm-chair in which he had been resting. "I'll be right back . . ." He left the room at a ponderous trot, an expression of such complete concern on his face that the three men, despite their individual fears, broke into high-pitched laughter, laughter as much expressing the strain and tension they had been under in the last few hours as their amusement at Harry's alarm.

Con McBride could recall only too well the way fortune had alternatively smiled and frowned at them during those last few hours. When their launch had churned away from the *Cockatoo*, he mused, the three men aboard had no time to spare for Flick's plight. Escape, from the wild shots being fired at them, from the lancing glare of the searchlight, was the sole concern.

Sailor had the throttle wide open, the palm of one hand beating a monotonous tattoo on the cockpit coaming as he muttered coaxing, blasphemous encouragement to his charge. McBride remembered how he had huddled grim and silent beside the seaman, eyes fixed on the widening gap between the two vessels.

Jacko, badly winded, more than a little bruised in his crazy backwards leap, still lay on his side on the cabin roof, breath coming in deep rasping gulps as he clung to the wood. The boat ducked on, dodging the light, being caught again in its hard brilliance, dodging once more by a savage turn to port, to finally lose the searching beam and gain the sweet shelter of the dark, a darkness mixed for the first time with sudden flurries of snow.

The flurries grew heavier, became drifting, blending clouds.

"Not much chance of them finding us in this," McBride had shouted above the engine roar. The helmsman, stony-faced, eased back the throttle to a quieter note before he answered.

"They won't find us. We're off the main channel now, heading up Loch Long. But it's going to be pretty rough for us too, trying to find the rendezvous. We'd better get Jacko down now—wait a minute and I'll help." He locked the steering-wheel, and, moving cautiously on the slippery deck, they quickly pulled the little Cockney down into the cockpit beside them.

"How do you feel, mate?" asked McBride.

"Ruddy—ruddy awful," gasped Jacko.

"Haul him into the cabin and make him lie down for a bit," advised Sailor. Head reeling, legs like rubber under him, Jacko made no protest as McBride slid a strong arm round him and helped him towards the narrow cabin hatchway.

"Might as well stay down there with him," said Travers. "I'll give you a shout when I need help. Just keep your fingers crossed—we're going to need some luck in this lot."

McBride gave a last glance towards the seaman, who had a white coating of snow gradually building up on his hair and shoulders, then helped Jacko through the hatchway. Stumbling in the dense blackness, he dragged the little man over to the bunk that lay along one side, and helped him on to it.

"Fag?" he asked.

"Thanks mate," replied Jacko. He was silent as the safeblower lit two cigarettes and handed one over. Then, "Gawd, what a wallop I took. They got Flick?"

"Uh huh. Last I saw they were swarming over him."

"Still got the stuff all right?"

"In my pockets," nodded McBride. "How about you? Any bones broken?"

Jacko gave a cautious wriggle, a soft "ouch" of pain, but answered, "Nope. Still in one piece, though I'll have a few beautiful bruises by daylight."

They sat silent in the damp-filled cabin. An hour passed, an hour during which the engine kept its steady beat, and then suddenly, so suddenly it came as a shock after the lulling, monotonous note, the motor died altogether.

McBride scrambled for the hatchway, followed by Jacko, who was still stiff and sore, but otherwise recovered. As they emerged from the cabin into the white-coated cockpit, they found Sailor peering anxiously out into the snow-muffled darkness. He silenced them with a wave of his hand . . . and as they stood silent, straining every sense, they understood the reason for his alarm. From some invisible point out there, obviously close at hand, they could hear the sound of waves breaking on rocks.

"We're close into the shore," said Sailor. "It's been snowing non-stop since you went below. I managed to pick out a small beacon light a while back as we ran up Loch Long, and between that and the compass I've been more or less steering this tub by the seat of my pants."

"How far we got to go?" asked Jacko.

"We should be nearly there. If this damn stuff would only stop falling for a moment, I might see far enough to spot some sort of a landmark. I reckon we're just inside the mouth of Loch Goil. The car's waiting on the west shore, about a mile up the loch—if only we can find it."

Shaking his head, he pressed the starter button, and, as the engine coughed to life, the launch gained way again and headed on, angling a little way out from the shore for safety.

After ten minutes, however, Sailor stopped the engine again, and once more the launch drifted.

"Well?" asked McBride.

"Damned if I know," admitted the helmsman. "We should be just about there."

"What will we do then?" demanded

Jacko. "We can't float around in this thing all day . . . the cops are bound to be charging all over the place looking for it."

McBride pursed his lips for a long moment before suggesting, "Start the motor again, Sailor."

"Where do you want to go?"

"Nowhere. But if your guess is right, then we are pretty close to where Harry is waiting. Start the motor, cut it, start it again, and cut it, and maybe he'll catch on to the fact that we're in trouble . . . if he's out there, that is."

"Good as anything else," agreed Sailor. "Hell, I'm damn near freezing. You'll need to thaw me out in an oven after this lot. My feet will probably fall off."

The engine bellowed, died, bellowed again, and finally cut. For long seconds the boat drifted, silent, all three men straining their eyes shorewards.

"There . . . look up there," gasped Jacko. The others followed his out-thrust arm. From a good quarter mile ahead, twin lights were winking on and off.

"It's Harry," exclaimed Jacko. "It must be. No other sod in his right mind would be hanging around here at this hour. My

God, Sailor, you're a ruddy marvel, chum."

The lights kept flashing. With a delighted yell, Sailor jumped to his engine, and the launch headed forward towards the point. With one hand he switched on the launch's navigation lights.

"We'll get in as close as we can," he declared. "Then we'll run the boat aground, and go the rest of the way in the other rubber boat. Drag it out, you two."

Spurred on by enthusiasm and relief, Jacko and McBride pulled the second collapsible out, and waited tensely. Sailor, hand firm on the wheel, peered ahead into the snow.

Ashore, waiting anxiously by the car, Harry decided the red and green navigation lamps were fairly close . . . and snapped the headlights on again, to leave them cutting into the dark. The launch was still too far away for the beams to give direct light, but by their diffused glow Sailor conned the little craft past a last outcropping reef of rock and swung the bow straight towards the shore.

With a grinding rumble, the keel struck

rock and shingle, rode up for a moment, then stopped, aground in the shallows.

A few minutes later the three had paddled ashore on the inflated boat, picked their way over the rocky foreshore, and had arrived at the road. The Zephyr's lights went out as they approached, and next minute Harry was beside them.

"Just three of you . . . what happened?" he asked. "Did something go wrong?"

"Plenty," replied McBride. "We'll tell you in the car. But we've got the jewels."

Harry gave a sigh of relief.

"Take the wheel just now, mate," said Jacko. "We're ruddy well frozen."

As they piled into the car and the doors slammed, Harry pulled a flask from the shelf underneath the dash. "That'll warm you up a bit," he offered, handing it over and starting the motor. "Now, what went wrong . . . how bad is it?"

As he drove, they told him, between nips of the blood-warming spirit. The wipers slapped busily away dealing with the snow trying to clot the windscreen, while the Ford ran silently on the deepening carpet beneath them. Things got worse as the journey went on. Twenty miles from the start of the journey, the car skidded wildly, and stalled.

"You'd better take over, Jacko," said the fat man, wiping his brow. "It's getting beyond me."

They changed places, and the car slithered onwards, along the narrow unfenced roadway. Dawn found them driving through wild savage country, tall bald mountains rearing cloudward, their peaks buried in dark grey. The speedometer fluttering around the twenty mark was in itself a tribute to the little driver's skill in fantastically difficult conditions. Twice they passed heavy lorries drawn into the roadside, cabs empty, the vehicles abandoned. Once, in the dawning, they saw a farm tractor striving forward on an adjoining road. But apart from that, an occasional sheep, bleating frantically as it huddled at the roadside, was the only sign of life. The snow had stopped. But dunelike drifts lay everywhere. And so they arrived at the house, lying in the mouth of a little glen that was formed by the hollow at the base of three savage peaks. And now, two hours later, they were there

146

together again, warm, comfortable . . . but trapped.

Wild rumours about the night's happenings aboard the *Cockatoo* had been sweeping through Dunoon most of the morning . . . and as a result the crowd which lined the football ground to see the start of the clan march was bigger than ever, reinforced by rubber-necking gossips anxious to see if the principals turned up —and if they did, whether their faces showed any sign of strain or worry to confirm the stories being so avidly circulated.

Exactly at 11.30 a.m. the first droning wails were heard as the pipers "warmed up". Then, within seconds, the grand march began. Twenty pipers, many of them from the local Boy Scout troop, led the way in a skirling wave of noise which, incomprehensible though it was to the watching tourists was, to the native ear, a spine-tingling rendering of "The Barren Rocks of Aden". Behind them, ignoring the slush and mud, forgetting even the cold north-east wind whistling round his bare white knees, came the Chief of Clan

Ronaldson, to be greeted with a roar of cheers as he strode on to the pitch. Dwyatt, a bonnet with the traditional chief's badge of three eagle feathers planted firmly on his head, was bursting with pride. His other troubles were temporarily forgotten as he strode along, kilt swinging. Six hundred other kilted Clan Ronaldson members followed behind in a tartan tide, displaying a weird and wonderful variety of shades and shapes of legs and knees as they strove to keep up with their fast-moving leader. Twice round the field they went, Dwyatt giving an ear-splitting grin as he passed Nicholas Malahne, who was juggling with a collection of cine and still camera equipment, lenses, filters, hoods and meters as he tried to capture the scene on film.

At the end of the second circuit, Dwyatt halted the procession with a wave of his hand and mounted a small rostrum. It had been knocked together for the occasion from half a dozen empty beer barrels and some planks of scrap wood, all covered in a rich-looking red cloth—one of the spare sets of screen curtains from the local cinema, borrowed for the occasion.

Another man climbed on the rostrum, a solemn white-haired figure, a voluminous Clan Ronaldson plaid thrown like a cloak round him, match-stick legs visible below his kilt.

"What's this we're getting now?" puzzled Bill Wilson, standing at the edge of the crowd, surrounded by Highlanders in tartans of every hue from strawberry roan to off-white.

"It iss the seannachaidh, sir—the bard of the clan," explained Constable MacLeod, an eager spectator by his side. "Now he will be introducing the chief to his people in the Gaelic."

The clan bard took fifteen freezing minutes to his introduction, a torrent of words which overwhelmed his listeners, flowed around them, and, by the time he was finished, left those not already numbed by cold reduced to a stage of limp relief.

"What did that add up to?" queried Wilson.

"He was chust saying that Mr. Ronaldson is the twenty-ninth chief of his clan," said Lachie MacLeod. "You won't have been hearing the Gaelic before, sir?"

"Heard it? Look, son, there may be a tribe of Iroquois Indians romping through my family tree, but I was brought up on the east coast of Canada, and believe me, the Scots there are more Scottish than you'll get anywhere. Clan societies, Highland dancing—we had the lot. Heck, they even used to sing hill-billy tunes in Gaelic over the radio half the day. I've heard it often enough—but any Gaelic my family ever had went out the window a few generations ago."

They watched while Ronaldson gave a brief reply to the bard, a reply which, even if not in the ancient tongue, was still sentimentally sincere—over sentimental, perhaps, to the outsider, but leaving a lump in the throats of his clansmen, most of whom usually saw their misty Highlands only in dreams—there was more money to be made among the city smoke. The pipe band struck up again . . . "Leaving Port Askaig" was their choice . . . and as the field began to clear, ready for the start of the day's sport, Sergeant Kearns materialized at Wilson's elbow. The sergeant, with two local plain-clothes men by his side, had been prowling through the gathering crowds, sifting out the few "hard cases" who were down in the seaside town in search of easy pickings.

"Business is brisk," he informed the inspector.

"What have you found so far, Rab?"

"Three pickpockets, two con men and a few of *les girls* down from the big city for the day," smiled Kearns. "The local lads have taken care of them. You know Big Elsie? She's down at the station now, swearing like a trooper and saying she just came down for a breath of fresh air!"

"Any more gen in about the robbery?"

"Well, they've moved the captain. But there's nothing much else, except that the newspaper boys are on to the story, and are running about daft."

A roar from the field signalled the start of the first competition, a tug o' war between the local fire brigade and a team of hefty farm labourers. Wilson turned to watch, grinning at the grunting, heaving teams . . . then found his attention wandering in the direction of an even more attractive proposition. Red-headed, slim, vivacious, cheeks bright in the chill air, right at that moment she was standing about four yards away, giving eager vocal encouragement to the firemen as they began to slowly but surely drag their opponents over the line.

"Five foot six, aged about 28, freckled complexion," registered her probable police description. "36—23—36, and a streamlined carriage," noted the off-duty department as Wilson ignoring all else, took in the perky wisp of a hat almost lost in the girl's long wavy hair, her neat-fitting smartly-styled ponyskin coat and her bronze leather shoes with their neat cuban heels—almost absurdly out of place in their surroundings of mud, brogues and boots. The farm men gave up as they were yanked over the line, and as they let go, the firemen, still pulling, collapsed in a heap on the ground. The red-head swung round, laughing, red lips wide to show neat pearl-white teeth. Bill Wilson grinned as their eyes met and held for a fraction of a second, thought he received an answering flash of amused interest, and then the girl turned away again, to join in the applause as the mud-covered victors left the field.

"Excuse my drooling," murmured

Wilson. "But did you see what I saw, Rab? A genuine peacherino . . . a treat for these tired old eyes. I'll join her clan any day."

Kearns, speaking from the disillusioned standpoint of a married man of some fifteen years duration, queried, "The girl with the furry coat?"

"Who else, for Pete's sake. I didn't know they built them like that around here. That's one case it would be a pleasure to investigate . . . still, I suppose we'll need to stick to work. I want to have another word with Ronaldson when he's clear."

He turned to look for the girl again. She had gone. But farther away, the Scots-Canadian spotted a figure which made him narrow his eyes for a totally different reason.

"Just a minute," he snapped. "There's a character over there who can help us. Let's go get him."

Skirting the edge of the crowd, he hurried to where a bearded young man in corduroys and an open-necked shirt of many hues was busily engaged with a pencil and a large sketching pad.

"Mind sparing me a minute?" asked Wilson, flashing his warrant card. The artist, a startled look visible under his rather patchy beard, opened his mouth, shut it again, nodded, and followed Wilson to the back of the crowd.

"I'm just making a few drawings," he began. "I'm an art student—I don't see what harm I'm doing."

"None whatever," soothed Wilson. "But look, if you want some real practice, and don't mind helping the police at the same time, then I'd be glad if you'd come along with us."

"No catch?" queried the bearded man. "I refuse to draw murals on the walls of the police cells. I understand the occupants usually prefer the dirty postcard technique."

"No catch," promised Wilson.

"Fair enough," shrugged the artist, falling into step with the detective. "Pity though—the country dancing's next, could have been one or two quite good studies in that."

They led him from the ground to the nearby hotel. Positive proof that Dwyatt Ronaldson was making it his headquarters

154

was given by the car that lay outside the entrance. A sleek American convertible, laden with chromium plate, it had its hood, upholstery, and even carpeting a sea of Ronaldson tartan. The clan chief had had the car specially "tailored" for the occasion—even the horn was a specially-made Swiss instrument that could blare the opening bar of the clan's march tune, "Revenge for the fallen".

"The Ronaldson rodeo," grinned Bill Wilson, as they walked past the car, their bearded companion giving a noticeable shudder at the way the red and green tartan clashed with the crimson cellulose. They found the hotel lounge a bedlam of flashbulbs, questioning reporters and protesting clansmen. Centre of the commotion was the clan chief . . . and the American was obviously finding the high-powered barrage being laid down by the newspapermen a harassing experience. Shoving his way through the throng, Wilson reached the American's side, waved down a fresh attack of photographers, and, as the clicking shutters of the cameras stopped for a moment dragged Ronaldson into a small side-room. Kearns and Lachie followed, the artist bobbing in their wake. As the door slammed behind them, Ronaldson slid into a chair with a sigh of relief, and happily accepted a cigarette.

"Boy," he said, "Am I glad that's over. They were pumping me silly about that jewel robbery."

"How much did you tell them?" asked Wilson.

"All I could, I suppose," admitted Ronaldson. "You know what it's like when these guys get started. They just soak you up like so many sponges. Still, it may do some good."

"They had to find out some time," nodded Wilson. "But I wouldn't say anything more without checking with us first. Newspaper stories sometimes help— but sometimes they tell the thieves as much about what we know as they tell the public about what's happened."

"Uh, OK, I'll try. Say, who's this? Another cop?" asked Ronaldson, nodding towards the bearded artist, who was already looking the clan chief over with a speculative eye.

Wilson explained, "He's not a

policeman—but he may be able to help us. Look, Mr.—'

"Burgoyne," volunteered the artist, "Deverent Burgoyne."

"Mr. Burgoyne. You can draw faces?" asked Wilson. "I mean draw them if you're just given a description of a man, without seeing him?"

Burgoyne scratched his beard with the point of a pencil. "I suppose so," he agreed. "I've never really tried, but it shouldn't be too hard."

"Then that's your task. Mr. Ronaldson, do you think you could gather some of your friends together? I mean the ones who saw these men last night?"

"Sure. Most of them are around the hotel, I guess. Nick Malahne's still taking pictures at the gathering. But will it take long? They're roasting an ox over a spit in about half an hour, barbecue style, and I don't want to miss that."

"We'll see you get there," promised the detective.

Ronaldson was as good as his word. He gathered some of his party and a few of the crew from different corners of the hotel, and sent messengers to fetch others, including Malahne, from the football field, where the Gathering sports were still in full swing. Continuing his search, the clan chief found Jonathan Russell. The tall Englishman was seated on a stool in the cocktail bar, deep in conversation with Valerie Van Kirken. The American girl, tall and with silky-blonde hair set in an old-fashioned but highly effective page-boy roll, was wearing a plain black wool dress with a pencil-slim skirt, its cut oozing quality in the way it followed every curve. She had tucked a crimson wisp of a silk scarf into the dress's deep V neck as a gesture towards her American host's favourite colour.

"Sorry to break it up, Jonathan," said Ronaldson. "But the police want to see us all again."

"I knew they'd catch up with this guy," laughed Valerie. "He's bin sitting here spinning me the most effective line I've heard in years . . . aw, don't look hurt, Jonathan, I think it's an extremely effective one."

Russell grinned. "Must I come right now?" he protested. "Well—all right. But I'll sue you if this woman isn't around when I get back." He gulped his drink, winked at his companion as she raised her glass in an ironic salute, and followed Ronaldson to the room where the corduroyed artist was getting down to work. Jonathan Russell was feeling on top of the world. What he had seen of the police prowling around the yacht had left him with a considerable respect for his own intelligence and planning, and little or none for their efforts at investigation. By now, he grinned to himself, Harry should be aboard the Dutch steamer at Aberdeen docks, and the jewels should be starting on their cross-water journey to the Continent. The operation hadn't, he admitted, gone exactly to plan—and the late unlamented Flick had been right, it had been his fault for not bashing the night guard hard enough. But the jewels were well away, the mask and cosh were now lying in a good few fathoms of water after being dropped out his cabin port-hole—and Valerie Van Kirk was proving a most attractive shipmate. His eyes glinted behind their glasses. The American girl, daughter of one of Ronaldson's business associates, knew her way around all right. It looked like being a very interesting evening.

"What goes on?" he asked Ronaldson as they waited beside the table, where the artist was busy with pad and pencil. A seaman was trying hard to put into words his recollections of the yacht raiders' appearances.

"Some stunt the police thought up," shrugged the American. "They're trying to get an idea of the boys that came visiting."

The sailor's place was taken by the next in line, Nicholas Malahne. Russell waited patiently behind him as the producer, arms waving, did his best.

"This is murder," groaned Malahne. "I never tried to describe anyone in such fine focus before—heck, his nose was kinda, you know—yeah, that's more like it."

The artist, listening patiently and from time to time sipping daintily at a pint of beer, roughed out three outlines before Malahne expressed satisfaction. It was Russell's turn next. And this, thought Russell, was the first annoying trace of originality his opponents had shown. Still, he'd better put as eager a face on things as he could. Pleasantly co-operative, but apologetically forgetful, he put on a display of chin-scratching and brow-grasping of which he felt quite proud. But, from the artist's point of view it added up to only a pale, almost featureless outline of a face Russell nodded to Wilson, murmured another apology to the American, then headed quickly for the cocktail bar.

"No handcuffs?" queried Valerie, pouting her neat red lips, hand on her hip to give deliberate emphasis to the sheath-like effect of her dress.

"No handcuffs," agreed Russell. "Another drink? Or do you want to revisit the Highland host?"

"All those bare legs make me feel cold," smiled the girl, giving her dress a flick to remove a trace of cigarette ash. "Dry Martini for me."

The artist threw his blunted pencil down on the table top with a clatter, wiped his hands on the worn knees of his corduroys, and exclaimed, "Finished . . . that's the best I can do from what I've been told. I've co-ordinated the lot into these."

Bill Wilson pounced on the two final

drawings that had emerged from a now crumpled collection of sketches, and whistled. "Say, you're not bad at that. Sergeant . . . take a look, will you? Do they ring any bells?"

Rab Kearns took the two sheets of paper, nodded slowly, and said, "This one, definitely. Name's Flick McKellar. A Glasgow 'ned' with a nasty record of violence. He's not long out of gaol. But he's never been in this sort of set-up before. All muscle and no brain, if you know what I mean."

"Flick McKellar," mused Wilson. "So that's the man who got left behind. How about the other one?"

Kearns shook his head. "'Fraid not. Mind you, it's not a very clear picture, Inspector."

"There wasn't a very clear description," sulked the artist.

"Take it easy, sonny," soothed Kearns. "It might be . . . no, I couldn't really tell. But the other's McKellar all right. Mind you, he's been quiet these last few months."

"Who does he hang about with?" asked Wilson, marvelling for the hundredth time at the filing-cabinet brain at work before him.

"Oh, the Ancroft boys, and the Mullen mob, sometimes. But nobody in particular. He's really round the fringes of some of the gangs, but never gets too firmly tied with any of them. Maybe Scotland Yard could say if he's been down south lately. I seem to remember a whisper that he'd become pals with some Englishman or other. No one could say anything for sure about it."

Bill Wilson turned to the artist, still patiently waiting. "Thanks a lot, Mr. Burgoyne. You did a pretty fine job. You'll want back to the Gathering now, I suppose?"

Burgoyne agreed, and wandered away, while the detectives set off to walk back along the slush-covered pavements to the police-station. Superintendent Melvin was awaiting them—and he had news which came close to matching the importance of the sketches they laid before him.

"We've found the launch," he announced. "It's hard ashore at the mouth of Loch Goil, about fourteen miles from here. Take a look at the map." He turned to a large wall chart as he spoke, and went on, "They must have headed north up the west side of Loch Long when they left. Then they ran the launch on to the rocks just about here—" his finger stabbed the map. "Notice anything special about the point they chose?"

Wilson peered closely at the map. "The road?" he ventured. "It seems to come close to the edge of the shore just where the launch came in, then to head north."

"Correct. And that means a car must have been waiting them there. Now, all we've got so far is a coastguard's sighting report. How about taking a trip out there? I'm tied up at the moment, between this ruddy gathering and the bunch of chancers your sergeant rounded up this morning. Take your choice how you go. There's a reasonable road from here for about two-thirds of the way, then a track for the last few miles. Mind you, this snow had made the going pretty grim. The snow-ploughs are out, of course, but the last section is almost certainly blocked. If you want, you can go by sea. Ronaldson's placed one of the *Cockatoo*'s launches at my disposal."

"We'll take the launch," decided

Wilson. "Sergeant Kearns won't mind—will you, Rab?"

Rab Kearns stared gloomily out of the police-station window. He said not a word. Glasgow, he thought, was never like this. A policeman could at least keep his two flat feet on the ground there, and not have to bob about in boats.

"That's settled, then," declared the superintendent. "Now . . ." he picked up the sketches before him. "Pretty good idea of yours, grabbing that artist. I'm beginning to appreciate how you've gathered your reputation, Inspector. And this is Flick McKellar, Sergeant Kearns?"

"That's right, sir," agreed Kearns. "Of course, it's only a drawing, but it's a very strong likeness. The scar wasn't much good on its own. We've an awful lot of 'neds' with needle-worked faces wandering around Glasgow. But that nose and mouth . . . that's McKellar all right."

"How about the other man? Any ideas there, Sergeant?"

"None at all, sir. The picture's pretty vague in outline. The witnesses only caught a glimpse of him as he scampered down the ladder."

165

"Mphh. Well, McKellar is the only link we have at the moment. No 'dabs' on the safe or anywhere else, I'm afraid, and no other clues at all."

"How about the boat that's been found, sir?" asked Wilson.

"It's called the *Tina*, registered at Gourock. We're checking on it now. Well, if you want to get a bite to eat before you go, you'd better move . . . I can recommend that wee restaurant down the road, the one with the brassware in the window . . . though you'll be lucky to get near it with all these damned clansmen in town. Meanwhile, I'll get this drawing copied and sent off on the afternoon boat to Glasgow. They can circulate it throughout the country, along with the list of jewellery."

"The list, sir? Could I see it?" asked Wilson.

"Aye," the superintendent slid it across the table. "The insurance rep here gave me it about an hour ago, and there are pictures of the stuff being flown up from the company's head office in London. They should be at Renfrew Airport now, and from there a Glasgow police-car's running them down to the boat. You should be able to see them when you get back."

"Wow . . . will you get a load of this . . ." Bill Wilson shoved his soft hat far back on his head as he glanced at the sheet of paper headed "International Fidelity Assurance". His sergeant came closer, gazed at the paper, and whistled in turn while Wilson read aloud:

"The following is the list of insured jewellery our client is understood to have had aboard the yacht, and which cannot now be traced.

"One set diamond ear-rings, brooch and clip to match. One necklace, pearl and emerald. One diamond and ruby watch and matching bracelet. Four rings—one ruby and sapphire, one large square cut emerald, one diamond (four stones), and one diamond and pearl." The Canadian glanced up with a surprised look on his face as he came to the next item, *"One atomic diamond brooch*—what the heck's that? Probably it caused an explosion when the guy that bought it had to foot the bill." He went on reading: *"Two bracelets; one diamond in platinum, one ruby and*

diamond in platinum; one necklace, three strings matched pearls. Various smaller items . . .

"The International Fidelity agent must be practically foaming at the mouth at the thought of his company paying for that lot. Incidentally, I'd like to meet him. Is he around at the moment, sir?"

Smothering something like a cough, Melvin, eyes twinkling, replied, "Not right now. But you'll no doubt meet in the afternoon. You've at least one common interest, getting that little lot back."

7

MAKING a good twelve knots, the *Cockatoo*'s launch sped up Loch Long, leaving a wide creaming wake snaking behind her. She reached the mouth of Loch Goil in just over an hour.

Sitting in the stern sheets, gazing shorewards, Bill Wilson didn't notice the grounded boat lying among the rocks until about a minute after the coxswain had throttled back the engine. The white-painted *Tina* was difficult to spot where she lay, hard under a snowy backdrop of bush and trees.

"I can't go too close in," said the helmsman. "But there's a line of rock running out to sea just beside her . . . I'll go close alongside the rock, you can jump across, and get to her from there."

"Fine," agreed Wilson. "Better roll your pants legs up boys, we're bound to get our feet wet." Ruefully, Kearns, MacLeod and the other two policemen in the party followed his example. The launch crept warily in, and backed water with a sudden roar, to drift only a yard from the smooth grey stone. It was easy to jump on to the rock ridge and scramble along it, then crunch down on to the shingle shore. They walked to the *Tina*, left high and dry by the receding tide, her rudder's base just touched by the waves.

Young McLeod was first aboard, then gave a hand as Detective-Sergeant Kearns puffed and levered himself up, followed by Wilson. A seagull fluttered from a corner of the deck as they boarded. It gave an angry, shrill scream, then headed out to sea, obviously indignant at being disturbed. Nothing else moved.

"We'd better just prowl about," decided Wilson. "That looks like the cabin hatch —mind your head, the beam's pretty low. And don't foul up any places where there might be fingerprints, young fellow."

A hail from along the shore stopped them. "We've found a rubber boat, sir," shouted one of the Argyll men. "It's still inflated, and the paddles are lying near it."

"Good enough," Wilson yelled back. "Keep looking around . . . we'll see what we can find here."

They ducked into the low-roofed cabin, and peered around in the grey light which filtered in through the small, grime-covered port-holes. It was bare and dull, the settee upholstery worn and dirty. A few cigarette stubs were on the board deck, damp and sodden.

"Take a look at this," exclaimed Kearns, pulling at a canvas bundle lying beside the port settee. "Here's another," he added, dragging out a second from beneath the couch. Young MacLeod helped him to spread them out on the deck.

"Boat packs," said Kearns. "Saw these often when I was in the RAF during the war. I wonder . . ." he turned over the canvas, searching for markings, found a set of faded stamps, and shook his head. "Just standard markings, I'm afraid, sir."

"Still, we may be able to trace them," encouraged Wilson. "Make a note of them . . . we'll get the covers taken back later, and these stubs collected. The boffins sometimes can make saliva tests on cigarette stubs."

"They can," agreed Kearns. "But I

don't know if they'll get much from damp specimens like these."

The cabin was otherwise bare. The cockpit, the deck . . . there was no trace of the *Tina*'s recent occupants apart from the stubs and the canvas bags.

They scrambled back on shore, past the finger-print expert who had come out with them. He was hard at work, blowing powder over the cockpit coaming in a painstaking search for prints. Bill Wilson led the way over to the other detective, standing patiently a few feet away from the rubber boat he had found. Bright red in colour, the boat was in startling contrast to the dazzling white carpet of snow that began only a few feet away. Spreading out, the four men moved off the beach, and began to explore the vague outline of the road beside it, their feet sinking in the soft, inches-deep snow. It was a useless search from the outset, but they continued to poke about the tinselled undergrowth on either side of the roadway for some minutes before Wilson finally declared, "Forget it. We're only wasting our time. If there were any tracks, this stuff's wiped them out long ago."

The finger-print man was still busy aboard the *Tina*. They left him and the other Argyll detective to guard the launch until high tide, when a boat was due to come out to try to refloat it and tow it back to Dunoon. Picking their way over the rocky ledge again, the three jumped back into the *Cockatoo*'s boat and settled down for the return journey. The sea was roughening a bit, white-capped waves buffeted the little craft, and Rab Kearns in particular was glad when Dunoon came in sight, its street-lights beginning to wink on in the dull early dusk. Once ashore, Wilson went straight to the police-station.

Superintendent Melvin, a paper bag of caramels by his side, was busy on the telephone as the Canadian opened his office door. Melvin waved him in, pointed to a chair, and continued his conversation. "He seems completely in the clear, then? Well, thanks for trying, anyhow. You'll let me know if you get anything on McKellar? Good. This end? Och, we're plodding away . . . but you know why they called your place Scotland Yard, don't you . . . all the best polis came from this part of the world." He chuckled at the retort that came over the wire. "Well, that's my story," he declared, "and I'm sticking to it. Cheerio."

Hanging up, Melvin turned, waving the caramel bag in one large paw. "Have a sweet. It's the only way I can cut down on smoking. All those scare stories have given me the willies . . ."

Wilson took a toffee from the bag, grinned, and asked, "Anything fresh, sir?"

"Aye, the *Tina's* owner has been traced in London. Very surprised to hear his boat had been stolen. And Scotland Yard's making a wee check on McKellar. By the way, a rubber boat's been washed ashore down the coast at Innellan."

"Bright red in colour?" asked Wilson, and as Melvin nodded, went on, "We found a twin beside the *Tina*. But nothing much else, I'm afraid."

"Not so good," said the superintendent, pursing his lips. "My boys have finished taking statements and the other routine stuff. Nothing there, either. We're up a bit of a gum tree. Here, though, I've a nice wee job right up your street . . . I think. This cocktail party aboard the *Cockatoo*. Better take a look in, and see that Ronaldson's got no more worries on his mind. And you can meet the insurance agent. She's out there now."

"She?" blinked Wilson.

"Aye, a Miss Paula Terry. Wouldn't do any harm to have a talk with her."

"Vinegary and about fifty, I suppose," sighed Wilson. "All right, Super, I'll go. My sergeant and Constable MacLeod are making out some reports, so I'll just shove off on my own." Cramming his hat on his head, he left the room. Melvin looked after him, and chuckled at something which amused him mightily.

Dunoon's boat hirers were obviously making a nice little off-season harvest ferrying guests from the shore to the *Cockatoo*. Wilson caught a boat as it returned from the yacht, and the owner, a lean, leathery West Highlander with a stub of clay pipe in his mouth, swung his little charge round and out again with practised ease.

The *Cockatoo* had seemingly recovered from its overnight shock. As the detective climbed the gangway to the deck, he could already hear the sound of music coming from a radiogram. A white-capped seaman escorted him 'tween decks to the main lounge, where a steward took his hat and coat and waved him in the direction of the babble of voices. The smoke-fogged room seemed crammed tighter than a sardine tin. Bill Wilson grabbed a sausage on a stick and a dry sherry from a tray which drifted under his nose, then tried to adjust his senses to the clamour around him.

"Hi, Inspector, come along for some fun?" queried a voice at his ear. "Don't turn round too quickly . . . unless you want my gin over your jacket." Nicholas Malahne was beside him. "Looking for Dwyatt? He's over in the far corner with his wife, or he was a few minutes ago. Boy, it's warm in here, nothing like packed humanity for generating heat." He wiped his brow with a white silk handkerchief, and asked, "Have you guys any theory yet about who you're looking for? My guess is some of the boys from back in the States have come over to pull this one. Reminds me of a movie I made once . . . let's see now, we had this girl who was trying to keep her boy-friend on the straight, but found he was mixed up in a bank stick-up . . ."

The crowd ebbed for a moment, and Wilson saw Dwyatt Ronaldson for the first time. Thankfully excusing himself, he battled his way over.

"Julie, we've got the cops back," said the American. "How's it going, Inspector? Wouldn't this give you a pain where the draught gets to in my kilt? This isn't my idea of fun . . . but, heck, it seems to be part of the procedure laid down by all the best clans, so who am I to argue?"

"Pay no attention to the big lug," smiled his wife, radiant in a high-waisted blue silk dress that obviously hadn't come off any peg. "He's just heard he's got to start off tonight's ball doing a solo waltz with me. And Dwy's main trouble as a dancer is that he's got two left feet."

Wilson grinned. "That makes two of us, Mr. Ronaldson. I like nothing better than a good old-fashioned jam session—but dance floors scare me. I came over to check that there wasn't anything you felt concerned about as far as tonight's dance goes. You know the police arrangements?"

"Uh-huh. But there ain't much sense

that I can see in bothering now. Heck, Julie's having to borrow a pair of earrings and a brooch from Miss Terry so that she won't look naked . . . and when you see the dress she'll be wearing you'll know just how true that is."

"Miss Terry? I've to have a talk with her while I'm out here," said Wilson. "Any idea where she is?"

"Coming over this way right now," said Julie. "Say, Miss Terry . . . can you spare a minute?"

Bill Wilson turned . . . and goggled. Vinegary and fifty, nothing . . . it was the girl from the Gathering. A shantung-green dress set off her smooth cream-and-freckles complexion, and her burnished red hair had been brushed to gleaming perfection. Her eyes brightened in recognition, then surprise, as Ronaldson made formal introduction.

"You're not what I pictured when I heard a Glasgow policeman was down," she admitted.

"You're rather a surprise yourself, Miss Terry," returned Wilson. That, he thought, ranks as the understatement of the year.

"We'll leave you two to talk cops and robbers," said Ronaldson. "Do what you like, as long as you get back Julie's stuff . . . or bring me that insurance cheque."

Paula Terry laughed as the American turned away, then in a business-like tone asked, "Well, Inspector, can I help you at all?"

"Huh . . ." Wilson pulled back to reality from his unconscious fascination with the girl's high but still interesting neckline. "Well . . . I didn't expect to find a woman on a job like this," he stammered.

"Don't let that worry you," said the red-head. "I've been in the insurance game for quite a little time now. I know my way around, though I must admit I haven't had a job as big as this land on my lap before."

"No slight intended," assured Wilson. "Look, we can't talk in this bedlam. Let's find somewhere quieter."

"Lead on," agreed the girl. "There's another small day-lounge down the corridor." They moved out of the smoke, into the passageway, and the detective opened the door the girl indicated. They stepped inside . . . and with a muffled exclamation the couple embracing by the port-hole over on the far side separated.

"Sorry," gulped Wilson, preparing to withdraw. "Didn't mean to intrude."

"No intrusion," said Jonathan Russell, wiping his glasses, which seemed to have become somewhat steamed. "Oh, it's you . . . Inspector Wilson, isn't it? You know Miss Van Kirken . . ." the flush-faced blonde at his side surreptitiously patted her hair back into place and forced a smile of greeting.

"This is Miss Terry," replied the Canadian. "Miss Terry's on the insurance end of this business. Well, we'd better be going."

"Not at all," Russell produced his cigarette case, offered it round. "How are things going, Inspector? Or are you getting angry at everyone asking you that?"

"Not at all," replied Wilson, blowing a slow cloud of smoke. "We've found the launch they got away in. It had run ashore some miles from here. There's no sign of the fellow who pulled you overboard, so far, though we've a good idea who he is."

"Oh?" Russell raised an eyebrow and

fished further. "The artist's drawings were a success?"

"Partly," said Wilson. "We think we know him, though of course we can't be definite until his body comes up. And we've found out how the gang got aboard so quietly. They used one of those ex-Air Force rubber boats. It's been washed ashore down the coast. A couple of kids found it a little while back."

Feeling more than a little perturbed, but still preserving an outward air of ease, Russell asked, "What are your duties in all this business, Miss Terry?"

"I'm the girl that'll have to pay out unless we recover the jewels," sighed the red-head. Then, a glint of humour just visible in her eyes, she asked, "How do you like it aboard, Miss Van Kirken . . . are you enjoying yourself? It seems a very nice boat."

"Very nice," agreed the blonde in icy tones. "Jonathan, be a dear and excuse me. I want to look out my dress for tonight . . . and I think I've got a slight headache coming on. Goodbye Miss . . . Teddy, isn't it?" She swept out with a glare that Paula countered with an amused lift of one eyebrow.

"I'll also need to move," excused Russell, following the blonde. As the door closed behind him, leaving Wilson and Paula alone in the room, the red-head chuckled. "Better knock the next time, Inspector," she said. "You know, my womanly instinct tells me we were most unwelcome."

Wilson grinned sheepishly. "Fair enough, Miss Terry," he agreed.

"Paula," corrected the girl. "You make me feel like someone's maiden aunt when you say Miss Terry in that voice."

"Paula," agreed Wilson. "Right, now what do you know about the jewels? I've seen the list, but it's background I'm after."

"The story's simple enough. My company—we operate on both sides of the Atlantic—have been covering Julie Martin's collection for some years now. The premiums for a year would pay for a good few months holiday for yours truly, and no scrimping. She's a very valuable customer, even if the collection is rather a big risk. There have been one or two attempts to get at them over the years, and that's why there are such tight rules about them being kept in a bank strongroom. And, of course, there's always an escort around when they're decorating their owner."

"You're quite happy about them being genuine?"

"Completely. Julie Martin's got a nice fat bank balance of her own, and Dwyatt Ronaldson, for all he looks like a sheep, makes more money than he knows what to do with.

"Like I was saying, we're usually pretty strict about the security arrangements for the jewellery. With a risk of £68,000 you can't blame the firm. But the powers in London thought that they'd be safe enough aboard the yacht." She grimaced. "My job was to keep an eye on Mrs. R. at the ball tonight . . . your policemen may be wonderful, but they can't go into the powder room every time Mrs. R. decides her nose is shiny. Say, will you be going to this shindig tonight?"

"I'll be hanging about somewhere, I suppose," agreed Wilson. "Unless, that is, something turns up. We're pretty well stymied at the moment, I'm afraid. This gang left nothing to chance."

Paula Terry was staying aboard the *Cockatoo* for a time. She had to see Julie Ronaldson again and hand over the jewellery she had promised to loan her.

"Don't get me wrong," she warned. "I'm only a working girl. But I've got some imitation diamond jewellery that'd pass muster anywhere. I got it in a gift from a man who paid for it thinking it was real. He got his money back because of a little job I did—and I got the synthetic sparklers."

Wilson got ashore in time to hear the newsboys shouting, "Terrible Dunoon robbery . . . clan chief's boat attacked." He bought a copy of the special edition of the *Evening View* which had been sent down by an early steamer, and glanced over the headline story. It took up the whole of the front page, leaked into page two, and even had a foothold in the back among the sporting gossip. There was a big spread of pictures, Ronaldson, his wife, a group of guests . . . he picked out Jonathan Russell, an arm raised to shield his face, as he had been caught by the photographer while at the hotel that morning.

Superintendent Melvin had the radio on at the police-station. The robbery gained a mention in the six o'clock general news, and had a much fuller report in the Scottish news that followed.

Flick McKellar's disappearance was summed up in a few brief sentences. "A man who had been detained in connection with the robbery fell from a boat which was conveying him to the shore. He was not seen again, and is believed drowned. A passenger on the yacht, who had been guarding this man, also fell into the water, but was rescued."

"And that," said Wilson, switching off the set, "is that. Where do we go from here, sir?"

"Damned if I know," growled Melvin. "So far, McKellar's our only real link. Yet that boat they stole from near Gourock . . . how did they come to pick one of the few boats in the whole area that was lying ready fuelled and fit for sea? At this time of the year most of the pleasure launches are either laid up or, if in the water, have their engines in bits and pieces. Usually the boating types don't get down to the job of getting their craft ready until about the end of April. It's a puzzle. And, talking of puzzles, I wonder if there's the slightest chance that McKellar made it ashore."

"Depends on whether he was much of a swimmer," said Wilson. "That water's darned cold just now, and remember, he had a bullet in one shoulder. No, I'm pretty certain he's still floating out there."

"Uh-huh, that's the most likely thing. Now, if we could find that body, there might be something in the pockets"—he grinned disarmingly—"och, not a signed confession or a list of names, or anything daft like that, but maybe just some wee thing that would help. At the moment we're up the proverbial creek. Er—did you see the insurance agent?"

The Canadian raised his eyes ceilingwards and shook his head slowly in mock embarrassment. "I did. And how!"

Jonathan Russell was alone in his cabin when he heard the bulletin over the ivorycoloured radio which was a standard fixture throughout the *Cockatoo*. He lay back in his arm-chair, a cigarette burning slowly between his lips, while the woman Regional newsreader went on to other items. He wasn't particularly worried about the police. Even if they had identified Flick, it shouldn't take them much farther. Like the rest, Flick had been well rehearsed, even if against his will, in the plan for the raid . . . and that included making sure that nothing was left, either in the bungalow, on the boat, or in their pockets that could yield any clue pointing to the others.

But how would the other four men react to the news of Flick's death? The radio hadn't mentioned his name. But the newspapers . . . his eyes rested on the paper lying on the floor by his side, with its glaring headlines and a story which included Ronaldson's account of the robbery, an account which gave considerable prominence to his own role and the "accident" in the boat when Flick had drowned.

Harry? He'd be all right. He had a ruthless drive concealed by his soft, fleshy body, a drive almost as ruthless as Russell himself. He'd understand, and probably approve.

Dan Travers? Russell thought he had the sailor's measure. He'd follow wherever he was led. His *forte* was the sea. Beyond that, he left the thinking to others.

McBride and Jacko? They were a different kettle of fish. McBride wouldn't like it . . . he had his own peculiar ethics about crime. But how far would that affect his attitude towards Russell? Jacko was pretty much the same as McBride. Harder, perhaps, more liable to see reason, and to appreciate the need for Flick's being silenced. And the little driver had had no love for the Gorbals "ned".

The soft buzz of the internal telephone interrupted his thoughts. He got up, lifted the cream-coloured receiver.

"Jonathan? It's Valerie . . . like to join me for a drink before dinner?"

"Fine. Can't think of anything better," said Russell. "It's a bit early, though."

"Not right now, silly. I'm not dressed yet . . . no, I don't mean that," she giggled. "I'm just going to change."

"Likewise," said Russell. "In half an hour?"

"An hour, my sweet . . . I want to put my best face on. 'Bye . . ."

Russell replaced the receiver, and pulled a small whisky flask from his drawer. He took a long, slow swig. It was a pity he had to leave the yacht in a few days' time, when it was due to sail. Valerie Van Kirken was one number it should be pretty easy to make, given time. Still, he would enjoy himself this evening . . . and to hell with the police, McBride and the rest.

Trapped and funnelled by the mountains, chilled by the carpet of snow over which it sped, the wind moaned unceasingly round the little cottage those many miles away from the *Cockatoo*. Huddled round the log fire, the four men gazed long at each other after the radio news bulletin finished. Then Harry moved, spun the dial to the Light programme, and the room throbbed with music.

"Blast you," snarled McBride, and in one pouncing step snapped the switch off. He stood there, brow furrowed. "I didn't like the little runt, but, well, he did his bit. Jacko and I wouldn't have got away but for him."

"Con's right," snapped Jacko. "Show some respect for the poor basket."

"If I remember rightly you said that the 'poor basket' would squeal on us as soon as the police laid hands on him," sneered the fat man.

"Not squeal," said Jacko. "He was just a mixture of bravado and stupidity. Any CID man with sense could trick and squeeze the truth out of him. But he's dead now."

"He's dead," agreed Harry. "And that removes a worry. It also, incidentally, means one more share to be split among us . . . another thousand or so apiece."

"I thought Russell always took care of his men," growled McBride. "Won't his cut go to his folks?"

"What folks? Flick's been on his own for years, as far as I know. His 'next of kin' is probably some coffee-stall doll with a soft spot for razor-boys. So relax. It's the best thing that could have happened, under the circumstances," said Harry. "One thing. Russell will still be in the clear. And we've got to get in touch with him."

Dan Travers, who had sat silent throughout the argument, raised his head. "How are you going to do that, mate?" he asked. "You told us you were to put an advertisement in the paper. We're stuck here."

"You don't need to get to a newspaper office, or even a newsagent to do that," said Harry. "If we could get to a phone we could fix it. Newspapers take adverts over the phone, whether you're speaking from your home or not. All you've got to do is give an address for the bill to be sent to."

"But where are we going to get a phone in this ruddy wilderness?" asked McBride. "We'd be lucky if there were a dozen houses within five miles of us, wouldn't we, let alone one with a phone. That's why this place was chosen, you told me yourself. And even if there was a house, the road's still blocked."

"Wait a minute . . ." Jacko broke in, a thoughtful note in his voice. "A phone . . . hang on a minute, I've an idea." He rose, and without another word left the room.

They heard the front door open a minute later.

The three men sat in puzzled silence. The little Cockney returned, carrying a small yellow-covered book in one hand. He rapidly flipped over the pages, stopped, peered closely at the paper, then announced, "Here's our phone." The others gathered round him as he explained, "This is an Automobile Association handbook. Great little book. Now take a look at this map. We're here . . ." he pointed to a spot on one finely marked road. "And here"—his finger moved—"here's the phone. It's an AA road-side box. They stick a lot of these phone boxes up in the wilds. This part of the world's humming with Yankee tourists in the summer."

"How far away?" asked McBride.

"Say—four miles."

"As the crow flies," grunted Harry. "How are we going to get there?"

"On our flat feet," retorted Jacko. "I've got a key to the boxes . . . got it a few years back when some pals of mine 'did' a house down south. It's come in handy before now."

"It's a damn good idea, Jacko," admitted McBride. "But four miles in that snow. Could we make it?"

"One man, no," admitted Jacko. "But two, yes."

"We could make snow-shoes," suggested Sailor. "Not real ones, but if you found some wood and rope, well, I'm pretty handy at making things."

"Get to it, then," exclaimed Jacko. "Here, Harry, you're the bloke who knew the code you were going to use. Get cracking on a message to explain the jam we're in. Con and I'll see what we can scrape together for a meal."

"Scrape a bit better than the last time," grunted the fat man. "That last thing you cooked is still giving my belly pains." But he pulled out a pencil and notebook, and set to work with new hope.

8

McBRIDE and company wakened early the next morning. It hadn't been planned that way—Jacko had simply forgotten to turn off the radio the previous night, and the set burst to life at 6.30 a.m.

Outside, the sky was still dull and heavy. At ground-level, clouds of rolling snow-dust swept over the featureless moorland to mist round the broad base of the mountains—mountains cruel in their white coverings, peaks lost in vapour. Cold, sleepy, ill-tempered, the four men hardly spoke until they had eaten. Harry made the meal, having taken over the task to save himself further suffering at the hands of the others, whose culinary efforts he described in two Anglo-Saxon words of short, crisp and unquestionable criticism.

They had decided their action. Jacko would drive the Zephyr as far along the road to the AA box as he could. Then Con McBride and Sailor would set out on foot across country, while Jacko waited. Harry had been ruled out, his frame obviously unsuited to the efforts ahead.

At 8 a.m. the Zephyr set off, churning, sliding, bucking over the snow which was ice-hard in some places, soft and treacherous in others. Jacko fought it through one and a half miles of country, guessing the line of the road half of the time, cursing the snow-crystals that were constantly swept across the windscreen. Then, inevitably, came disaster. The Zephyr crunched across a fairly level stretch of snow, a sudden gaping hole was gouged by the front off-side tyre, and with a jarring bang the car settled in a deep ditch. A clogging curtain of gorse and grass had stopped the snow from seeping through, to constitute as neat a trap as any hunter could have contrived. On the dashboard, a light blazed its green alarm as oil pumped out through a hole torn in the sump, spreading over the snow in a dark warm flood.

Jacko smashed a fist on his knee in frustrated rage, then switched off the engine and got out to inspect the damage. He came back into the car in less than a minute. "We've had this crate," he grimaced. "Sorry boys, but from here on you're on your own. And there's still two and a half miles to go."

"Can't you do anything with it?" asked McBride.

Slowly, the little Cockney shook his head. "The sump's smashed. We wouldn't get more than a couple of hundred yards before the engine seized solid—even if we could get the damn thing out of this ditch."

Reluctantly, McBride and Sailor left the Zephyr, shivering as the wind hit them for the first time, cutting through the layers of extra clothing in which they were muffled. Quickly they tied the crude snowshoes to their feet, odd-shaped triangles of wood and rope, and made a few clumsy trial steps. With a lopsided grin, McBride suggested, "Not much chance of us being in the next Olympics." Then, giving a last wave to Jacko, still standing despairingly beside the disabled car, they set off on their floundering way. The little driver watched their painfully slow progress for a few minutes, then got back into the car, slammed the doors, and thought how lucky he was to only have to sit, hope, and wait.

McBride and Sailor lost count of time as they trudged along, kicking first one foot then the other ahead of them in a splay-footed gait. The snow-shoes were awkward, unfamiliar, but without them they would have had to struggle every step of the way. Sometimes they fell, and one would help the other to his feet. A grunt was the only thanks exchanged—neither had energy nor concentration to spare for anything but the task of moving first one foot, then the other. The cold, reflected light from the glittering white all around ate at their eyes, making their heads throb, forcing them to try to seek relief by shutting their eyelids. But when they did, they overbalanced, and fell again into the cold, wet, yet somehow welcoming snow.

The men, like insects against a vast, crumpled linen sheet, slowly skirted the shoulder of the big bald mountain which was their landmark. Once, losing the road, they plunged into a snow-filled gulley where the soft drift collapsed beneath their weight. Sailor, the heavier of the two, sank to his waist with cry of alarm. McBride found himself held by the thighs, and felt himself slowly sinking.

"Fight it, for God's sake fight it," he shouted. "If you don't beat the stuff you're a dead man. Fight it, Sailor." Scraping with their hands, kicking, crawling, faces stung by wind-driven particles, they dragged themselves clear. McBride looked anxiously at his companion, who was obviously nearing exhaustion. "Got to keep moving," he gasped. "Can't be far."

"Feel—feel sick," croaked Sailor. "I'll try . . . but I can't go on much farther."

Their body heat melted the flakes that clung to them as they struggled on, the moisture soaking their clothes. Then the wind chilled and froze again, and the sodden garments clung in agonizing discomfort, while lungs and stomach seemed to contract in mute protest.

The AA box, a solitary feature on the lonely landscape, came into sight as a blurred outline not a moment too soon. Somehow they made across the last downhill quarter-mile to its shelter, used their snow-shoes to shovel away the small drift that piled against its walls, and unlocked the door. The box was small, its concrete floor icy cold, but once inside, with the door shut, the two shivering, gasping men felt safe. McBride used his teeth to pull off his gloves then, fishing deep in his clothing with one numbed hand for the scrap of paper on which Harry had written the coded advertisement, lifted the telephone.

The soft Highland voice of the woman operator answered within seconds. A couple of minutes' delay, and he was speaking to the newspaper, long miles away in Glasgow. Quickly, efficiently, a "tele-ads" girl took down the advertisement, and promised it would appear in the next morning's paper. The bill, she said, would be sent on.

McBride replaced the phone. Reluctant to leave the shelter, they smoked a cigarette, found half a dozen small reasons to delay. But finally, silently, McBride opened the door, and they plunged out once more. The journey back to the car, following their old tracks, was another nightmare, cold, chill, seemingly never-ending. But at last they staggered up towards the Zephyr to collapse, exhausted, on the ground beside it. Jacko dragged the two men inside, forced whisky down their throats, and watched grim-faced as the raw spirit burned its way through their chilled bodies, bringing a new fit of trembling to them.

Two hours had passed from the time they left to their exhausted return.

Another half hour passed in the car, a half-hour in which McBride and Sailor Travers experienced the agony of the return of circulation to half-frozen limbs, a half-hour in which the car windows steamed up and the atmosphere grew fetid but almost warm, before they could face the last stage in their journey. Then, at a snail's pace, they trudged back along the car tracks, tired in mind, exhausted in limb, but frightened to stop. The grim procession reached the cottage, and sanctuary.

Aboard the *Cockatoo*, still at her moorings in the Holy Loch, Jonathan Russell lay asleep till nearly ten that Friday morning. It had been 3 a.m. before he returned to his cabin, peeled off his dinner jacket, ripped off his black bow tie and thankfully prepared for bed.

The Clan Ronaldson ball had been glittering and gay despite the overhanging knowledge of the jewel raid. Ronaldson and his wife had shown no sign of their worries as they led off the first dance. Julie was radiant in a rich white poult gown with a halter neck and pleated bodice falling away to a wide sweeping skirt, a perfect contrast to the Ronaldson tartan sash she wore over her shoulder. The sash was held by a huge silver thistle brooch which had been a surprise gift from her husband's clansmen.

Within fifteen minutes of the first formalities the bar was besieged by perspiring clansmen. Cornering a waiter and obtaining liquor from him was a feat that demanded almost superhuman effort . . . and all the time the band brayed and blew in the background. Russell left Valerie Van Kirken at their corner table and entered the fray. It took fifteen minutes to organize two Martinis, and he returned with the precious freight just as the girl collapsed in her chair after a tussle round the floor with a giant six-footer who wore the uniform of the Argyll and Sutherland Highlanders.

"Hi again," she smiled. "Where'd you disappear to?"

"Bar's a madhouse," he explained. They sat sipping their drinks in silence, danced, danced again. Russell made another expedition to the bar, and a third.

"Still got that bottle in your cabin?" he asked. She looked long and quietly at him, then nodded. They rose, left the hotel, and drove back along the shore road in his Jaguar. Valerie pressed close beside him, eyes glowing, hand resting on his arm . . . the signals, decided Russell, of a coming interesting experience.

Dressing that Friday morning, he thought that it had been very handy that the *Cockatoo* had been almost deserted when they boarded her. In the American girl's cabin he had had an itchy-fingered moment as he gently helped her to unfasten the diamond necklace at her throat and slid the matching clips from her dress. But, mused Russell, never mix business with pleasure. And pleasure had been the theme, without a doubt.

Shrugging his sports jacket on to his shoulders, he left his cabin, walked smartly along the passageway to the main lounge, and pounced on the pile of newspapers laid out on the table. "*Gazette . . . Gazette . . .* here it is." Quickly he thumbed through the pages until he found the "small ads." section, and ran one well manicured finger down the "Articles for Sale" list. His face darkened. "What the hell . . ." he exclaimed, checking again, slowly and systematically going through each item. With a curse, he threw the paper down.

"That how you feel, friend? My head's got at least three wheels that aren't meshing this morning," complained Nick Malahne, who had entered the lounge unheard. "That Highland hospitality takes a hell of a lot of beating. I met up with a guy who stays close to here, he's got a sheep ranch or somethin'. So he says, 'come on out for a drink,' and I go along with him. Drink . . . My Gawdalmighty! It looked harmless enough, but it was sheer liquid dynamite. Then he tells me he's got his own still. 'Chust Highland enterprise,' he calls it. Brother, back in Prohibition days the liquor barons in the States would have paid the guy a fortune for that stuff. A teaspoonful in a bottle of water would give most of our barflies a kick! Hey, Jonathan, you aren't listening —what's the matter?"

Russell, lips pursed, one forefinger rubbing over his pencil moustache, was making no pretence of interest. "Nothing, Nick, nothing," he shrugged. "I'm going to get some breakfast." And, turning on his heel, he walked out, leaving the puzzled American staring after him, indignant at the brusque treatment he had received.

The dining-room was deserted, the other *Cockatoo* passengers either still asleep after the night's celebration, or already finished their meal. Russell had some orange juice, nibbled at toast, and drank a couple of cups of strong black coffee. Then, shoving back his chair, he nodded curtly to the attentive steward and headed for the companionway. He had to think, think alone. Had the plan misfired? It could be just a simple delay in the advertisement . . . or had something happened to prevent Harry getting to that boat at Aberdeen? By now he had imagined the fat man safely on his way to Holland.

He stood on the boat deck, staring out over the grey, restless water. Did the non-appearance of the message mean that the gang had turned against him because of Flick's death? No, that must be ruled out. Harry should have been aboard the ship at Aberdeen and the message should have been in the newspaper office long before the story of the raid broke in the papers.

For once, Russell felt indecision, an irritating sense of his own inability to discover what was going on. This, he told himself, was the second time those beautifully neat, foolproof plans had come unstuck. He had thought his preparation as painstaking as it had ever been. "I'm damned if I know," he grated aloud. "It's as if there was a jinx on this job."

The launch cutting out across the water caught his eye. As it drew near, obviously heading for the *Cockatoo*, Russell made out a familiar figure standing at its stern. Detective-Inspector Wilson was coming calling. On an impulse, Russell went towards the head of the gangway and waited on the party coming aboard. Sergeant Kearns puffed up the gangway first, Paula Terry close behind, then Wilson, and finally young MacLeod.

"Morning, Mr. Russell," greeted the girl. "I didn't see much of you at the dance last night. You must have left pretty early." There was a faint hint of frost behind the smile she gave. Russell choked down the sarcastic reply on the tip of his tongue, and answered her almost mildly.

"Yes, I did. Miss Van Kirken and I went for a drive, if you must know. We felt the place was almost overpoweringly crowded. Satisfied?"

"No need to be touchy," chided the girl. "Still, maybe I was being nosey. Actually, it's my tall, dark and something or other friend here who wants to see you . . . I'm looking for Mrs. Ronaldson."

"Why do you want me, Inspector? Surely I've told you all you can possibly want by now?"

Wilson nodded, "You've helped a lot, Mr. Russell. But I'd like you to come ashore with me, if you don't mind. Mr. Ronaldson as well. A man's body was found in the Firth today. The morning steamer came across it, and I'm afraid the result isn't too pleasant a sight. He got caught up with the propellers. I want you both to come and see if you can identify the man. We think it's the fellow who fell overboard."

Russell frowned, then nodded assent, and, appearing to relax a little, asked, "Any further developments, Inspector?"

Wilson slowly shook his head. "We're moving. 'Investigations are proceeding apace' is the normal phrase that covers it over here. Back home in Canada we'd probably sum it up as the vacuum-cleaner treatment . . . suck everything and everybody up, whether good, bad or indifferent, and put the lot under the microscope."

"Including me?"

"Including everybody, Mr. Russell."

They found Ronaldson in his "den", a pair of thick horn-rimmed reading glasses perched on his nose as he read the morning papers. "C'me on in," he invited, sweeping off the horn-rims and tossing them on the table top. Waving ruefully towards the pile of newspapers he said, "I suppose this is what you call having a good Press. I reckon there's about one inch devoted to the Gathering to every twelve giving the latest on the robbery."

"That's the way it goes," replied Wilson. "There's nothing newspaper readers like better than a nice juicy crime —and the Press boys are really sinking their teeth into this one." He explained the reason for his visit.

"Sure, I'll come," said Ronaldson. "But how about a drink first?"

"Too early for us," thanked Wilson. "Paula—Miss Terry here—wants to have a word with your wife, if she may, while we're gone."

"That's more than I can have," said Ronaldson ruefully. "I got hell for disappearin' into the bar last night. She isn't exactly speakin' to me this morning. You'll find her down in our private sitting-room, I guess, Miss Terry."

"I'll try to heal the breach then," said Paula. "And I know just what she means. This gentleman"—she pointed to Wilson —"asks me to dance, then disappears halfway through and doesn't come back for a couple of hours."

"Heck, I told you," protested Wilson embarrassedly conscious of Rab Kearns's sardonic grin and young MacLeod's poker-faced interest. "It was business. Sergeant

Kearns found one of his 'friends' . . . a con man named Kincaid . . . had gate-crashed the party, and we had to escort the gent off the premises."

"And that took two hours?"

"The inspector's right, miss," supported Kearns. "And he was straining at the bit to get back all the time." Even young MacLeod could hardly suppress a grin at the look that came across Wilson's face. Hurriedly changing the subject, the detective asked, "Can you come right now, then, Mr. Ronaldson?"

"This minute," agreed the American. "How about you, Jonathan?" Russell, who had been a silent spectator, nodded bored agreement.

Paula found Julie Ronaldson engaged in the delicate task of painting her toe-nails a bright pink. "'Morning, honey," greeted Julie. "Dump your coat somewhere . . . be an angel and press that bell for me, then grab yourself a seat."

As Paula obeyed, Julie went on, brow furrowed in concentration as she guided the lacquer-soaked brush, "Painting toe-nails is my favourite relaxer. It's so darned silly, but it gives me a kinda spiritual uplift." Tongue between her teeth, she made a finishing stroke, then asked, "Any more word of my jewels? No? I'm sure goin' to miss them. Sure, I'll be able to replace the stuff all right once International pay out on my claim . . . but you know how it is, sentimental value and that kind of thing. The pearls, for instance . . . Dwy gave me them the day I quit my last Broadway show." She waved one neat foot in the air to speed the lacquer's drying. "Say, that reminds me, I've got your brooch and things to give back. You know, Paula, they may be fakes as you say, but believe me, they look as good as anything I've ever seen."

There was a knock on the cabin door, and a steward entered. "Bring some coffee, Jimmy, will you?" asked Julie. "And see if you can find some really sticky cakes." As the man left, she confided, "Knocks hell out of my figure, but a girl's got to enjoy herself somehow. How's that husband of mine, incidentally?"

"He's going ashore in a minute or two with Inspector Wilson. They've found the body of the man who was caught after the raid."

"Poor old Dwy. He's in the doghouse this morning. How about you, honey? How's that big handsome cop? No need to look startled, I'm just a naturally meddlesome dame, and I saw the way he was gawpin' at you."

"The cop," said Paula, "is fine. But also in the doghouse."

"Keep him there, honey. It does them all a lot of good to have a spell being sorry for themselves." She stopped as the steward returned, carrying a laden silver tray. As they settled down again, Julie, again waving her foot in the air and speaking through a mouthful of cake, asked, "Wha' brings you here an'way?"

"The inspector," said Paula. "He asked me to have a talk with you. He thought you might have some ideas about what happened when the jewels disappeared."

"You're out of luck," sighed the American. "I only wish I had."

"How about your crew, the guests . . . isn't there any of them that you're wondering about? Even the smallest thing?"

211

Julie's eyes lost a little of their friendliness. "Now look, honey, we don't want to fall out. Dwy and I have both been asked this before. And the answer's the same. The crew's 100 per cent, and as for the other people aboard, heck, they're our friends. We've known most of them for years."

"I know. And I'm sorry. But we've got to poke and pry. The police don't think this could have happened without someone aboard helping. And, looking at it from the hard cash angle, my company have a lot of money at stake. We've got to ask questions that may seem pretty nasty. Please think, Mrs. Ronaldson, isn't there any little incident that you can remember that might help?"

"Nothing. You're on the wrong track, Paula. If you ask me, the night guard was probably fast asleep, and these thugs just climbed aboard on their own."

"They couldn't have, Mrs. Ronaldson. That ladder was lowered to them. And how did they know exactly where to go when they did come aboard.

"How the hell should I know . . ." Julie, flushed, halted in mid-sentence and apologized. "I'm sorry, honey. Guess my nerves have been shaken up more than a little, though I don't like to admit it. The captain lying in hospital, still unconscious; that man drowned, Jonathan Russell nearly drowned . . . it's been horrible." She took a cigarette from the enamelled box on the table beside her, snapped a slim gold lighter. Taking a deep breath of smoke, she went on, "The whole thing's crazy. But I don't want Dwy to know how I feel—he's upset enough about the whole business already, though he's trying not to show it either. And after all, we're sailing from here in a few days for the Mediterranean, and I don't want this hanging over our heads to spoil it all."

"Will all your guests be staying on?" asked Paula, sipping her coffee.

"Some of them. Nick Malahne's coming, Valerie, a couple of the others. We've a bunch of new faces coming aboard at Monte Carlo."

"Valerie Van Kirken—that's the blonde girl . . . I met her yesterday with Mr. Russell," said Paula.

Julie nodded agreement, and lowering her voice, went on, "I don't want to sound like an 'advice to the lovelorn' column, but she's really fallen for Jonathan. He's certainly acting up to her, but . . . you know they left the dance pretty early last night? Valerie's old enough to look after herself, yet . . . heck, I suppose I'm just a dirty-minded matron, and Jonathan's too nice a guy." She lapsed into silence.

"You met him on the plane coming over here, I believe," fished Paula.

"That's right. The poor guy was having trouble making up his mind about the time. He didn't know whether to put his wrist-watch back or forward, and I don't blame him. These time-changes are confusing when you're flying.

"After that, Dwy got talking to him about boats . . . they're both crazy about sailing. We met him a couple times more after we'd been in London a few days and, well, it ended with us inviting him up. Dwy thinks a lot of him, and I like him too. But I just can't figure this business with Valerie."

"Didn't he have any trouble getting away from business to come up to the *Cockatoo*?"

"Heck, no. He was going off on holiday

on his own, and well, Dwy and I thought it would be nice to ask him up. He's his own boss, and he needed a rest. Poor Jonathan . . . twice Dwy's been set to take him sailing, and twice Jonathan's been called away to Glasgow on some business that his London office said needed urgent attention."

"I supposed you arranged to meet again when you were coming over on the plane?"

"Not exactly. We made a sort of hazy arrangement . . . you know how it is. Then one day he came into a restaurant where we were having a meal, we fixed up to go out for a night . . ." She stopped, stared suspiciously at the girl, and demanded, "Why so interested anyway? If you think he's in on this, you're crazy. The poor guy nearly got drowned when he was pulled overboard by that thug."

"I was just being curious," said Paula. "Let's change the subject. You know, your jewellery looks beautiful, really beautiful, though I've only seen photographs of it. There's one piece in particular that looks just out of this world —that lovely diamond brooch. That's the one that's described as 'atomic'. What does that mean?"

"It's a beauty of a brooch all right," agreed Julie. "That was Dwy's wedding present to me . . . the most valuable thing I had, in more ways than one. There must be all of 200 stones in it, and it cost about thirty thousand dollars—say ten thousand pounds." Her face saddened. "I don't suppose I'll ever see it again. The atomic part is simple. The stones are put in some kind of a nuclear reactor, and they can be made into all kinds of colours—blue, green, brownish red, whatever you fancy. They'd only just started doing it back in 1955, and when Dwy gave me it there wasn't another brooch like it in the world." She brightened a little at the memory of a half-forgotten joke as she went on, "I was scared at first, in case it might be radio-active. But Dwy just laughed, and told me how they actually check the stones with a Geiger counter every day for a week or so after the process until any radiation's disappeared."

It was noon when Paula got back on shore. She went to her hotel, and spent nearly half an hour on the telephone to London. Then, stopping only to repair her face, she went along to the police-station, where she found Bill Wilson and Superintendent Melvin in conference.

"How'd it go, Paula?" asked Wilson. "Did Mrs. Ronaldson have anything constructive to tell you?"

"I don't know," frowned the redhead. "Russell seems to be the odd man out in this party. Mind you, that's just a personal opinion. There's something about him I just don't like."

"That's not a ground for arrest, I'm afraid," commented Melvin. "We've had a look at his background, like all the other passengers, more so in fact because of his so recent friendship. Everything seems all right—nice little business in London, no record, a normal citizen by all counts."

The girl shrugged. "What's been happening at this end, Superintendent?"

"The stolen launch gave us a faint lead. We had men rummage around the Gourock area with copies of Flick McKellar's photograph. He was one of a group of men staying at a bungalow on the outskirts of the town. A shopkeeper remembered seeing him, and from that our men traced the house. It's deserted now— was rented by a Mr. Smith who paid cash down to the agents. The owners are abroad. And, unfortunately, the agents have only a vague memory of Mr. Smith —a rather tubby middle-aged man. The local CID have gone over the bungalow, but haven't found anything much in the way of prints or other sign."

"These men—four or five of them— kept very much to themselves," chipped in Wilson. "The neighbours saw little of them, and it's one of those districts where people pride themselves in having nothing to do with incomers till they've been settled a couple of generations. All they could really say is that they had a Ford Zephyr, registration unknown. As for the body, it's our man all right. Ronaldson and Russell identified him, and we sent the body's finger-prints up to Glasgow for cross-checking with the files."

"Its prints?" Paula shuddered. "That must have been nasty."

"Rab Kearns did the job," said Wilson. "Didn't seem to bother him much. Right now, he's on his way up to Glasgow on some mysterious idea of his own. Mumbled something about a name he remembered that might give a lead, but that he probably couldn't do anything till about midnight. He'll be back down in the morning."

"Now you know it all," said Melvin. "We've been sitting here wondering what to do next. Any ideas?"

The girl looked quizzically from one to the other. "You could buy me my lunch," she suggested.

The men grinned. "The lassie's right," boomed Melvin. "And we'll let our Glasgow visitor foot the bill. Let's go, Inspector Wllson, I could eat a horse."

"And that, I hope," murmured Paula, "isn't a warning of what's coming our way."

9

IN their mountain hideout that night four men suffered an agony of uncertainty and knew to the full the terrible wild loneliness of winter in the unfriendly north. At the same time the man they mentally envied was pacing like a caged tiger in his cabin aboard the *Cockatoo*. Restless, uneasy, Russell was equally lonely and uncertain yet wanting none of the gaiety and companionship that existed only a few yards away in the yacht's lounge. Worry besieged his every thought. He chainsmoked till his lips felt raw and sore, concentrating on the problem before him. God alone knew what the next knock on his door might bring—would it be the police? Seeing Flick McKellar's body had been a major shock. He felt no remorse at the sight of the wet corpse, savagely mutilated by the propeller blades which had hacked it. But its recovery might start a chain reaction . . . and chain reactions had a nasty habit of ending in a colossal explosion. Flick had had to die—but even in death he might prove as compromising as he would have been alive.

Russell pressed his forehead against the cool glass of the cabin port-hole, and stared blindly at the glitter of the lights ashore.

One fragment of the sparkling brilliance came from the police-station. White-shaded electric bulbs glared down on unceasing activity. Telephones were the major links in the relentless pursuit of fact. The wires hummed as the flow of inquiries went out and a tide of answers returned. Check . . . check . . . double-check, and at the same time the detectives had the additional task of "parcelling up" the smaller fish caught in their net. Spivs and con-men, prostitutes and pick-pockets, the "neds" who had come to the Gathering in search of easy pickings had to be charged, statements prepared, their court appearance arranged.

"Blast all these Highland shenanigans," exploded Melvin as, at nearly 10 p.m., he began to near the end of his mountain of work. "Maybe my grandfather was a

221

Campbell, but any more tartan epidemics like this, and I resign."

Wilson looked up from the desk opposite. "Never mind," he soothed. "Think of what Edinburgh must be like whenever the Festival comes round. All those hysterical culture vultures and bogus longhairs—give me Glasgow at pub closing time on a Saturday night any time!"

"When's that sergeant of yours going to phone?" asked Melvin.

"Rab? He moves in his own mysterious way. He told me that if he didn't contact me by early evening I wouldn't hear from him till tomorrow. Right now he's probably tenement-bashing round Glasgow, looking for some pet 'grass' or other."

"And your red-headed lady?"

"Come off it, Super. Paula got darned miserable hanging around, and went off to the local cinema. She says she's only seen the film twice before. That girl's up to something, though . . . she was on the phone to London twice again this afternoon. She told me she didn't know enough yet to be ready to say anything, but that she thought she'd be able to give us some real help by the morning if what she was after materialized."

"Has she still got this bee in her bonnet about friend Russell?" asked Melvin. "Mind you, he's as likely a candidate as any, I must admit. The crew, for instance, are all pretty straight. Two or three of them have been 'up' for waterfront brawls or getting sozzled . . . the cook's got a wonderful conviction for being drunk in charge of a horse and cart that I must ask him about some day. But there's not a real hard case among them. And the guests? Scotland Yard have been checking on some of them through the FBI in America. They're all strictly top-drawer stuff. That fellow Malahne even holds an honorary deputy sheriff's star in Texas . . . he must have made a picture there.

"Aye, I can't blame the lassie," continued Melvin. "She's no fool. But you know, there just isn't a thing to really tie Russell in. I even sent his finger-prints down to London—we got them off a wine-glass he used at the dance—and the Yard still say he's in the clear. Ach, I'm damned if I know. I just hope either your sergeant or the girl manages to turn up something, or by this time tomorrow we'll be chasing our tails, and the Chief Constable will be getting ready to chew me."

"I know what you mean," said Wilson. "I can see me being shipped back home to Canada at this rate. I'd hoped that when we found McKellar's body there might have been a lead there—but there wasn't a thing on him that would help."

Melvin thumped the bell-switch on his desk. "Coffee," he told the orderly who answered. "Hot, strong and sweet. And if any reporters show up looking for a statement, tell them to—to go jump in the Clyde."

When morning struggled up over the Cowal hills the next day the grey clouds had temporarily disappeared and the pale, watery yellow sun managed to cast enough heat to soften the texture of the snow that lay everywhere. A thin skin of icy water formed on its surface—but beneath, rotting in places, still earth-hard in others, the vast remainder of the white blanket lay untouched.

Bill Wilson was in the middle of a very interesting dream in which a red-head flimsily clad in an accident insurance policy played the major role. He decided to take firm hold of that policy . . . and then came a rattle of shots.

He jerked awake . . . and the rattle became a persistent thumping on his hotel door. Yawning, he crawled out of the warm cocoon of blankets and opened the door to find Rab Kearns waiting impatiently outside. The detective-sergeant, muffled to the eyes in his coat and scarf, came into the room rubbing his hands fiercely together and complaining bitterly of the cold. "I feel like a brass monkey," he declared, teeth chattering. "D'you mind if I put on that electric fire in the corner?"

"Help yourself," said Wilson. "As long as you've got a shilling to put in the meter in the other corner first."

Kearns glared, but fumbled in his pockets for the coin, then crouched over the fire as it began to glow. "Didn't get to my bed until about three this morning," he complained. "And I had to be away again at the back of six to catch the boat. Wife's kicking up hell, too—I wakened her coming in, and then I woke her up again going out."

Stripping off his pyjama jacket and beginning to wash in the little basin, Wilson asked, "Was the trip worth it? You could have stayed home till a later boat if you wanted."

"Aye, I suppose so. But I thought I'd better get back down and tell you about last night." Kearns paused, and threw over the towel for which his companion was blindly groping. "I had an idea when I saw McKellar's body yesterday—I remembered seeing him with a girl—one of the coffee-stall crowd. She'd been with him once or twice a few years back, before he was sent away for his last stretch. Anyway, I went looking for her, and you know how difficult it is to find those judies —about the nearest they've got to a regular address is the fines office at the Divisional police court. Eventually I had to wait around until the 'neds' began to gather about midnight. Then I finally got to her. She was pretty mad at first—she was just lining up a customer, a Yankee sailor."

"Spare me the horrible details," begged

Wilson, rubbing shaving cream on his face and reaching for his safety-razor.

"Fair enough," shrugged the sergeant. "Well, she wouldn't say anything at first, but after I'd rubbed home how dead Flick was, and had threatened to book her for the usual, she told me all she knew. Flick had been living with her for a few months after he got out—they both went out to work at night, so it seemed a pretty good arrangement. Anyway, he told her he was being lined up for a big job, though he didn't know what it was. All he let slip was that someone called Harry, a fat man, was the go-between. She never saw Harry herself. Then about a week ago Flick packed up and left, saying he was going to Gourock and that the job would be pretty soon. He promised her they'd head south for the fleshpots as soon as he got his cut."

Wilson whistled softly. Finishing shaving, he began to pull on a shirt as Kearns continued, "The girl got a letter from him—just a scrawl. She showed it to me—for a quid. It was just one sheet of paper. But it said there were four others in the outfit, and that he had met the boss —'a swanky—with glasses and a wee

227

moustache, like a ruddy Hitler!'—and that this character was running the whole job from the inside."

"Hell and Hallelujah . . ." Wilson, still dressing quickly, was visibly shaken. "That sounds like only one man, Paula Terry's favourite candidate—Russell."

"Aye." Kearns, inwardly pleased at the effect of his news, frowned as a sudden important thought struck him. "Eh—will they have started serving breakfast at this place yet, sir? I could do fine with a meal."

"Food?" Wilson stared, bewildered for a moment. "Later," he declared. "We'll need to chase round to Superintendent Melvin's home and bring him up to date on this." As he spoke, however, there came another series of knocks on the door.

"Who the hell can that be?" he asked. "This place is getting like the Central Station at rush hour." He pulled on his jacket as the sergeant opened the door. From the corridor a familiar gruff growl asked, "You decent in there, Wilson? Doesn't matter to me, but the lady seems to care." Melvin and Paula Terry came in, the girl flushed with excitement.

"Super—that's a bit of luck. We were

just going to look for you. Sergeant Kearns has turned up something pretty important," said Wilson.

"So has the lassie," replied Melvin. "That's why we're here. She dragged me out of bed—or at least my wife did—about half an hour ago. Tell him about it, Miss Terry."

Paula fished in her tan leather handbag and brought out a folded sheet of paper. "This message came by phone to my hotel this morning," she explained. "Someone in our London office has been working overtime to get the information, but I think—well, listen." Running her tongue over her lips in a quick nervous movement, she began:

"Query Russell. New York office report airline check shows made last-minute booking on Trans-Atlantic flight to London. Was offered seat on earlier plane, but declined. Spent two weeks in New York, appears to have made only a few business movements. Little known of actual activities.

"London files query show no claim our firm, but check with Viking

Assurance lists man Jonathan Russell as lodging £100 claim for property stolen from safe in house where he was guest in Sussex during 1954. One of several guests who lost property, including haul of £23,000 in jewellery and £6,000 in silver plate. Viking lists show Russell had not known householder, came down as invitee of another guest. Dominant Insurance list man Russell as claimant in warehouse blaze in 1949 when £8,000 worth goods destroyed in mystery fire. Cause not ascertained."

She stopped, and looked triumphantly at the three men. "He may have no police record, but the insurance companies have him listed," she told them.

"It could easily happen," agreed Melvin. "He wouldn't be on our files unless he had actually been charged with an offence. It adds up to a smart bit of work on your people's part, Miss Terry. What do you say, Wilson?"

"Pretty cute," agreed the Canadian. He lifted his cigarettes from the bedside table, handed them round, and declared, "Now it's our turn. Take a seat on the bed, and listen to what Sergeant Kearns has been up to." Quickly, he explained about the Glasgow woman and her letter from McKellar, while Melvin, nodding slowly, asked an occasional question. When he finished, they sat silent for a moment.

Melvin was first to break the silence. "Mr. Russell has obviously got himself into a spot," he remarked mildly.

"A spot?" chorused Paula. "That's an understatement. What do we do now, that's what I want to know."

"Do?" said Melvin. "I'm not very sure. Wait a bit—a wee thought's just struck me. Remember when you told me about seeing Mrs. Ronaldson? Didn't she tell you that Russell had had to go off to Glasgow?"

"On two different days," agreed Paula. "He missed going sailing with Dwyatt Ronaldson as a result."

"Can you remember the dates?"

"No—" she wrinkled her brow in thought. "But she did say that he had stayed overnight at a hotel in Glasgow."

"I catch on now," exclaimed Wilson. "You're getting at the fact that Russell probably isn't a sailor, and was trying to dodge going out with Ronaldson. And—say, did he actually stay in Glasgow when he went away?"

"Exactly," nodded Melvin. "And something more. Depending on the dates he went away, it would link him a bit more closely with Gourock. Can you remember the date on that letter the girl showed you, Sergeant?"

Kearns, without a moment's hesitation, rattled it off. "March 16, sir, a Thursday."

"If we can find out that one of the days Russell was away was March 15, then we can take it pretty much for granted he's our man." Melvin grimaced. "All we've got to do then is prove it."

Wilson blew a long cloud of smoke through his nostrils. "That's it, sir. Prove it . . . and if he's been as clever as it looks, then he'll be a hell of a slippery customer to nail. He must have killed McKellar for fear he talked. McKellar being caught was probably the one real slip in the whole set-up. But won't the autopsy show if McKellar was dead when he hit the water?"

"It would if he had been," said the superintendent. "But the post-mortem showed the lungs had been full of water. He was probably unconscious, and was held under, if Russell did what we think he did—and I don't see it any other way now." He stood up. "I'm going to start some phoning. I'll get Glasgow to check on the hotel side, and ask Scotland Yard to try and find out if any of Russell's pals knew him as a yachtsman—or if, in fact, he had any interest at all in boats. When the replies come back, I think we'll take a little trip out to the *Cockatoo*. But in the meantime," he shrugged, "The best thing we can do is wait."

Sergeant Kearns cleared his throat in noisy fashion. Wilson grinned. "Wait and eat," he suggested. "Rab here is wearing away to a shadow of his bulky self. Will you join us, sir?"

"As soon as I've finished phoning," promised the superintendent. "But don't order porridge for me—I hate the stuff. Bacon and egg and a pot of tea will suit fine."

Even with radio, fast squad cars and all the wonders of science at their disposal, policemen can't work miracles. The speed of inquiries is often governed by the rate at which two feet can climb a long dark stair, the length of time it takes before a certain telephone number stops giving the "engaged" tone, or the time it takes to sift through scores—perhaps hundreds—of pages of data.

It was fully 10.30 a.m. before Lachie MacLeod bustled into the hotel with the news that Superintendent Melvin was waiting for. Breathlessly, the young constable handed over the two message forms. Scratching the tip of his nose in an unconscious indication of inward tension, Melvin read the messages through, and raised his head to meet three pairs of eyes.

"We're right," he said quietly. "Russell's business acquaintances have never heard him talk of sailing. He went to Glasgow on the two days he left the *Cockatoo*. But he left the hotel immediately after booking in, and didn't return until the late evening. And the first night he was away was March 15 . . . the evening previous to McKellar writing his letter."

He rose, grimly determined. "It's time we asked Mr. Russell a few very pertinent questions," he declared. "I'm going to the *Cockatoo*—coming along?"

They crowded into Wilson's Sunbeam, and, Kearns at the wheel, Paula beside him, Wilson, Melvin and an uncomfortably crushed Lachie MacLeod in the rear, they set off for the slipway. A hire launch was lying there, just finished a ferry crossing to the Cloch shore. Its helmsman quickly abandoned his flask of tea, cast off his boat and took them across the water to the *Cockatoo's* moorings. As the little boat came alongside, one of the *Cockatoo's* crew appeared on the gangway platform and caught the line thrown to him. The launch touched, and they scrambled across, then, Melvin in the lead, went slowly but purposefully up the gangway. The sailor followed them up.

"Tell Mr. Ronaldson the police are back," ordered Melvin. "And ask Mr. Russell if he'll come to see us."

"The boss is somewhere aboard," drawled the crewman. "I'll find him for you. But you're right out of luck with Mr. Russell. He left about half an hour ago."

"Left?" barked Bill Wilson. "You mean he's gone ashore for a spell?"

"Nope. He isn't comin' back. I helped carry his baggage down to the launch myself—he said he'd been called away unexpectedly."

Superintendent Melvin's face was strained and a little grey. But he said nothing, merely nodded, and followed the seaman to the day-lounge. As the man left to find Ronaldson, Paula raised an expressive eyebrow. "Looks like the bird's flown," she commented.

"There must be something more to it," contended Wilson. "He couldn't know how close our inquiries were getting."

"Maybe he just got the wind up, sir," suggested Sergeant Kearns. "Some of these birds are like that. The pressure gets too much for them, and they've got to clear out."

"We'll find out in a minute," sighed Melvin. "Here comes Ronaldson."

Dwyatt Ronaldson breezed into the cabin, dressed in flannels and a gay multi-coloured jersey. "Believe it or not, I was down peeking at the engines—" he began, then stopped as he sensed the air of tension around him. "What's up?" he asked.

"I'm not sure yet," replied Melvin. "I believe Jonathan Russell has left your yacht, Mr. Ronaldson?"

"Yeah. 'Bout half an hour back. He's got to return to London pretty quickly . . . he got a telegram from his office this morning. Why? Is there anything I can do instead?"

Melvin slowly shook his head. "This telegram . . . did you see it?"

"Point of fact, I did. Jonathan brought it to me when he came to say he'd have to leave. It was a rotten thing to happen— he'd planned on staying for a couple of days more."

"What did it say . . . I've a good reason for asking."

"Nothin' special," said Ronaldson, obviously puzzled. "Let's see now . . . 'Return immediately, imperative negotiate personally German export contract.' It came from his London office."

Wilson, catching Melvin's eye and receiving a nod of permission, asked, "Did you see the office of origin—you know, the top of the telegram where it shows the place it was sent from."

"Nope. Can't say I did . . . Jonathan

had it in his hand, and I just glanced at the message. Say, what the heck is this all about anyway? What's Jonathan been up to . . ." Then, suddenly, anxiously, Ronaldson asked, "There hasn't been an accident?"

"Not that we know of," said Superintendent Melvin. "The only accident is that we didn't get here before Mr. Russell left. I'll tell you straight, sir, we want to ask him some pretty personal questions regarding his movements. We've discovered some extremely pertinent details about Mr. Russell that need some explaining." He silenced a protest he saw framed on Ronaldson's lips. "I'm sorry, Mr. Ronaldson, but there are facts, indisputable facts, which make it look as though Mr. Russell knows a lot more about the gang that raided your yacht than he's said so far.

"Try to believe us—and help us. What have you seen of the man this morning?"

Ronaldson, obviously shaken by the vehemence in the policeman's tone, stood silent for a moment. Then he answered, "Not very much. He stayed in his cabin most of last night—he said he had a hell of a migraine headache. This morning, well, we had breakfast together pretty early, he went ashore for a spell to hunt up a drugstore—he said he wanted some special prescription for his headache—and came back in about, say, forty minutes. I didn't see him after that until he brought the telegram to me. Our launch brought it back with the ordinary mail at about 10 a.m. He'd packed and left within the hour."

"One last point, Mr. Ronaldson. How was he planning to travel?"

"By car. He was going to get his Jaguar out of the garage, and drive down. The snow-ploughs are supposed to have cleared the road through to Glasgow, and he said he preferred that to going over by boat."

"Aye, I can believe that," said Melvin in grim tones. "Well, we'll need to move, Mr. Ronaldson. We want to find Mr. Russell, and find him pretty quickly. Thank you for your help—and believe me, we don't rate this as a wild-goose chase."

Back on shore, they moved quickly but at last surely. This stage, at any rate, was routine. From Dunoon, a phone message went to county headquarters at Lochgilphead, a score of miles north. Minutes later, that message was being relayed by radio to all the Argyll police-cars. Police-operators began passing it by phone to the network of tiny stations scattered throughout the lonely Highland area, many of them tiny cottages manned by one policeman. Often the man was out, and his wife took the message.

The same word, sent to Glasgow's police information room, was soon being relayed to forces throughout Scotland as a general alert.

"Special search requested for a dark-grey Jaguar car, may be heading for London. Occupant Jonathan Russell to be detained for questioning re Dunoon jewel theft. Argyll CID to be informed."

As Melvin continued his task of casting a country-wide net, Bill Wilson laid down a telephone in the police-office, and turned to Paula, sitting on the desk-top beside him.

"That clinches it," he said. "The local Post Office say the telegram was phoned in from a public call-box in Sandbank, just along the road from Dunoon. The girl who took the telegram said the sender was a man named Smith. He seemed worried about how long it would take to deliver the telegram, and kept insisting that it was a very urgent message.

"As long as they get a name and address to send the message to, plus the right amount of money put in the coin boxes, the Post Office ask for nothing more."

"Then Mr. Russell beats it back to the *Cockatoo*, and sits around waiting for his telegram to arrive," nodded Paula. "But why? Why cut and run when he was due to go away in a couple of days at any rate?"

"Maybe he caught on to us," shrugged Wilson. "Doesn't matter much, anyhow. We've got to find him again. One thing's in our favour, thank the Lord. The weather should slow him down. Half the ruddy highways are either blocked or like sheets of glass with the ice that's on them."

Jonathan Russell was driving north as Wilson spoke, driving over roads where the tarmac was buried deep under hard-packed snow, snow forced back to the verges in places by ploughs, or dug slowly and painfully away by shovels. The cut-back drifts were like walls on either side, reaching above the car at times. In the back seat of the Jaguar lay his hastily-packed suitcases. In one pocket of his coat was a folded newspaper—the newspaper that had decided his departure, that had made him go ashore and send the telegram.

It was a simple little advertisement. "For Sale. Four genuine cottage-type stoves. Must sell urgently. Personal inquiries only. Box 364." If Harry had made it, the notice would have read, "Owner going abroad." Instead, he realized from its wording that Harry, the others—and most important, the jewels— were still at the cottage. Going away might arouse suspicion . . . the telegram had been at best a clumsy ruse.

But Jonathan Russell, that specialist in neat and tidy planning, knew that the fabric of his camouflage had become worn and thin in places. His meticulous planning had failed for once—and as long as the stolen jewellery and the other men remained in the country, that long did he remain in constant danger of discovery and arrest.

10

ALL six cylinders of the Jaguar's three-and-a-half litre engine purred sweetly as Russell took the car quickly but gently north. Delicate handling was the secret of driving in snow, he had long known, and the great flexible heart of the Jaguar responded to his light caress with a steady flow of power. The snow-ploughs had done their job well. Mile after mile trickled past as he headed up the length of Loch Eck, some stretches almost approaching normal condition where a liberal coating of sand and salt had been scattered by Council roadmen. Luck was with him. The Jaguar burbled through Strachur three minutes before the village police-station received its warning. At the next hamlet, the solitary constable was out helping a shepherd rescue a score of sheep buried but still alive under a deep drift. The vital message lay on his cottage mantelpiece, waiting his return.

Along Loch Fyneside and still north the

car headed, the mountains growing taller and more bleak, the road narrower as it struck inland again. The snow-ploughs had not reached as far as this. Only a few deep ruts left by heavy lorries aided the Jaguar's passage, the trip recorder moved slowly now on the dash, each tenth of a mile that came up representing an individual test of skill and stamina. A vast flurry of snow, like a miniature cloud across the roadway, appeared ahead, and, puzzled, Russell slowed the car to little more than a walking pace. Then he relaxed. A huge rotary snow-plough, taking giant bites of snow, digesting it to powder, then flinging it to the side, was eating its way down the highway from the north. He pulled into the road-side until the giant machine had passed, then drove on over the cleared surface. The car sped past an Automobile Association road-side box which had a motor-cycle combination parked close beside it. There was no sign of the patrolman. "Probably inside, keeping out of the cold," thought Russell. "Wise man."

Not far now . . . he swung the steering wheel to the right at the next road junction, and the wheels crunched into virgin snow once more. Three hundred yards up the side-road the Jaguar stalled for the first time, held in a shallow but clogging drift. In the sudden silence, Russell heard the faint hiss of snow melting and steaming as it came in contact with the hot surface of the engine block and exhaust pipe. Tight-lipped, he flipped the gear lever into neutral, started the engine again, then reversed back a score of yards before taking another tilt at the white dune. The car pressed on a little farther than the last time, then stalled once more. He repeated the process . . . and this time the Jaguar burst through. Fighting wheel-spin, choosing his path, Russell moved on again, and for nearly ten minutes kept the car at a steady gait. Then, nearly two miles up the road, the Jaguar hit another deep patch and stopped, rear wheels spinning furiously as they failed to find a grip in the soft surface. With a curse he threw open the car door and got out. Pulling open the luggage boot, he seized a length of tow-rope and began slashing at it with his penknife. Then, fingers numb and swollen with the cold, he tied the cut strips on to the tyres, muttering another string of oaths as his fumbling fingers sought to thread the rope through the wheel rims' narrow slots. At last the makeshift snow-chains were in position, and he slammed shut the boot door and tumbled back into the car again.

The ropes bit as the wheels began turning, the car moved slowly—slowly—and was clear, travelling once more over the white waste. It swung round the shoulder of the rise ahead, and Russell suddenly had to resist slamming his brakes at the sudden sight of the black Zephyr lying deserted by the roadside, a fresh coating of snowdust building over its lines. If he had touched that brake pedal the Jaguar would have joined the other car in the ditch . . . instead, he squeezed it past the Ford, then increased his pace a little.

Soon the cottage came into view, and at last he switched off the engine and let the car coast the last few yards, to come to a standstill at the front of the low stone building.

Four men boiled out of the cottage door as he left the car. "You made it, be damned," cried Harry, pumping him by the hand in welcome. "We didn't think there was much chance—but you ruddy well did it!"

Brushing aside the greetings, Russell led the men back into the house. Not until, coat off, whisky in hand, he was seated before the fire, did he speak. "What went wrong?" he demanded. "Why didn't you make the boat?"

"The weather," said Jacko. "In case you haven't noticed, it's been ruddy well snowing since the moment we pulled the job. The road's blocked to the north, and we couldn't get out. We couldn't even get back the way we'd come. I don't know how the hell you managed to wriggle through."

"The snow-ploughs have been out," said Russell. "Main road's all right, it's only this blasted back road that's trouble-some. I passed the Zephyr on the way up."

"She's a write-off until she can get to a garage," grunted Jacko. "Sorry, mate—nothing I could do 'bout it. But you can thank Con and Sailor for getting that blasted advert in the paper, even if it was a day late. They walked miles over moorland, ruddy mountain and worse to get it in."

"That's about the only constructive thing you four have done," sneered Russell. "Whatever we're going to do, we'll need to do fast. They've found Flick's body."

"We heard on the radio that he had been drowned," nodded Harry. "That was a bad break—though it always means more lolly for those left, if you look on the bright side." He stuck a thumb in each arm-hole of his waistcoat and let his stomach rock with silent laughter.

"It'll mean gaol unless things go a bit more smoother than they have been . . . where's McBride got to?" frowned Russell.

"Right here," said a low-pitched voice. McBride stood in the door of the room, glaring at Russell. In one hand he held an opened newspaper. "So you did for Flick —killed the poor little mug." He turned to the others. "I saw this paper sticking out of his coat pocket. Just thought I'd have a look, seeing we hadn't had sight of one for three days. Here it is—'Mr.

Jonathan Russell, who was rescued after being dragged into the water as the man tried to escape from the small boat, went to the mortuary to help identify the recovered body.' God, I knew you were hard, Russell, but—" he took a step forward, hands clenched. "Who's next, Russell? Who'll be next for the chopper . . . me, or Jacko . . . or Sailor? How about your pal Harry? Are his fat guts sacred?" He glowered across the room.

Russell toyed with his drink, sank a little farther back in the arm-chair, then, poker-faced, but with a razor-sharp undertone in his voice, demanded, "What would you have done? Let him sing to the police? That's what he threatened. Either I got him loose, or he sang. There wasn't a snowball's chance of getting him away . . . so I killed him. What did you expect me to do, pat him on the head and say it didn't matter?"

"It was the only thing to do," agreed Harry. "Hell, Con, we could have been in gaol right now if Flick had talked. Even Jacko agreed that was likely to happen."

"Would we?" snapped McBride. "Russell, yes. But the rest of us? Flick didn't know where this place was. Russell saved his own skin, and nobody else's. He could have promised to help Flick, or cut and run with him. For my money, I'd rather do a stretch than have a man's life on my account sheet."

"Hark at Sir Lancelot," sneered Harry. "You . . . ugh . . ." The fat man gasped as McBride hit him hard across the mouth with his open hand. "Damn you, McBride," he quivered. "If you can't face facts, I can—and I back the boss."

"That's no surprise," murmured Jacko. "I think it was a pretty foul deal," he went on. "I'll give you it straight, Russell, I'm watching my back from now on. It's done, and that's an end to it. But I wouldn't try it again. The next time your little scheme may back-fire, and they may fish the wrong man out of the water—if you see what I mean."

McBride, ignoring the half-frightened, half-angry Harry, still standing white-faced beside him, grunted agreement at Jacko's words. Then he demanded, "Well, what are we going to do now? How are you going to get us out of this mess?"

Russell swallowed the remainder of his

drink, rose, and warming his back by the fire, said, "First, we've got to get that jewellery out. That's still Harry's job. I'll take him out in the Jaguar this afternoon, and drive to Renfrew Airport, beside Glasgow. He can get from there by plane to Belfast, work down to Dublin, then get across from Shannon Airport to Holland. His passport's OK for the Ireland-Holland trip, and there should be no trouble getting to Belfast. The police don't know who they're looking for yet."

Dan Travers, who had been bewildered by the speed of events, had come to life at the mention of the journey. "How'll he get the jewellery through the Customs, Mr. Russell?" he asked. "The Dutch are pretty hot stuff on Customs checking, I know. I remember once, a few years back, I got nailed by the Dutch Customs trying to smuggle in a load of Yankee fags when the tramp steamer I was on docked at Rotterdam . . . and I had them in a cert hiding-place, in one of the engine-room ventilators."

"Don't worry, Sailor," assured Russell. "The solution's simple. We use a carrier —Harry knows who to contact in Dublin to get that arranged. A nice homely house-wife with shabby luggage and a brand new passport will get on the plane . . . with the stuff hidden in her clothing. Harry'll be on the same plane, and get the stuff back after they've gone through Customs."

"Won't they search her?"

"Why should they? If they searched even one in a hundred passengers travelling by air without having definite cause there would be an international outcry. One in a thousand's nearer the mark . . . and that's long enough odds against."

"How about the rest of us?" growled McBride. "Will you come back here?"

"No. I left the yacht on the excuse that I had to attend to a German export contract that had come up. So after I've taken Harry to the airport I'll get on the London plane, then go on to Germany from London. From there, I can travel up and join him in Holland. Don't worry, I'm not running out on you . . . I'll be back. But I think the wisest thing for you, Jacko and Sailor is to continue to lie low here. No one knows you're here, and even if they got Harry or myself there still would be no direct lead to this area . . . we don't talk. As far as the locals are concerned, or if anyone comes along, well, you're just three men having a winter holiday."

"Sounds all right," agreed Jacko. "But remember, Russell, any funny business and . . . well, we've plenty of friends who could take care of you even if we were otherwise engaged. When will you leave?"

"Let's see, it's coming up for one now. We'll have something to eat, and get on our way immediately afterwards."

Sullen and uneasy, McBride stood watching as the others bustled about. Russell had disappeared into another room with Harry to work out the details of their plan. Jacko was helping Dan Travers to open some tins of food and brew the inevitable tea.

The safe-blower had never had a high regard for Russell. The man's link with McBride's now-dead friend and the impression of fair dealing had "sold" him on the job. But now, with an almost pathological distrust, McBride realized that the rimless spectacles the Englishman wore covered a ruthless gaze on the world—Russell would sacrifice anyone and everything to suit his own purpose. To work with him, he thought, was like going for a stroll with a tiger. As long as the tiger was content, the walk might be pleasant. But the slightest disturbance might lead to full ferocity being turned on any accomplice.

He was convinced that Russell couldn't be trusted, especially in the present mess. They were going to be left high and dry, with a smashed car and no communication with the outside world. But was there any alternative? Without Russell and that bloated swine with him they could have no hope of cashing the loot. The whole job had been slickly organized, too, he had to admit. Russell had made a craftsmanlike plan of action—but if, as it had said in that newspaper, the alarm had been raised by the night guard, then Russell, peerless in the theoretical sphere, had fallen flat on his face when it came to actual action.

We're like ruddy prisoners, he thought. Yet short of packing in their share of the money and hiking out there wasn't a thing they could do. He stared gloomily into the fire, wishing he'd stayed at that dog-track and ignored the message that summoned him north.

While the police search web was still being hastily spun into being, and after he had discovered that Russell's recall telegram was a fake, Bill Wilson had sat chewing on a pencil, trying to figure out the fugitive's possible moves. Would Russell head for London? But was that where the other members of the gang were? The stolen launch had gone ashore on the west shore of Loch Goil where, obviously, a car had been waiting to pick up its occupants. Why there? Why, if the men were heading for England, hadn't the *Tina* been steered back across the Firth to Gourock, or even to the Ayrshire coast, giving a clear run south?

He got up from the desk and walked over to the wall-map. He traced the road from Loch Goil with his finger, and began whistling softly. From the west shore of the loch there appeared only one reasonable direction to travel . . . north.

Guessing his thoughts with telepathic accuracy, Superintendent Melvin, who moved to the Canadian's side, commented,

"Aye, that's my own feeling. He's heading north, to link up with his pals. That big car of his will probably get through too, barring our men spotting it. Most of the main roads are pretty well opened up by now, even if the side-roads are badly drifted. It's how to find him that's the problem. Looking for a needle in a haystack would be simple compared with trying to find a man in that wilderness, especially at this time of the year. There are damn few people living up that way, in the real Highlands. Oh, they notice strangers quickly enough. But if a man can dodge them, and some place to get shelter —well, he can stay hidden for a long, long time and no one any the wiser."

They stood looking at the map for another long moment. Then the Canadian ran one hand through his hair, shrugged, and asked, "You thinking the same as me?"

"What's that?"

"That we might as well get moving after him, on the chance that he's heading that way?"

"Go if you want," said Melvin. "But it won't be at all comfortable up there, you know. It'll be cold as hell—damn silly phrase though that is—and a damn sight more lonely."

Wilson shook his head. "I hate to mention it again, but I'm Canadian, and believe me, when they talk about the wide open spaces, that's Canada. It gets so cold out there that . . . well," he grinned. "I'll be OK. Give me a pair of heavy boots and some winter kit in case I have to walk— oh, plus a set of chains for the Sunbeam —and I'll be happy. Can I take Constable MacLeod?"

"You'd better," said Melvin. "He knows most of the country up there. It's his home territory. How about your sergeant?"

"Rab? He'll moan like fury, but he'll come along all right."

"And where do I fit in in this little outing?" Paula Terry cut in. She had re-entered the room, and had been standing unobserved behind them, listening.

"It's no' exactly the job for a lady," pointed out Melvin. "Besides, surely your job ends filling in the claim form for the company?"

"Don't you believe it," she disagreed.

"I stay with the job, right through. I'm sure the Inspector won't mind me using the fourth seat in his car—will you, Bill?"

"Nothing doing," exploded Wilson. "If I do find this character, the last thing I want around me is a woman. Stay here, and we'll tidy up this bit of the job." More gently, as he noted the warlike glint coming into the girl's eye, "You've been a grand help. But this isn't your line. Heck, girl, show some sense. Say, look, stay here and when I get back we'll—we'll have some dinner together or somethin'."

"Thank you, kind sir," mocked the red-head. "Come off it. Are you going to take me with you or not?"

"No."

Paula Terry pursed her lips. "You," she said slowly and quietly, "are a double-barrelled stinker." Then she turned and swept from the room. Melvin roared with laughter. "She's got a—hoo-hoo—a temper to match her hair, Inspector," he declared. "Still, the lassie's away, anyway. We'll get this organized, but quickly."

Twenty minutes later the Sunbeam sped away from the police-station, snow-chains clattering. Kearns drove it swiftly over the road out of town, though slush at first, then into white snow again. Along Loch Eckside they went, then on towards Strachur. They came to a road fork, Wilson nodded, and the Sunbeam took the right-hand route, heading north. Twice on the way they drew in at road-side phone boxes and Wilson checked back with Melvin at Dunoon. There was no word of the Jaguar . . . it might have disappeared into thin air for all the trace of it that could be found. But at the second call, Wilson was told something which injected fresh urgency to his task. Vinator, the captain of the *Cockatoo*, had died in hospital while undergoing an emergency brain operation —died without regaining consciousness. He was the second man to die in the *Cockatoo* crime—and for the first time a definite murder charge could be added to the list against the raiders.

They drove on again with a new grim resolve, the lonely miles slipping past until, just beyond a tiny collection of cottages, they caught up with a roadwork gang. The men were crouched in a small canvas shelter beside their lorry, taking a brief rest from their job of sprinkling grit over the road surface, already roughly cleared by a snow-plough team ahead.

"Seen any cars going through?" hailed Wilson. A burly ganger threw the tea-slops from his can into the ditch, and answered, "Aye, a few, mister . . . why?"

"One of them a Jaguar?"

"Aye." The roadman raised an inquisitive eyebrow.

"Can you remember the colour—or the registration number?" shouted the detective. The ganger shook his head, turned back to his companions, and asked them if they could help. He re-emerged from the shelter, shaking his head. "Ah think it wus black," he declared. "But two o' the boys are sure it wus grey. We've been too busy tae pay much attention, mister."

Wilson waved acknowledgement, and the Sunbeam went on. "Not positive," he admitted. "But good enough. How far now to problem corner, Lachie?"

"Another three miles it will be, sir," declared young MacLeod. "Are you not awful sure what to do, sir?"

"That's an understatement." Wilson sat silent for a moment, then said, "Spinning a coin would probably be as good as

261

following my hunch. But I guess north is still the best bet. Ah, to hell with it . . . here, have a cigarette."

Sergeant Kearns took a hand off the wheel and, without looking, felt for the packet and clawed a cigarette out and towards his lips in one swift movement. "Sometimes I think you've got built-in radar in that head of yours—when it comes to finding cigarettes at any rate," cracked Wilson. "Here, Lachie . . ." he offered.

"I don't smoke, sir," said the policeman. "It iss unhealthy, I believe." Kearns cackled, Wilson gave a look of surprise, then told the youngster, "You're probably right . . . I've stopped scores of times myself," and snapped his lighter.

The snow-covered landscape slid past. And now they were at Glen Kinglas—and the problem junction. To the left, the road wound north, north to where the first of the towering Grampian mountains could be seen, awesome, white, and indistinct, a misty haze, vague and grey, marrying their peaks to the sky. On the right, up the glen, the other road also headed for a range of high, cloud-clawing peaks. But beyond them, the men knew, lay the gateway to the Lowlands and the road south.

From the rear, MacLeod cleared his throat and said, "Eh . . . maybe I could be helping you a wee bit, sir."

Wilson swung round, one arm on the back of his seat. "Help? If you've any ideas, speak up lad. I'll grab any straw going, believe me."

"Well," MacLeod began, diffidently. "If this motor car was going up the north road, then I think I know someone who would have spotted it. Och, indeed, that iss about all the poor wee soul does all day, spot cars. He's an invalid lad who stays in a cottage two miles along the way. Johnny iss kept in bed most of the time, and he hass his bed pulled over by the window. He lies there, and watches the road and the cars that go by—in fact, he's got note-books chust crammed full of car regis-tration numbers."

They headed up the road, through a huge slush-pond which sent a wave of half-frozen water drenching over the car. Wilson snapped on the windscreen wipers to clear the blinded glass, in time to reveal the Sunbeam heading for a solid-looking stone dyke. Kearns bellowed like a bull, and swung the car clear.

The house, smoke curling lazily from its chimneys, stood near a curve in the road. As they approached it, MacLeod leaned forward to point to the large first-floor window. Behind the glass, they could just make out a pale, eager little face. "That's Johnny," said the policeman. "He will be taking our number right now."

"Like a train-spotter," said Wilson.

"Chust so, sir—though I don't suppose he will have effer seen a train in his life. It iss a good distance from here to the nearest railway, and even then the people go by the bus—the trains are verry expensive, you know."

The boy gave them a cheery "good morning" when his mother showed the three men into his room. Propped up in bed by three fat cushions, he gazed at them in awe as Lachie MacLeod explained the reason for their visit.

"So if you haff been watching the cars today, Johnny, you can be helping these gentlemen and myself quite a bit."

"Gosh, will I get a reward?" asked the

boy, one thin hand grabbing the notebook lying on his quilt.

"We'll arrange something, I imagine," smiled Wilson. "How many cars have you seen going through today?"

"Well . . ." the boy pondered. "I don't count the regulars—Mr. MacDonald the milkman, or the doctor, or Miss Anderson, who stays in the big house. And there haven't been as many as usual because of the snow." He counted the column of entries in his book. "Twenty-three, that's counting the lorries."

"Have you got a Jaguar among them . . . here's its registration number . . ." Wilson handed him a slip of paper.

Frowning, the boy checked his list. "Och yes, it passed only about two hours ago. It has a London registration number, the first of that series I've got. See"—he pointed—"here it is, and then there are one, two, three . . . eight others, and then your own car."

Wilson pulled out his wallet, and solemnly extracted a ten shilling note. "This is the first instalment of the reward," he told the boy. "There'll be something more later, Johnny . . . and thanks again."

There was another car parked beside their Sunbeam when the policemen left the little house—a bright red Morris Minor. Paula Terry, alone in the car, gave a self-satisfied "toot" on its horn as Wilson strode towards her. Winding down the window, she beamed, "Hallo, Bill, are we on the right track?"

"You're on the wrong one, at any rate," growled Wilson. "I thought I left you back at Dunoon."

"You thought wrong, then. I knew you were planning to take the north road, so I got out my car—it's got snow-chains like yours—and here I am!" She gazed mockingly into his eyes.

Wilson flushed, began to say something, changed his mind, and sighed, "You win. But I want to warn you, this is a dangerous game. Captain Vinator's dead—he died in hospital a little while ago. Won't you change your mind?"

The girl turned pale, but shook her head firmly and finally. "I'm sorry, Bill, but it doesn't alter things."

"All right," the Canadian reluctantly

266

agreed. "Look, I'd better stay in the Sunbeam with Rab. Do you mind if young MacLeod travels with you?"

Paula shook her head. "Send him over," she invited. "I'll be glad to have him."

The two cars set off again, the Sunbeam in the lead. On and on they went, over the churned snow. Wilson shivered despite the warmth of the car as he saw a mountain stream which normally dropped some eight feet down a rock face beside the road. It had frozen, and long icicles hung from the stone, reflecting the sunlight from their mirror-smooth surfaces. Just past it, Kearns slowed the Sunbeam, the Morris pulling in tight behind their tail, as a yellow-painted motor cycle combination came towards them, heading south.

"It's an AA outfit," said the sergeant.

"Flash him down," ordered Wilson. "He might have seen some trace of the Jaguar." Kearns quickly snapped the headlamp switch on and off a couple of times, and the motor cyclist gave a wave then stopped a few yards ahead. Wilson got out of the car, and met the patrolman as he walked towards them. "Seen anything of a grey Jaguar saloon?" he asked. "We're police, and we want to get hold of the driver."

The patrolman slapped his gauntleted hands across his yellow oilskins and shook his head. "'Fraid not, sir," he replied. "I've been busy this morning, what with road condition reports to headquarters and helping all the blokes who've got stuck in ditches. The road's not very long open, though. The snow-ploughs only got it clear a short while back, and very little traffic won through before that."

"Our man would have passed in the last couple of hours," said Wilson, stamping his feet as he felt the chill seeping through the soles of his shoes. "Wouldn't you have seen him if he'd come this way?"

The AA man shook his head. "He could have passed when I was in our telephone box up the road," he admitted. "I've been trying to do a bit of detective work myself this morning—nothing in your line, sir, but a right puzzle all the same. I just don't understand it at all."

The detective, natural curiosity aroused, asked, "What sort of puzzle?"

"Well, look, sir, this road was blocked, really blocked, by heavy drifts—five feet deep some of them—down at the south end all Thursday and most of yesterday, and it was the same a few miles up at the north end, where it runs through a kind of ravine. This stretch in between was pretty bad too. Nothing could have got through until last night—and even this morning there was still this pretty tough stretch in the middle until the snow-ploughs cleared it. They've been clearing the Glasgow road and some of the more important ones first, you understand. Yet someone gets through to my box up there, and makes a phone call yesterday morning . . . and didn't pay for it either. The money's not what is really bothering me. What I want to know, sir, is how did he get there? He must have walked miles to do it."

"You mean someone's stuck out there somewhere, and was phoning for help?"

"Devil a bit of it. Effie at the switch-board in the village was telling me when I phoned in just now. She was kidding me that some people could get through the snow all right, even when the AA was stuck. So I took a look at the register in the box—there's a ledger on which members are supposed to put down their calls, and what they cost. There's no entry there at all."

"Where did the man—it was a man I suppose?"—the patrolman nodded—"where did the man telephone to?"

"That's the funniest bit of all. Effie doesn't listen into the calls, you know—the Post Office are very strict about privacy. But she was just checking that he got through all right, it being quiet like. This fellow was phoning a newspaper in Glasgow and giving an advertisement to them. Some daft thing about wanting to sell stoves. Imagine walking through this ruddy snow just to put an advert in the papers!"

Wilson rubbed his chin thoughtfully. "It does seem pretty queer." He thought to himself that it seemed even queerer it should happen on the road that Russell had almost definitely taken. "Look, how far away is this box of yours?"

"Four miles or so up the road, sir," said the patrolman. "But I didn't mean to bother you about a silly wee matter like someone not paying for a phone call."

"There's a chance this phone call may

have something to do with why we're here," explained Wilson. "Can you turn and go back to this post of yours, and we'll follow?"

The patrolman nodded, and went back to his machine. It started at the first kick, and he swung the combination round in the roadway. The two cars started off in his wake.

"So you see, Rab," said Wilson. "There might be a tie-up between this queer phone call and Russell heading this way."

Nursing the car over a slippery stretch of road, Kearns nodded slowly. "You mean it might have been a code message, or something like that?"

"That's the general idea. I'll check at the AA box. Best thing to do would be to phone the newspaper and find out if the advert was in this morning's issue. If it was, then that would account for Russell leaving. He got a message from his pals saying he was wanted, and took off as soon as he could. Ah . . . there's the box up ahead. I'll go in when we get there . . . explain things to Paula, will you, and I'll bring you all up to date when I get through."

He was in the AA box for nearly twenty minutes. Coming out, he spoke to the patrolman again, then, as the latter re-entered the box, the detective came over to the Morris and climbed in. Kearns was already in the back seat, beside Lachie MacLeod. Slamming the door behind him, Wilson turned towards Paula, and his eyes widened. "Hell's teeth, what's this, a ruddy tea-party?"

She handed him a paper cup filled with steaming tea and gestured towards a parcel of sandwiches lying in the dashboard pocket. "This is called a woman's touch, Bill," she explained. "Trust men to go tearing off into the wilds without a bite of food. I picked up a couple of vacuum flasks and the sandwiches before I set out."

Munching happily in the back, Kearns declared. "Well, I'm glad you came, anyway, miss."

Wilson sipped the cup. "I'd have been happier if you hadn't put sugar in the stuff," he complained. "All right—I'm only trying to be funny."

"Don't burst anything in the effort," replied the red-head sarcastically. "Well, don't keep us in suspense, what happened?"

"Mmmh . . ." Wilson took a deep bite at an egg sandwich, munched for a moment, then began, "It looks like we're really on to something. The advert went from here to the *Daily Gazette* in Glasgow. Effie at the switchboard—I gather she's pretty sweet on our AA friend—looked back the number. I checked with the newspaper office, and the notice appeared today all right. I've got a note of it . . ." He fumbled in his pocket for his notebook, opened it, and read, "'For Sale—Four genuine cottage-type stoves, must sell urgently. Personal inquiries only.' The man who phoned had an English accent, says the girl who took the advert. And he was desperately anxious that it made the next day's paper. Asked her twice to confirm it, in fact."

"Did he give an address?" asked Paula.

"Name and address," nodded Wilson. "They're sending the bill there. John Robinson, and an address in Inverness. It's almost certainly a fake. The patrolman says he's never heard of the street-name . . . and he was stationed there for three years."

Paula poured more tea from her flask into his cup, and asked, "So what do we do now?"

"This Automobile Association man's drawing up a little map of the district. He says there's only about half a dozen houses within as many miles. When we get the list, we split up, check the lot, then meet back here. He's agreed to stay by the box until we return, and to keep in touch by phone with Melvin at Dunoon."

"That's all very well, Bill, but we can't just go up to house doors and ask, 'Please, are you hiding a gang of crooks,' can we?" said Paula, frowning.

"We're looking for that Jaguar," Wilson patiently explained. "We may bump into trouble, but I doubt it. They won't show their hand unless forced to, and if we see anything suspicious we come away and shout for reinforcements. If you want, though, you can stay here with the AA man."

"Not on your life," declared the girl, tossing her head. "I can look after myself, and that includes knowing a few judo holds. And besides," she dived into her handbag, "I've got this . . ." She produced a stubby little ·25 pistol.

"Put it away," begged the detective. "I don't trust women with guns. This is just a reconnaissance trip. The road scout's coming over now . . . he must have the list made up."

The patrolman had. There were, he explained, exactly five places in the neighbourhood where there were no telephones.

"These three," he passed over one slip of paper, "are all pretty close together. The other two on this piece are farther away. The first three, well, there's two shepherd's cottages and an old mansion house that the youth hostels people run. On this other piece of paper I've listed the remaining two—they're both shooting lodges. There's a gamekeeper living at the first one, and the other, Craigmore, has been taken by some retired city man."

"Fine." Wilson took the lists, and turned to the others in the car. "Lachie, I want you to go with Sergeant Kearns in the Sunbeam and check on the first three. The youth hostel might be a good bet,

Rab. Two or three men posing as climbers might easily get a bed for a few nights without the warden suspecting anything wrong. Paula, I'll come with you if it's OK, and we'll check the other two."

"I'm swooning at the thought," declared the girl. "Just wait till I give this man some tea . . ."

"Don't worry about me, miss," twinkled the khaki-clad scout. "These sidecars on our bikes aren't completely filled by breakdown equipment, you know."

After a last route-check on the patrolman's maps, the two cars set off. The Sunbeam soon turned off the main road, the Morris kept on. The first house on Wilson's list lay only a quarter mile off the main road, but the rough road to it taxed the little car to the limit as it slogged through the snow. Reluctantly, Bill Wilson told the girl to stop when they had covered only half the distance. "I'll walk the rest," he volunteered. Fifteen minutes later he returned, shivering with cold. "W-waste of time," he declared. "The gamekeeper's out, and his wife's a deaf old dame . . . I had a shouting match before she understood me, and then there was nothing doing. Next stop, Craigmore."

"I thought I heard you say a while back that the weather was mild here compared with the land of the Maple Leaf," joked the red-head.

Rubbing his hands together, trying to restore the circulation, Wilson protested, "So it is. But you've got a damp cold here that sneaks in at the bones. The actual temperature isn't so bad. You'd see what I meant if you went up those mountains. It'd be a damn sight colder up there than down here, yet you wouldn't feel it so badly."

With difficulty the girl turned the car and, to much wheel-spinning and sliding, headed it back down to the main road, sighing with relief as the wheels reached the smoother surface. The Morris motored quietly for a while.

Wilson stared gloomily through the windscreen, sick of the endless white snow around them. "Paula . . . how'd you ever get into this business?"

"Sheer noseyness on my part," said the girl. "I was living with Mum and Dad down at Fenchurch. One night I came home late from a dance, and saw a local pillar of the church carrying a load of stuff out of his shop and loading it into his car. The next night the place went on fire, and burned to the ground. Then I found out that he owed money at the local bookie's —the bookie's son told me. After that, I went to the insurance company—I got their name from the policeman's son. The company saved a bit of money, I got a job, and that's all there is to tell."

"What about the future?" asked Wilson, glancing at her out of the corner of his eye.

"Oh, one day I'll get married, I suppose, and give some man a load of worry—better watch, or I might decide on you. More important, though, isn't that our junction ahead?"

The detective grunted in disgust. "That's it. What . . . ah, never mind. Hey, watch it, this looks pretty deep." The Morris floundered into the half-frozen surface and bucked slowly forward amid occasional agonized whines from the rear wheels as one then the other hit a soft patch of snow.

"Want me to take the wheel?" asked Wilson.

"I'll . . . manage," gasped Paula, concentrating on her task. "We . . . wouldn't get very . . . far without those chains. Oops . . ." The car swung practically sideways, then corrected. Tensed in his seat, Wilson warned, "Look out . . . there's another car ahead—it's in the ditch."

"Can't see anyone in it," said Paula. "They must have walked the rest of the way though I noticed a set of car tracks quite plainly in the snow as we . . . came up." The Morris slithered past the abandoned Ford, and bumped onwards.

"There's the house ahead," said Wilson. "That Ford in the ditch must have come from it. If it did, the driver had a long walk back."

"Let's hope we don't . . . have to . . . do the same," gritted Paula. Then, as she slowed the Morris to a crawl, and finally halted outside the cottage, "Whew, you can drive back with pleasure. Wait a bit and I'll come to the house with you this time. I'll need to change my shoes first. I always drive in these pumps, but I've got my good old fur boots behind the seat." She struggled into the boots, zipped them close, then got out, wrapping her coat tightly around her. They walked up to the cottage door, and knocked.

Jacko was trying to coax some music out of the radio when the knock came. Loud, insistent, repeated, it shocked the five men to sudden silence, consternation visible on each and every face. Russell was the first to recover. He slipped over to the nearest window and peered out the side of the curtain, then turned, the colour gone from his face.

"Police," he hissed. "It's a fellow Wilson—he was at the *Cockatoo*. And a girl, an insurance rep."

Harry slid a squat black automatic from his jacket pocket and asked a silent question. Russell shook his head. "My car's well out of sight?" he demanded. Harry nodded. "Jacko took it round to the shed at the back. They won't spot it."

Another knock came at the door.

"See if we can play them along," ordered Russell. "I'll go in the back room. Jacko, you answer the door. Act dumb." He moved swiftly across to the other room, closing the partition door behind

him until it was only open a slit. The little
driver made a face at his companions then
went towards the hall way in a slouching
walk.

11

THE green door of the cottage swung open, and a small, tweedy man gazed inquiringly at Wilson and Paula.

"'Afternoon" drawled Wilson. "Sorry to bother you. I'm a police officer"—he flashed his warrant card in an automatic gesture—"and I'm making some inquiries around here."

"Police?" queried Jacko. "Up here? Has there been an accident in the snow? Are there climbers missing on the mountains again?"

"Not exactly," chipped in Paula, impatiently. "Do you mind if we come in out of the cold for a moment?" She shivered.

The little man hesitated, then stood back and waved them in. "Of course, of course," he fussed. "Forgive me Miss—Constable—what does one call a lady policeman?" As the two squeezed past him, Jacko decided that his carefully learned country gentleman routine was certainly just as smooth as ever.

"Miss Terry is an insurance investigator," explained Wilson, following the girl into the hall way. "My name's Wilson —Inspector Wilson."

"Raeburn, John Raeburn," volunteered Jacko, tongue in cheek. "I'm up from the city with three friends, having a quiet little holiday—won't you come through?" He ushered them into the living-room where McBride, Sailor and Harry stood in an awkward little group near the blazing fire. "Mr.—Smithers, Mr. Johnston and Mr. Ellis," he introduced. "We've got visitors, gentlemen—the police, I'm afraid. Have any of you been robbing banks lately?" He giggled and Harry gave a half-hearted grin in reply.

"What brings you here, Inspector?" asked Jacko, turning towards his "visitors" again.

Relaxed, easy-mannered, the Canadian replied, "We've been searching the area for a Jaguar car we believe may have headed this way . . . do any of you gentlemen know anything of it?"

Jacko shook his head. "You're out of

luck, Inspector. Frankly, your car is the first we've seen for days . . . the road's been blocked you know. In fact, as we haven't the telephone, we're quite cut off. All we've had to keep us in touch with the outside world has been our little wireless," he waved in the direction of the radio set on the small shelf beside the fire.

"Don't you have a car of your own?" asked Wilson. "We passed a Ford Zephyr down the road . . ."

"That's ours," agreed Jacko. "Mr. Ellis and Mr. Johnston tried to drive through the snow yesterday, but they ended up in the ditch, I'm afraid . . . isn't that right, Mr. Ellis?"

McBride, seizing his cue, hastily nodded his head and declared, "Things were very bad, very bad indeed. How did you manage to get through, Inspector?"

"The snow-ploughs have been out on the main road," shrugged Wilson. "But as for the rest of it, Miss Terry deserves a medal for her driving. On today's form she'd win the Monte Carlo rally hands down."

"Good show," congratulated Jacko . . . ouch, he thought, don't overdo the accent, clown. In more moderated tones, he queried, "This car, Inspector . . . I'm sorry I can't help you. But what case is it you're investigating?"

"The *Cockatoo* robbery," said Wilson. "Though perhaps you haven't heard of it, being blocked by snowdrifts as you have."

"We've heard, all right," chipped in Harry, thumbs in his waistcoat. "The Scottish news bulletin on the radio gave a pretty full account of it. How's the case progressing?"

"The bunch that pulled the job were clever, very clever," said Wilson. "But like every gang of crooks they made a few mistakes. We're coming along slowly but surely."

"And this Jaguar car you're looking for —is it linked with the robbery?"

"We think so. We thought it would have headed to somewhere around here, and we're checking in the hope that someone may have seen it pass. But if, as you gentlemen say, no traffic has come through since the storm began, well, we'll just get on our way."

"But Bill . . ." Paula began, then flushed a little as Wilson interrupted her to say, "Of course, if you see or remember anything, Mr. Raeburn, we'd appreciate it if you contacted us."

"Of course, Inspector," agreed Jacko. "By the way, we don't want you to give away secrets, you know, but how is that unfortunate captain who was attacked in the raid?"

"Captain Vinator? He's dead," said Wilson, in a hard flat voice. "He died just after noon today . . . so you see, we've a lot to do. The *Cockatoo* case is now a murder hunt. Good-bye, gentlemen, and thanks again." He took Paula's arm and, grasping it firmly, steered her towards the door. Jacko followed hard on their heels to the outer doorway.

"Don't worry, Inspector," he declared. "If we see or hear anything, we'll let you know . . . oh, and don't bother about our car. We've plenty of foodstuffs, you know, and we'll get the Ford taken care of as soon as the snow goes down. It shouldn't last more than a few days. Good-bye . . ."

As the green door slammed shut behind them, Wilson, hand still tight on Paula's arm, muttered, "Don't argue, walk . . .

slowly, but straight towards our car. Don't look back." The girl obeyed. This time Wilson took the driving seat. He started the engine, turned the Morris, and sent it crawling back down the road they had come.

"What's going on?" queried Paula. "Why did you shut me up in there . . . I wanted to ask them about those car tracks. we saw in the snow. I'm darned sure they weren't made as far back as yesterday morning. No tracks could have stayed so clear and distinct in all the snow that's been drifting with the wind."

"Quite right," agreed Wilson. "That's why I shut you up . . . that and the fact that there's a copy of today's paper lying on the table in that room. It just happens to be the Gazette—the one that had the mystery advert in it. How did today's *Gazette* get there if that cottage has been cut off for days? That little fellow— Raeburn he called himself—was a plausible enough character, but I didn't like the look of his friends. Confucius, he say, 'Wise man get out smartly!' Look, I'm driving round this next curve in the road, and stopping the car as soon as we're out of sight of that house."

"And?"

"Then I'm going back to have a scout around on foot. These car-tracks seemed to lead round to the back of the house. I want to see what's there—and I think it's an odds-on chance there's a grey Jaguar lying hidden. You stay with the Morris till I return. Give me half an hour, and if I'm not back by then, head for the AA box and bring up the cavalry."

Paula sat silent, a strange expression in her eyes. Then as the Morris slowed and stopped, she quietly said, "Don't do anything foolish, Bill . . . I don't want anything to happen to you."

Wilson looked at the girl for a moment, then silently nodded. He gave her hand a quick squeeze, and stepped out of the car. Without a backward glance, he began to plough a floundering way across the deep, smooth moorland snow.

A scowl sat like a poker-mask on Jonathan Russell's face as he emerged from hiding seconds after the front door of the cottage had banged shut.

"Make sure they're clear," he barked, and Sailor hurried over to peer out the side of the curtained window. "They're going, boss," he declared. "The car's just turning —it's driving off."

Jacko, hands trembling a little as he lit a cigarette, re-entered the room and asked, "Did you hear what he said about the captain? He's dead. God, Flick must have really belted him one with that cosh."

Russell nodded, grim-faced. It was just one more item in the catalogue of disaster that seemed to be compiling . . . Wilson not only looking for him, but knowing that he had headed north instead of towards the Lowlands. And even knowing the exact area to search . . . was the soft-spoken detective a magician, he wondered bitterly. How much did the police know? How tightly had they sewn him into his place in the pattern of the *Cockatoo* raid?

McBride, gauging Russell's stony silence as indecision, demanded, "And now? It looks as though we'll all need to get moving. That cop'll be more of a mug than I think he is if he doesn't do some more checking around here. He'll be back . . .

and the next time he may be a ruddy sight more nosey."

"He's right, boss," declared Harry nervously. "We can't hang around here."

"How did they strike on us here, Russell?" goaded McBride. A cold glint in his eyes, he suggested, "It couldn't be that they got a little tip too early—one they weren't supposed to get until, say, tomorrow, when we were here but you'd gone?"

Russell flushed red with rage. "Have you gone completely crazy?" he demanded, voice almost incoherent with anger. "Stop trying to push me, McBride. I've had just about all I can take from you. And by God, when we get out of this we're . . ."

He stopped, staring at the coffee table, the blood draining from his face. "Harry . . . that table . . . was that newspaper on it when Wilson was here?"

The fat man, puzzled, looked blank for a moment, then nodded.

Russell collapsed into a chair, one hand plucking nervously at his moustache. "If Wilson saw it, we're done for. And this time, McBride, do you know who's shopped us? You, you thick-skulled fool. Do you know why? Because it's today's paper . . . the one you took from my coat pocket. Yet you all told Wilson that no one had got through for the last three days."

He got up, pacing the floor in savage fury, the others struck silent by the threat he had revealed. "Wilson'll be back all right," he snapped. "In fact, he's probably making his way back right now for a second look around before going for help. Harry, you and Sailor get round to the back. Get outside and under cover . . . and stay there until I tell you to move. I don't give a damn how cold it gets . . . stay there. McBride . . . you get to that front window, and watch the road. Jacko, your post's by the car. If anything happens to the Jaguar, well, we've had our lot. I'll stay here and gather our stuff together, ready to move off."

It was wet, exhausting going through the deep, clinging snow, and Wilson unhappily conscious of his vulnerability against the white backcloth—"like a plug for somebody's soap powder"—crouched, crawled and stumbled from scanty cover

291

to cover. He could feel the damp seeping through every inch of his clothing. His breath came out in warm, steamy clouds, yet each freezing gulp of air he took seemed to scrape at his lungs like so many little knives. He was thankful to reach his goal, the shelter of a low stone dyke which ran over the moorland to close by the back of the cottage. With infinite caution he peered over the inches thick snow that crowned the rough stone top. The rear of the house and the old, barn-like shed that stood near it seemed deserted, the only sign of life the slow curling smoke rising from the cottage chimney. Slowly the detective crawled his way down the length of the dyke wall, keeping below its shelter. When at last he raised his head again, he was looking down into the backyard of the cottage. Only a gentle downhill slope, perhaps twenty yards in length—the cottage drying green—separated him from that shed.

If the car was there, he decided, he'd get away again as quickly as possible, without prying further. From where he crouched, the shed masked all but one of the cottage windows, and that was blank and uncurtained, the kitchen by the look of it. Breathing a quick prayer for success, he swung one leg over the dyke, wincing at an unexpected cramp in the limb, but forcing the muscles to complete their task. Grunting, he slid over the wall and, limping slightly, ran across the short stretch of ground, falling to his knees again as he gained the protection of the shed wall. Heart thumping madly, ears strained for the slightest sound, he waited. Only the faint moaning of the rising wind, carrying flecks of snow in its grasp as it sped down from the mountain slope, disturbed the silence.

Slowly, Wilson rose to his feet again, crept to the corner of the shed, and peered round. The wide double-section door was ajar. He listened again, then stepped out and gently prised one half of the door. It creaked back on its hinges—he saw the grey bulk of the Jaguar lying just within the entrance.

And from behind him a voice said, "It's there all right, mister. Now turn round— slowly. I've got a gun here. Right, Jacko . . ."

Wilson, obeying, saw a faint flickering

movement as a man emerged from his hiding place beside the Jaguar's bonnet. Then he was staring across the yard to where "Mr. Smithers and Mr. Johnston" were standing, hard-faced and watchful, a few feet from the tangled stack of logs which had given them cover. The trap was sprung . . . and Wilson felt a hand fall on his shoulder from behind.

"Sorry mate," said Jacko. "But you would come back. Just take it easy, and everything will be fine. Remember, though, I've a monkey-wrench in my other fist."

Harry, a Luger automatic hanging slackly in one podgy hand, came across. "Head for the house," he ordered. "Move . . . we haven't got all day."

Cursing at the foolhardy way he'd walked into such an obvious reception, Wilson allowed himself to be pushed over to the kitchen door, was shoved through it, then marched by the three men into the living-room he had seen such a short time before. Jonathan Russell stood by the fireplace, his silence more ominous than any words. For long minutes, it seemed, he stood like that, sombre-faced, staring at a spot a few inches above the detective's head. Finally, still avoiding looking directly at the man before him, he said, "Sailor . . . get back outside and keep an eye open. Go with him, Jacko."

Harry, hefting the Luger, pushed Wilson a little farther forward into the room. The detective looked over to the window, where McBride stood, an unlit cigarette dangling from his lips, an unhappy expression on his face, then back again to Russell, once more silent and lost in thought.

"You might at least say hallo," he declared. "After all, I've come quite a way to see you . . . and how about letting me nearer that fire. It's cold walking through the snow, I can tell you."

A faint grin appeared on McBride's face. Russell took off his glasses, and began slowly polishing the lenses. "I'm trying to make up my mind just what to do with you," he said in a low, soft voice. "Obviously you've been just too clever, Mr. Wilson. I admire clever people as a rule. But frankly, this time . . ." He shrugged his shoulders, finished the almost mechanical polishing, and returned the spectacles to his face. Then, "As a first step . . ." leisurely, steadily, his hand slid into his jacket and slowly emerged grasping a twin of Harry's weapon.

Wilson tensed, unable to drag his eyes away from the menace of the cold black muzzle. His throat seemed suddenly dry. Russell squinted slowly along the line of the barrel, nodded, and ordered, "Tie his hands, Harry. You'll find some electrical flex in the top drawer of that sideboard, I think."

The fat man, moving with amazingly light step, rummaged for a moment then returned. Careful not to get into the line of the Luger, he pulled Wilson's hands behind him and quickly, expertly, lashed them together with the plastic-coated wire. With a satisfied grunt he finished the task, then pulled a small twist of string from his pocket and bound the detective's thumbs together. The prisoner winced with pain as the cord sunk into the flesh.

Russell nodded satisfaction, and slid the gun back out of sight into its jacket holster. "I take it we haven't got very much time before your friends arrive?" he asked.

"Stick around and find out," snapped Wilson. "You and your pals"—he glared at McBride and the fat man—"have caused two deaths so far, one of them in your own gang. That's two counts of murder . . . and the law says every man jack involved in a job like this is equally guilty."

McBride's face twitched nervously at his words. Harry contented himself with a push which sent his prisoner off balance and sprawling awkwardly into the nearby arm-chair.

"What's the idea, Russell?" asked McBride. "We going to leave the cop here? I'll tell Jacko to get the car out . . ."

"In a little while," said Russell in the same soft, deadly voice. "Right now there are a few things I want to find out. How did you obtain the lead to us, Wilson? It wasn't at the yacht, was it?"

"Does it matter?" pleaded McBride. "Look, for God's sake, Russell, let's get moving. There may be a score of his pals heading up the road right now."

"They might, but I don't think they are," purred Russell. "I'm waiting, Wilson."

"You can ruddy well wait," said the prisoner, squirming into a more upright position. "I promise, though, you'll hear every detail soon . . . along with the judge and jury."

His face an angry red, Russell stepped forward, clenched fist raised. But a sudden commotion from the rear of the house stopped the blow in mid-air. Wilson, craning his neck, gave a low whistle of dismay as the room door swung open and a tousled Paula Terry, one sleeve half-torn from her coat, was hustled in. Sailor released his tight grip on her arm, and gingerly examined his wrist. "The witch bit me," he complained.

Jacko, leaning against the doorpost and casually searching through the girl's handbag, explained, "She was hiding behind the dyke wall. You could spot that red mop of hair a mile away, though, and she didn't keep quite low enough." He whistled, "Nice girl . . ." and scooped out the tiny ·25 pistol which had been nestling beside the powder compact in the bag. "Just as well we grabbed her first go," he declared.

"Over here with that," ordered Russell.

Jacko raised an eyebrow at his tone, but obeyed, tossing the little weapon across the room. Russell caught it neatly. "The rest of the flex, Harry," he gestured. The fat man leered, and in his peculiarly light, yet lumbering gait, crossed over to the girl. "Neat little wrists," he declared, showing his teeth in an unpleasant grin and stroking her arm. He howled in dismay the next second as the girl's foot flicked backward and rapped his shin.

"Get on with the job," rapped Russell, and Harry, scowling, grabbed Paula's wrists again, muttering to himself.

"You solve a puzzle for me, Miss Terry," declared Russell, arms folded across his chest. "When you came in, I was wondering how best to dispose of your detective friend. Now, I think we have the solution. You see, you and he are the only two people who can link our little group together, and I've a feeling that though you may have friends nearby it will be some little time before they actually come looking for you. I see I'm right . . ." He smiled dangerously as the girl's eyes widened perceptibly. "Your car should be up the road a little way, I think. We'll bring it back down here, and park it neatly outside the cottage . . . where everyone can see it, I assure you. But then, when your friends do come, they'll find there's been a little accident—a fire. You and the zealous Mr. Wilson were so busy searching the cellar. It was such a pity that you dropped the oil lamp you need down there . . . we haven't electric light down below, I'm afraid. And the fire . . . there's such a lot of inflammable material in that cellar, it's a positive danger. Why the paraffin tank alone . . ." He shook his head in mock horror.

White-faced, Wilson told him, "As a plan it smells. They'd see through it quickly enough, and be after you again."

"Would they? Perhaps after a little while. But it will give our little party sufficiently long to get well away to a nice safe place," said Russell in that same soft voice. "Get him up from that chair, Sailor."

Slowly, uncertainly, Sailor moved towards Wilson. He put a hand on the detective's shoulder, and hauled him to his feet.

"Don't be a ruddy maniac, Russell,"

McBride, eyes wide with horror, stormed across the room. "You can't do it . . . my God, man, they'd hang us so fast we wouldn't have time to say a prayer. Tie them up and dump them in the cellar if you want, but leave it at that."

"Move them," said Russell, ignoring the plea. "Harry, bring that oil lamp, will you?"

McBride, face twisted in a mixture of passion and disgust, seized Russell by the jacket lapels and pulled him to within a few inches of his face. "No . . ." he roared.

Russell slammed his arms upwards and inside the safe-blower's grasp with such force that he broke the grip and sent McBride staggering. At the same time, his right foot danced behind the other man's leg . . . and his opponent crashed backwards on to the carpeted floor.

Shoving a lock of his dark hair back from his eyes, McBride scrambled to his feet giving a strange, animal-like growl. With one hand he scooped up the whisky bottle lying on the table, and with a quick movement smashed its base against the wood. Whisky and splinters of glass sprayed over the table . . . and, the savage, jagged remains of the bottle held a little way before him, he came forward again.

"I said no," he snarled. "We're in a big enough jam thanks to you already, Rus—" The whip-crack of a shot cut him short. McBride halted in mid-stride, one hand clasping his side, lips drawn back in a grin of pain. Then his legs buckled under him, and he collapsed to the floor.

A little curl of blue smoke wisped from Russell's hand, and he tossed Paula Terry's tiny pistol on to the chair beside him. Taking a step nearer the moaning man he lifted his foot and kicked twice. The first sent the smashed bottle careering across the carpet. The second took McBride slam in the face. With a faint sob Paula turned her head away.

"Anyone else?" asked Russell, hoarsely. Sobbing with pain, blood dribbling from the corner of his mouth, McBride began to drag himself into a sitting position, hand still clutching the wound in his side. As he did, Russell stood back a little and again began to swing his foot back, eye measuring the distance.

"Don't do it, Russell," said Jacko, his voice challenging and deliberate, his right hand going inside his jacket. Even as it got there, a dull, heavier explosion rang out. The little man jerked to his full height, mouth opening, then, slowly at first then in sudden collapse, crumpled to the floor. His right arm was crooked in front of his head . . . and a cigarette case lay inches away, dragged from his pocket even as he fell. It didn't need an expert to declare he was dead. The wide, raggedly round hole in his temple, the open but unseeing eyes, were ample proof.

Hand shaking violently, Harry stared in fascination at the Luger in his hand. The sharp tang of exploded cordite was acrid in the air. "I thought he was going for a gun," he almost whispered. "He . . . he had the other automatic. He took it from me just before he went on the launch to go out to the *Cockatoo* . . . I . . ." The trembling seemed to be spreading over his whole body. He looked round the room . . . at the girl, her face still turned away in horror . . . at Wilson, grim, tightlipped . . . at Sailor, shocked and bewildered. Lastly he turned to Russell, still standing by McBride, sunk back on the floor and suddenly quiet. "I thought he was going for a gun," pleaded the fat man again, now shaking like a jelly.

Russell licked his lips, then rubbed a finger over his moustache. "It was . . . unfortunate," he commented. "But maybe . . . yes, in a way it helps quite a lot." Supposing Wilson and the girl were found burned to death, their hands still tied. And supposing Jacko's body was found, obviously killed before the fire gutted the cottage.

If McBride's body was found with Wilson and the girl, and it bore a wound from the girl's gun—

The situation that would be suggested would be that Wilson and the girl had come to the cottage and had been surprised by the two men, but not before Paula Terry wounded one with her little pistol. And then? Perhaps the investigators, trying to piece together the clues remaining, would decide that there had been a quarrel, that McBride had shot Jacko, and had been about to imprison Wilson and Paula in the cellar when they were all trapped by the fire. For added realism, he could toss down both the guns just before he shut the cellar door. The Morris left outside the house would help, as if McBride had planned to use it to escape.

He turned to Sailor, who was still grasping Bill Wilson's shoulder. "Sailor, do you want to stay with Harry and I? I'll double your cut in the kitty."

Sailor, the uncertain look still on his face, swallowed, then nodded slowly.

"Good man. Know how to drive a car?" The man nodded again. "Right, then walk up the road till you find that Morris and bring it back down here. It shouldn't be far away. Wait a bit . . ." Russell strode over to where the girl's handbag was lying, and pulled the car keys from it. "There you are. Now get going, and be as fast as you can about it. Everything will be tidied up by the time you get back, and we'll be ready to leave."

Slowly, a trifle reluctantly, Sailor obeyed.

"Russell, listen to me," Wilson pleaded earnestly. "I don't know what crazy idea you're working up now, but if you've any sense you'll call the whole business off right now. Pack it in, man. At the moment, there's just a chance you might still only draw a long prison sentence. But start monkeying with us, and it's the rope . . . a long chill walk some morning at 8 a.m., then the black flag flying over the prison . . . while every warder in the place is banging doors to drown the noise of the gallows trap from the other prisoners!"

"Shut up," Russell bellowed across the room. "You and the girl got yourself into this mess by being too damned nosey. Do you think I'm going to throw away a fortune in precious stones—stones that'll take Harry and I anywhere in the world—just so that you can have the pleasure of arresting me?"

"It was my fault . . . please . . ." pleaded Paula. "My company found out from records that you'd been a guest at some other parties where there were robberies, and we just checked on from there. That's as much why we're here as anything else. You can't just shovel the blame on to Bill. Three people have died so far because of those jewels . . . can't you see how insane it is, how futile to start killing again?"

"At the moment, Miss Terry, I only know that the police have me marked—perhaps not enough to actually arrest me and stop me leaving the country, even if they find me. I'm getting out, right now. That means abandoning my business, most of the other assets I've got . . . but not these jewels. Now you and your friend, unfortunately, can identify me with not only those two on the floor, but my colleague Harry and our remaining assistant. Your friends outside the glen probably have a fairly reasonable idea as to the area you're in . . . it wouldn't take them many hours to find you, and if you were still alive, that would be me finished. It's a shame to waste a good-looking wench, but . . ." He shrugged, and turned away to bend over Jacko's body. Feeling rapidly over the dead man's clothes, he lifted the tail of the jacket . . . the missing Luger was beneath, held in a makeshift holster attached to the man's trouser belt. He pulled it free, then turned to McBride.

The safe-blower made an effort to drag himself to his feet as the tall, ruthless figure approached. Gun in one hand, Russell pulled him upright with the other,

307

then pushed the man towards the wall. McBride bit his lip hard at the stabbing agony the sudden movement caused to his wound, and gave an animal-like grunt of pain as Russell smashed the muzzle of the Luger into his unprotected stomach. "Stay still, you pig," growled his tormentor, searching him with his free hand. "What's . . ." His eyes narrowed as he felt in McBride's jacket pocket, then a sneering grin came on to his face as he brought out a small silver drinking flask. "Keep it," he jeered, ramming the flask back into the man's pocket "With luck, you may manage a last drink before it's all over. Harry . . . get the cellar hatch open, and that oil lamp lit. Then move that chest of drawers down until it's opposite the hatch."

He turned to the three left in the room. "It's very simple. McBride here took you prisoner, you see. But when you were all down in the cellar there was this terrible accident . . . you couldn't get back to the cellar hatch because the flames were so fierce. But just in case, by some strange miracle, you manage to get back up the stairs and try to open the hatchway, we're going to overturn the chest on top of the lid. The cottage will burn like a torch— these old buildings are all pitch-pine except the walls, and the place should go up as if soaked in petrol. If anything of the chest remains, well, it'll look just as if it fell over as the floorboards began to burn."

"You're crazy mad," growled Wilson, taking a step forward, and straining at the bonds that held his arms fast. "You can't force us down there . . . and if we stop a bullet it spoils your plan."

"True," admitted Russell, eyes narrow and bright behind their lenses. "But would you like to see your girl pistol-whipped? Not knocked out, just hit and hit again, perhaps ripped across the mouth with the sight-piece of this Luger . . . maybe another drag just above the eyes? It takes a little time, and it isn't as clean as a razor message. One of Laval's French Fascist boy's told me about it towards the end of the war. He wasn't a Fascist any more of course, it wasn't healthy. But I gathered he'd had some experience in the art." He raised the automatic threateningly. Paula, ashen, shut her eyes. Beaten, Wilson stopped in his tracks. Lip twisting in sardonic amusement, Russell turned and shouted, "Harry . . . are you ready yet?"

"Just moving . . . the . . . damn chest," came the reply from the hallway. There was a fresh creak of wood on wood, then the fat man, sweat beading on his forehead, reappeared "Lamp's lit," he reported. "I left it just outside the cellar hatch. And Sailor's coming down the road with the Morris."

"We'll wait till he gets in," said Russell. Three minutes later, as the man came back into the room, he found fresh instructions waiting. "Gather up our things, and get them out to the Jaguar. Then bring it from the shed and round to the front of the house . . . the keys are in the ignition lock." The man departed, and Russell, taking a last look around, said, "Time's up. Take McBride, Harry . . . I'll bring these two. The wounded man pushed along in the lead, they left the room and went into the gloom of the hall.

The cellar hatchway, lying at the back of the hall, gaped open. From its square shape a flight of wooden steps led downward into the darkness. Picking up the bright-burning oil lamp lying on the floor, the fat man forced McBride down and, three steps from the bottom, gave him a push in the small of the back which sent the safe-blower staggering. Feet scuffing the stone floor, hazed on by the pistol, he dragged himself towards the dark of the farthest corner, and sank down.

Russell dealt more gently with his two captives, but still pushed them down and over beside McBride, next to a miscellaneous collection of boxes, tins and old furniture.

He appeared almost sad as he looked at them by the light of the lamp. "This is it," he declared. "I don't like it having to be this way, but . . ." He shook his head, then, while Harry kept his gun covering the trio, moved across to the big twenty-gallon tank of paraffin, standing to the left of the steps. As he turned the tap at its foot, the pink liquid came gurgling out in a fast-flowing jet which spread in a dark pool over the floor, soaking round the foot of the stairway then, still spreading, beginning to reach out towards the nearest wall.

Russell, satisfied, turned the flow off again.

"Back now, Harry," he ordered. The fat man withdrew to the foot of the stairway, gun still at the ready.

"Russell . . . don't leave us to roast," croaked McBride. "These two won't give you away if you let them live . . . and I won't open my mouth, I swear."

"Too late," snapped Russell. "Up the stairs, Harry, then cover me from the top."

The fat man obeyed. Then, holding the lamp in one hand, Russell slowly mounted the stairway himself. He paused at the top, set down the lamp for a moment, and quickly but carefully wiped both Paula's tiny pistol and Harry's Luger while the fat man trained the gun taken from Jacko's body.

Then, moving rapidly, Russell tossed the two guns far into the cellar, picked up the oil lamp, and threw it down into the middle of the pool of paraffin. The glass smashed against the stone floor . . . there was a sudden blinding wave of heat and flame . . . and the cellar door shut with a bang. Even above the roar of the fire the three could hear the rumble as the heavy chest was pushed over the trap.

The scorching flames licked nearer every second.

313

12

AS the first blast of exploding heat receded in the cellar, a spreading, popping crackle of burning wood took its place, telling only too plainly how effective the spilled paraffin had been. And when the heat penetrated the temporary shield formed by the metal of the twenty-gallon tank . . . Wilson shuddered at the thought, and struggled afresh with his bonds. Then he felt strong, firm fingers on the flex, the touch of cold steel at his thumbs . . . and suddenly he was free.

"Cut the girl loose," gasped McBride. "Then come and help me." The flickering orange flames lighting the cellar showed beads of sweat already pouring down the man's face in the intense heat. He pressed an opened pen-knife into Wilson's hand, and gave a faint smile of encouragement.

"Cheer up, mate, we may get out yet . . ."

Wilson, already cutting at the flex binding Paula's wrists, shouted above the noise of the flames, "What do you mean? The cellar hatch? No hope . . . and it's the only way out."

Shielding her face from the scorching heat, Paula began massaging the circulation back into her wrists, the red glare playing strange tricks on her hair. Smoke billowing through the underground room nipped her eyes till the tears streamed down her cheeks. She was vaguely aware that, every step a dragging effort, one hand pressed hard against the wound in his side, McBride was scanning the upper section of the cellar wall. Suddenly he gave a shout, "Hey, copper . . . jump to it!"

Wilson scrambled to his side. The man bellowed in his ear. "There's our way out . . . that metal ventilation grill up above." He pointed to the grill, black with dirt and rust, tiny pinholes of light filtering through the tightly meshed metal. "I saw it from outside this morning, that's two feet above ground level."

"It's locked solid," shouted Wilson. "Built into the stone. No use . . . we've had it."

"Not on your ruddy life," snarled the safe-blower. "See this . . ." He held up the silver flask. "Look, you drag that big box over so you can reach that grill . . . don't argue."

Paula helped him shove the box across, the girl glancing apprehensively over her shoulder at the rapidly spreading flames, already licking dangerously close to the base of the paraffin tank.

"Up on it," shouted McBride. "Here . . ." He had the flask in his hands again, but it was a strange, unusual flask, realized Wilson. The base had been released, and out of the interior McBride was sliding what looked like a torch battery. "Hold that . . . carefully," he ordered. "It's gelignite. My 'first aid kit' I call it. Only way you can carry the stuff in safety—the container's got padded sides." He was unscrewing the stopper as he spoke. Out tumbled a tiny copper tube, just an inch long, and a short length of cord. "Detonator and twenty second fuse," he shouted, hurriedly placing the fuse in the hole at the top of the detonator, then crimping down the copper edges with his teeth. "Stick . . ." Wilson handed back the gelignite and McBride swiftly pushed the detonator home. He glanced wildly around, then seized a piece of the cut flex from the floor. "Lash the stick tight against the grill," he instructed. "Tight now . . . our lives depend on it." Coughing, spluttering in the dense smoke, tormented by the building heat, Wilson obeyed. "Now this," yelled McBride, grunting with pain as he dragged over a heavy block of wood he had found. "Jam it behind the gelignite. Got a match?"

In the face of the approaching inferno, the query for a match was almost humorous. But Wilson nodded.

"Light the fuse . . . then get the hell down here," shouted McBride. Wilson scraped a match against the stone wall, lit the short length of fuse, then jumped down through the dense, swirling smoke.

"In the corner, face down," instructed McBride between racking coughs. The three crouched side by side.

In the confined space, the blast battered and thundered against their ear-drums. They were conscious of small fragments of stone, wood and other pieces of material peppering around them. When they looked again, the grill was free at one end, and daylight streaming in. Wilson jumped back on the box and, exerting every ounce of strength left in his frame, wrenched the whole structure backwards and inwards.

"Girl first," he gasped, and seized Paula by the waist to give her an upward boost. She scraped and tore her way through the narrow hole. "You next," he gasped, turning to McBride. The safe-blower waved him on. "No ruddy heroics. Get up," ground Wilson. McBride pulled himself on to the box, reached up, grabbed the stone sill of the grill, then let go with a groan. "No use," he moaned. "Pain. Can't."

"Try, man," sweated Wilson, conscious of the flames now eating at the wooden trestles of the paraffin tank. It should blow any second. "Up . . ." McBride made another grab, pulled, then Wilson got his shoulder under the man's bulk and strained upwards. Suddenly, the man was through, and the inspector scrambled at his heels, ignoring the stone that barked his knees and shoulders, the smashed, jagged metal that tore at his clothes.

Out . . . he staggered a few yards, then fell face down on the wet snow, head reeling, every muscle shouting protest, throat a red agony. And a dull boom and fresh wave of heat signalled the explosion of the paraffin tank, while the tinkle of glass and clatter of slates told of the blast's effect on the cottage. Rolling over on his side, he blinked through red-rimmed eyes at the building. Smoke and flames were ripping from nearly every window.

"Confucius say, 'Wise man get out smartly,'" gulped a slightly hysterical voice in his ear. Then Paula, smoke-grimed, her clothes torn and blackened, was in his arms, sobbing as she buried her face in his shoulder.

Rab Kearns and young Lachie found them an hour later. The police Sunbeam came over the treacherous road surface at a mad rate, its driver spurred on by the ominous column of black smoke soaring into the sky from the still burning skeleton of the cottage.

The two men tumbled from the car, and were gazing in horror at the gutted shell of the building when Wilson hailed them. A welcoming white-toothed grin split his smoke-blackened face as they hurried across to the side of the house, passing

Paula's car, cellulose heat-blistered but otherwise intact.

"What in God's name's been happening, sir?" blurted the sergeant, his normal phlegmatic manner shaken. "Are you all right—how about the lassie?"

"Round the back," gestured Wilson. "We're OK, Rab, but we've been a darn sight closer to the Pearly Gates than I ever want to be again." He led them towards the backyard shed, still standing though a few blackened patches on its roof showed where sparks from the cottage had burned and smouldered. "We got in here for shelter . . . I thought it was going up too, a couple of times. But," he gave a ghost of a smile, "I threw snowballs at the flames."

"We waited around the AA box for a bit," said Kearns. "Then we thought you'd maybe gone off the road, or got stuck in a drift, and came looking. Thank God we did."

As the three men entered the gloom of the shed, Paula rose to her feet with a tired smile of welcome. Beside her, covered with Wilson's coat and lying on the rear seat squab ripped from the Morris, lay the man who had saved her life. Pale and weak from loss of blood, it was with an effort he raised his head to peer at the approaching figures. Kearns bent low over him, eyes widening in surprise.

"Con McBride . . . no wonder that safe on the *Cockatoo* was opened so neatly. This fellow's top in his class, sir, though I haven't heard of him operating in Scotland before. So far he's only been a photograph in *Police Gazette* notices."

"He's top of his class in more ways than one," said Wilson. "McBride blasted a hole out of that cottage cellar, or you would have been sifting ashes right now to find what was left of us. He's told me all he knows about the raid and the man behind it."

"Russell?" queried the sergeant.

"Russell. He's on the loose again in his Jaguar with two members of the gang. This was their headquarters . . . there's another one of them lying somewhere in that cottage with a bullet in him, shot by one of his pals."

"That's right, copper," said McBride, looking up from his makeshift couch. "The swine organized the whole *Cockatoo* job, and a dirty blood-stained job he made

321

of it too. He's trying to make a break for it now . . . trying to get the loot to Ireland as first stage out of the country to Holland."

"They won't make it, chum," said Kearns. He turned to Wilson. "I was phoning Superintendent Melvin again. We've got road-blocks on every highway in the West of Scotland, plus mobile patrols. A ruddy bicycle couldn't get through, let alone that Jaguar."

"Think you can squeeze us all into the Sunbeam, Rab?" queried Wilson. "McBride here will need the back seat to himself, I'm afraid, and the keys of the Morris are either in Russell's pocket or somewhere in the cottage."

"Aye, we'll manage somehow . . . if Miss Terry doesn't mind sitting on your knee in the front," he twinkled. "The young fellow here," he nodded to Lachie MacLeod, "can get on the floor at the back."

"First stage towards the judge and jury, I suppose," winced McBride as, gently, they began to help him round from the shed to the Sunbeam. "Well, I knew I was chancing a preventive detention stretch when I took on the job."

"Once that wound mends you'll have to face the courts," agreed Wilson. "But this I promise, McBride, you won't lack friends to speak up for you . . . things won't be too bad. Hell, man, we can't send a ruddy hero to jug for the maximum term."

They settled him as comfortably as possible, stretched out on the rear seat. Then slowly, carefully, the loaded car headed back through the white drifts to the main road . . . and only young Lachie MacLeod saw the way the safe-blower's teeth clamped tight in pain as the Sunbeam swayed and bumped. Once on the main road, however. Progress was smoother and quicker, and in a very few minutes they reached the Automobile Association box, where the khaki-clad road scout was still waiting. He had company—the crew of an Argyll police car which had arrived about half an hour before.

Wilson went straight to the telephone in the road-side box. "Effie?" He asked the operator. "Good. Get me Dunoon police . . . and Effie, be a good girl this time . . .

you know what I mean." The connexion took only a minute. Effie was doing her best to please. Swiftly but leaving out no pertinent detail, he told Melvin what had happened at the cottage.

"I'm sending McBride down in your police-car. He'll need to go straight into hospital . . . and he deserves the best. Oh, and we could use some police and firemen up at that cottage. There's that body to bring out, among other things . . . one Jacko Bright. The charge for that killing is against Russell's junior partner, Harry Vogt. Flick McKellar killed Vinator."

"Hmm." Even over the telephone wires Wilson could hear the faint tapping of a pencil on a desk-top. "That brings us to the score against Russell," said the superintendent. "I make it one charge of murder—Flick McKellar—though we'll have a job proving it. Then there's three of attempted murder, for the fire-raising job, one of shooting McBride, one of assault on the *Cockatoo* watchman—not counting his part in the actual robbery. This boy's going to be in trouble, isn't he," he concluded drily. "What are you planning to do now?"

"I'm damned if I rightly know. Head for the nearest hotel, I suppose, get a wash-and-brush-up, a couple of stiff drinks and a square meal. Paula needs a rest . . . in fact, I wanted to send her back down with McBride, but she's still as stubborn as a mule."

"Fair enough. Take my tip, laddie, and head for the Ross Arms," said Melvin. "It's about nine miles from where you are, and as good as they come in the Highlands. I'll grab a car and run up to join you . . . and I'll leave orders for any 'gen' that comes in to be pushed on to the hotel. That's a blank area you're in, as far as radio reception's concerned, so the car sets are useless. But unless these three are hiding in a ditch somewhere we should soon hear of them bumping into a road-block somewhere."

They did.

At 4.55 p.m., according to the official police occurrence report filed later, Russell's grey Jaguar came along the quiet loch-side road straight towards the arms of a waiting police check-point crew.

Russell was at the wheel, Harry by his

side clutching the precious briefcase containing the *Cockatoo* gems, while Sailor hunched miserably in the soft luxury of the rear seat. For nearly two hours they had been on the road. Already there had been two hairsbreadth escapes from police patrols. In the first, Russell managed to skid the car off the road and behind some trees till an approaching car had passed. In the second, they had seen a road-block ahead just as the Jaguar came slowly over the brow of a hill. The police at the block were talking to a lorryman whom they had stopped—and Russell managed to reverse back out of sight without being spotted.

Ploughing once more through the sea of slush, ice and crusting snow, seldom seeing a house in all that wasteland of mountain and glen, they seemed at last to be slipping through the fine mesh of the net. So far, though, they had put only twenty miles between themselves and the cottage, and it was small consolation, thought Russell, that Wilson and the others should now be scorched, almost unidentifiable corpses. He hadn't expected a full-scale hunt to be mounted so quickly. Obviously he had been wrong when he had imagined that the police were only suspicious. They wanted him—wanted him badly. Still, if the car could wriggle through, there was no one living who could link Harry with the raid. He could still get away with the haul on the round-about journey to the Hague. Sailor, too, could skip out . . . and Russell himself could probably chance heading for London if he shaved off his moustache and dyed his hair—two small items sufficient to drastically alter any appearance. It would have helped even more if he could have shed his glasses—but without them his myopic eyes could pick up only a blurred image of the world around. The two changes must do—and once he got to London he could quickly organize an escape route.

It was comparatively easy going on the loch-side. The snow was smoother, thinner, on the road surface, thanks to the combined action of wind and water. The Jaguar was rolling along at a steady 45 m.p.h. over the slippery surface. Across the grey, still waters the pale sun was glinting, and there was hardly a cloud in the dull blue sky.

And they saw the road-block. The Jaguar had just swung round a curve in the highway where the road, following the line of the loch, was hacked out of the living rock. The police-car, a Riley, lay about two hundred yards on, swung across the breadth of the highway. One man was at the wheel, the other standing a little way in front and already waving them to slow down.

Cigarette clamped tight between his lips, Russell dropped the Jaguar down a gear, gauged the gap between the bonnet of the Riley ahead and the unfenced edge of the drop to the loch. His foot smashed the accelerator down to the floorboard, and the engine's six cylinders bellowed in an orgy of power. The grey car shot forward towards the now wildly waving policeman. Thirty yards . . . twenty . . . the man had drawn his baton . . . ten . . . Russell eased the wheel over a fraction. There was a splintering crash and the windscreen starred before him as the hurled baton hit the glass. The fat man gave a cry of fear, Sailor, hypnotized by the rushing loch-side, began fumbling with the rear door-handle. Only inches to spare, the Jaguar slid past the Riley's radiator while Russell peered through the cracked, distorted glass and swung the steering wheel back. Pitching wildly over the rough verge, nearside wheels inches from space, the car swung back towards the road again . . . and the wildly skidding rear wheel hit a low, snow-cloaked boulder.

The whole ton and a half of car seemed thrown into the air, then came down again with a crash. Sailor bounced across the compartment like a rubber ball . . . hit the nearside door, and, as it burst open, disappeared through it in a shrieking tangle of arms and legs.

For nearly two hundred yards more the Jaguar zig-zagged down the road, Russell sawing at the wheel, unable to brake, to accelerate, to do anything but try to steer it away from the plunge into the waiting loch waters. Then at last the car slowed its mad way, he recaptured the "feel" of the controls and, rear door still swaying gently backwards and forwards, the car got under way again.

Beside him, Harry was being noisily sick on the floor. Russell himself was trembling like a leaf. But they were through . . . and still free.

The police car radioed Dunoon a few minutes later. "We picked up the man who was thrown out," said the crewman. "He's a bit mangled . . . looks like a smashed pelvis among other things. Went straight over the edge, bounced on some rocks, then plopped into the water, he did. We'll need an ambulance . . . daren't move him the way he is. Over."

"Roger, K16," crackled control. "We'll send a wagon immediately and pass the word. Over."

"K16 to control. That Jag won't get far. She's spouting petrol from her tank. Must have holed it as she went over that boulder. And that smashed windscreen won't help either."

For all of three miles Jonathan Russell drove at that same breakneck pace, the rear door still flapping, before he dared slow the car, assured that the police patrol was not on his tail. Only in the last mile had he become conscious of the falling needle on the dashboard petrol gauge, a gauge now registering only two gallons in one of the car's twin tanks, none in the other. Beside him, Harry Vogt was gradually beginning to recover something approaching composure again.

Russell curled his lip in disgust at the man's weakness. "I'm stopping the car. Try and get that mess cleaned up before I get back," he growled, pulling the Jaguar in beside an overhanging rock and stepping out. Gratefully, he stretched his arms in luxurious fashion, feeling the cold clean mountain air filling his lungs, the cathedral-like hush of the wintry Highland scene soothing his jangled nerves. The wind had dropped. Nothing moved in the whole white stillness.

He walked round to the back of the car, the odour of petrol fumes coming to his nostrils as, carefully stubbing his cigarette in the snow, he bent to examine the underside of the tail. A slow trickle of fuel was still coming from the gashed nearside tank. That left only the offside twin . . . and he'd been running on that all day. "Two gallons," he swore. "That won't take us far . . ." Rising, Russell launched an ill-tempered kick at the nearest tyre, slammed shut the half-open rear door, and returned to his seat. He lit another cigarette, and sat back, completely ignoring the fat man. Sailor and the car . . . was there to be no end to it at all?

He began to polish his glasses in unconscious habit. "We'll need to get another car, Harry. Anything. The Jaguar sticks out like a sore thumb now, and it wouldn't take us much farther anyway."

Colour just beginning to return to his cheeks, Harry Vogt took a long time answering. The world was a grey, miserable place just then, even the satchel of jewellery held little attraction. He almost wished the car had gone over the lochside . . . things would at least have finished, then and there. Slowly he moistened his dry lips and asked, "If we get a car, what do we do then? Keep heading south?" He almost sobbed. "We're bound to be picked up, Russell, we're bound to be . . . my God, what a hellish mess, what a mess we're in."

"Belt up," snarled Russell. "What do you want to do? Give yourself up to the police? Stop blubbering, and shove over that map again."

Russell snatched the printed sheet from

him, and spread it open in a crackle of paper. "We want somewhere where we can lie up overnight . . . perhaps even all day tomorrow," he declared. "If we can do that, then the police will think we've slipped through, they'll call off some of their men, and we'll stand at least an even chance." He pored over the map, with its mass of brown mountain contours, only occasionally relieved by the blue of water and the thin tracings of green glens. As he stared, the faint glimmer of an idea began to emerge, the green and brown and blue became a swimming haze before him as his mind toyed and twisted with possibilities. Somewhere we can lie up overnight . . . somewhere not likely to be searched, yet where we can get warmth, food.

There was a harder, familiar set about his mouth as he declared, "Snap out of it, Harry. You'll maybe get that holiday in Monte Carlo yet. Once we've found a new car, well, we'll see . . ."

Angus Wright, crofter, was humming happily at the wheel of his elderly Austin. It had been a good day . . . hadn't he managed that little piece of business about the sheep subsidy to the confusion of that Civil Service mannie, with a nice little cheque due to come along in a few weeks . . . and wasn't he now going home, ready to celebrate the occasion, the comforting bulge of a half-bottle of his old friend Dugal's triple-run elixir in his jacket pocket?

Only another four miles to home, and the roads were a wee bit better than they had been in the morning . . . Lizzie would have the tea about ready, he thought comfortably. Hallo . . . there was a big car stopped ahead, and two men waving. Windscreen smashed too. Still humming happily, he braked to a gradual halt beside the other car.

"Would you be in trouble, now?" he hailed the tall, worried-looking stranger coming across. "Can I be helping you with a run down the road?"

The stranger smiled. "It's really quite simple," he said . . . and in two swift movements wrenched open the car door and dragged the surprised crofter from behind the wheel and half into the road.

"Take your great hands off," spluttered Angus. "I'll be losing tempe . . . r," he faded into silence at the sight of the gun in the second man's hand, pointed fair and square towards him.

"You won't be harmed," soothed the tall stranger. "Just come out of the car quietly. We want to borrow it for a while." Hypnotized by their menacing attitudes, the crofter climbed the rest of the way out of the Austin.

Quickly checking the car's petrol gauge, standing at just below full, Russell said, "Now just start walking down the road apiece, and nothing'll happen to you."

"But how am I to be getting home?" wailed Angus.

"On your two flat feet, I'm afraid," sighed Russell. Then, losing his patience, "Get moving." He shoved the little man away from the car, and Angus, losing his balance, crashed to the ground. A look of horror spread over his face as he rose, one hand feeling his side. "My bottle . . . my bottle is smashed . . . och the triple-run . . . you black devils." The men took a step nearer. "I'm going. All right, I'm going," he moaned.

A faint dribble of finest still-juice was coming from Angus's pocket as he hobbled

335

away into the gathering dusk, mumbling to himself. The two men looked at each other, then, for the first time in many hours, burst into fits of uncontrollable laughter. The sound carried far . . . and Angus, still making his way down the road, turned to shake his fist.

Tears of mirth in his eyes, Harry raised the Luger and fired over the crofter's head. The man's pace accelerated into a clumsy gallop, and the two by the car went into fresh roars of laughter, almost hysterical in degree. Russell clung helplessly to the side of the old Austin. But at last, he stopped and, still shaking with mirth and freed tension, declared, "Come on, transfer over . . . and don't forget that satchel, Harry."

They drove off in the rusty old car, heading west, back into the wild, cloud-hung mountains.

13

SURROUNDED by a high, unclimbable fence, the squat, harsh jumble of wires and metal, red man-high porcelain insulators and skeletal grey towers was like a science-fiction nightmare, a Martian mirage. In fact, it was a prosaic electricity board post serving as giant meter and fuse-box for the hydro scheme twenty miles north.

Sheltering behind Ben Vonnach's massive west shoulder, the station took in the set of high-voltage cables that ran by pylon from the hydro scheme, checked its current, and fed it out again in two directions—the main towards the national grid, a tiny portion eight miles to Ardvare power station, to serve a dozen small villages in West Argyll.

Lit by a battery of powerful outside lamps, the rectangle of ground formed a bright beacon in the darkness. In its centre was the low single-storey station building, built of grey native granite, where the duty engineer went about his systematic tasks. The station was a startling construction to find in the desolate, lonely mountain land, but already, although it had been built for only three summers, even the shy deer accepted it as much a part of their lives as the rocks and burns. They passed by without fear or interest.

But this night it was not deer that watched the station. Jonathan Russell and the last of his helpers took in the bright, yet lonely scene with grim satisfaction.

"There's our shelter," said Russell, sitting in the car, all lights extinguished, some five hundred yards away from the building. "As long as the power keeps flowing nobody's likely to bother checking the place. Two, maybe three men at the most working in it . . . see that little house in the far corner of the compound? And this road leads straight down to the main gate . . . in fact that looks like the only gate."

"What if it is locked?" asked Harry, hands buried in his overcoat pockets in an attempt to keep warm.

"Then we ask them to open up. We can say we've been lost in the mountain roads, stuck in the snow, and will they put us up for the night. Then, when we're inside . . ." Russell's lips drew back in a wolfish grin, and he pushed the starter button. Lights out, engine little more than ticking over, the old car began to roll down the gentle incline towards the station. Swishing over the carpet of snow, the Austin swept towards the high, concrete fence posts with their jutting crown of barbed wire, and stopped at the long swing of the spike-topped gate.

"Get out and try it," grunted Russell. Harry heaved himself out of the car, and padded across. Next instant he gave a quick thumbs up sign, and began to swing open the heavy gate. The Austin came quietly forward and through, to stop just within the compound. Russell got out, and the two men moved silently forward. All around they could feel, as much as hear, the humming, pulsating power as a hundred and fifty thousand volts poured their silent path. It was a strange, eerie feeling. The very hair on their heads seemed to prickle with the unseen energy.

They reached the door of the station and quietly tried the massive brass handle. It turned smoothly, and they tiptoed into a cream-painted corridor where the air was warm with the heat of a score of radiator pipes. The humming had grown to a buzzing, the faint click of relay switches and meter instruments coming from all around. Russell made a warning gesture to his companion, and crept down the corridor to where a brown wooden door stood ajar. He peeped inside, into a large room in which a row of filing cabinets and a large instrument panel occupied two walls. An elderly, balding man was seated at a desk in the middle, busy writing in a logbook. Drawing the Luger from his jacket pocket and stepping into the doorway, Russell ordered, "Just stay right there . . . don't move, don't touch anything."

The operator gave a startled gasp and half-rose from his seat. He saw the gun, and sank slowly back into the chair, eyes opening wide. Russell stepped forward, Harry, gun also drawn, hard on his heels.

"Anyone else here?" demanded Russell.

"No . . . not here," gasped the engineer. "Jim's at . . . I mean . . ."

"Jim's where?" snapped Russell,

moving towards the telephone on the desk. He seized the cord, and wrenched the instrument wire bodily from its junction. The man sat silent, mouth open, watching the gun. "Jim's where?" came the question again. "Don't keep me waiting. We're not playing at games."

"At . . . at the cottage," blurted the man. "He's off duty just now. He'll be resting."

"Anyone else? Families?"

The man shook his head. "Just the two of us live here."

Russell's eyes gleamed bright behind his spectacle lenses. "Fetch him, Harry," he ordered. The fat man slid from the room. Prowling round the desk, Russell seized a cake of chocolate lying beside the logbook. Between munches he asked, "What do you do at this place?"

"Make sure the power supply keeps operating properly . . . we keep a check on quantity, the wires and things like that. It's a sort of safety switch-box, mister. What . . . what are you wanting with us . . . are you the IRA?"

Russell shook his head. "Don't worry. We don't want to blow up your power station, or whatever it is. We're going to stay here tonight, maybe tomorrow, then move on. You'll go about your normal routine work, we'll tie you up when we leave—and that'll be the end of it. You won't be harmed—if you do as you're told."

The outer door banged open, and next minute Harry prodded a sleepy-eyed youngster into the room. "Here's Jim," he declared. "And I picked this up while I was at it . . ." he slapped a whisky bottle on the table. Russell flicked the cap off one-handed, and took a long swig. He laid the bottle down again, wiping his mouth with the back of his hand.

"Well, young Jim," he said. "I've been telling your friend here we're going to be your guests for a day or so. Nothing to worry about . . . though we'll tie you up for a start." One by one he jerked open the drawers of the filing cabinets, and finally threw a coiled length of thin cable from one across the room to Harry. The fat man obliged, leaving the youngster trussed like a chicken, perched uncomfortably on a hard wooden chair.

Peeling off his already unbuttoned coat,

and throwing it carelessly on top of a cabinet, Russell said, "I'll look after our other friend . . . what's your name, anyway?"

Sullenly, the older of the two operators muttered, "Mitchell."

"I'll look after Mr. Mitchell. You bring the car up to the building, and see if you can gather some food down at the house. We'll have the key of the main gate, Mitchell."

Silently, the sub-station operator took the heavy key from his desk drawer and passed it over.

"That's a good Mitchell. On your way, Harry. Lock the gate while you're at it."

The jewel satchel on the desk, they were eating thick bread-and-meat sandwiches backed by an enamel pot of tea when from somewhere out in the corridor a bell rang two long peals. "What's that?" demanded Russell, jerking upright and seizing the pistol from where he had laid it, inches from his hand.

"It's Ardvare power station," said the operator, a gleam of hope in his eye. "It's time for our nightly check call with them."

"Check call? On that?" asked Russell, pointing to the useless telephone.

"No . . . we've a carrier telephone system that works on the power lines. They check through every night, to confirm meter readings. There's a headphone set on one of the panels in the main meter room." The bell shrilled again, loud, insistent.

"Answer it then," ordered Russell. "But I'm right behind you. Say what you have to, and no more."

The man gave a despairing glance to his bound companion, nodded wearily, and, rising, walked into the corridor and through another door into the huge, high-ceilinged meter room. Rubber matting running the length of the floor, the brick-walled room was lined with black enamelled cabinets, all packed with electronic devices automatically measuring and watching the slightest variation in the power flow amidst a constant clucking, buzzing and clicking of instruments. Rows of dials stared out, their indicator needles steady . . . and everywhere that soft penetrating hum. The operator flipped open a panel-cover and, under Russell's suspicious gaze, connected up a headphone set with practised ease. Russell, prodding him gently in the back with the gun, mouthed, "Go ahead."

"Hallo Ardvare," said the older man. "Vonnach here."

"Hallo Vonnach," came the metallic voice of his counterpart, from over the miles. "Everything OK? You took a time getting there."

Russell scowled a warning. "I—I was out in the compound doing a maintenance job," explained his prisoner. "Sorry . . . do you want to check the readings?"

"Aye, Sandy . . . I've a fresh pot of tea on the brew, so let's get it over with," said the Ardvare operator. For the next couple of minutes they exchanged long, complicated sets of key figures. Then, with a cheery "'Night man," the Ardvare operator shut down.

"Is this the only apparatus for this kind of talking?" asked Russell. The man bit his lip, then nodded. Russell pulled the headset from his grip, and stuffed the clumsy shape inside his jacket, then demanded, "When's your next check due?"

"Ten o'clock tomorrow morning," muttered the man. "See here, mister," he became more spirited. "You canny just run about waving guns like this an' shoving me and the lad about. This is an electricity board station—Government property."

Casually, without his expression changing a fraction, Russell smashed the back of his hand across the operator's mouth. The man's head jerked back, a red weal on his face, a thin trickle of blood beginning to ooze from a cut lip.

"Listen, little man. Listen carefully. We're on the run. Out there somewhere are an awful lot of policemen. But we're in here, where there are no policemen. And we've got these—" he hefted the Luger. "You keep your ruddy power-house running, and just leave the worries to us. Now, just in case you've any ideas . . ." He moved to the opened panel, gazed at the mass of circuits of tiny valves, hesitated, then cautiously removed two of the little glass-topped components from their sockets. "I'll keep these till the morning," he declared. "You'll get them back for 10 a.m., and if they happen to try to call you between times . . . well, you tell them tomorrow that there was a minor fault and you had a difficult time repairing it."

The operator hesitated.

"Well? Let's get back."

"I—I can't. There's some work to be done. I've got to check the current flow. If I don't then a fault might develop in the lines."

It was Russell's turn to hesitate, faced with the unknown. At last he agreed, "Go ahead. But just do your job . . . no tricks."

The operator moved towards a bank of panels, and, under Russell's hawk-like gaze, began slowly adjusting dials and switches. At last he turned. "It's done," he nodded. "But I'll need to do it again in another half-hour. It's done every half-hour."

Uneasy, but determined to avoid anything which might cause suspicion in the outside world, Russell agreed. "You can do it. Just keep things running, and stay out of trouble . . . that's all we want. Now get the hell back to the office."

Head lowered, the man obeyed.

The "private" sign hung on the resident's lounge door wasn't really necessary. Casual visitors were few and far between during the off-season at the Ross Arms, and a couple of shepherds gossiping over a pint in the public bar were the only other customers that night.

Behind the shut door, Superintendent Melvin, relaxed after a satisfying meal, took his time filling a battered pipe from an equally battered-looking pouch. On the couch opposite him sat Bill Wilson and Paula Terry. Sergeant Kearns and Lachie MacLeod were sitting a little distance away. Awestruck, the young constable was listening to the Glasgow man's account of some of his early adventures as a beat cop among the big city's "neds" and hoodlums. Striking a match, Melvin puffed carefully at his pipe, got it burning to his satisfaction, and gave another satisfied sigh. "Och well, I suppose we'd better get down to work," he declared. "Though I must admit I don't feel at all inclined."

"That makes two of us," yawned Paula.

"I could curl up and go to sleep here and now. What's the time, Bill?"

Wilson glanced at his wrist-watch. "Leaving eight-thirty, I make it. The night's young yet. Say, I wonder what that character Russell's up to right now. It's what, nearly two hours since that last report came in."

"Aye," nodded Melvin. "I told them to phone me the moment there was any trace of that old Austin Russell's pinched."

"Do you think they could have got through and away?" asked Paula.

Melvin grunted, and settled back in his arm-chair. "No' much chance of that, lassie," he declared. "It could have happened, of course, switching cars the way they did. But every policeman we can squeeze is out there on the lookout. And as soon as that doctor brought Angus what's his name down to Ardvare village and told how he'd found him walking along the road, crying for his car and his bottle, we put that new alarm out. Incidentally, I sent a man away with a breakdown team to bring the Jaguar back."

"That fellow Travers is lucky to be alive

349

after the tumble he took," declared Wilson.

"Aye, Inspector, he is that," Melvin stopped, frowning, as the light in the room flickered, died for a second, leaving them in firelight, then came back to full brilliance. It flickered again, then resumed its steady glow. "Something wrong with the power," he shrugged. "Little wonder in weather like this—it's freezing hard outside. Anyway, as I was saying, Sailor Travers must have fallen from that car like a drunk man—completely relaxed, hardly knowing what was happening to him—to avoid being killed on the rocks. Mind you, he was smashed up quite a bit. It'll be a while before he can stand trial."

Paula gave a stretch and crossed her ankles, feeling almost back to her usual self after the bath and change of clothing provided by the hotelier's wife. "And he's got no idea where they were heading for?" she asked.

Wilson took a deep pull at his pipe, the tobacco glowing red in the bowl. "No. They were still trying to get down south, that's all he knows. Och, we could theorize all night and get nowhere. Either they're sitting in that Austin somewhere in the mountains, damn near freezing, or they're bowling down the Glasgow road . . . and for all we know they might be in yet another car. But they seldom get away, lass, always remember that. There's an awful lot of policemen in this wee world of ours, and they don't give up easily."

They sat silent for a spell, staring at the glowing fire, each with their own private thoughts.

Melvin's were purely professional. Russell and the man Harry Vogt could have got through the cordon all right. There were plenty of side roads, and however ubiquitous the police under his control might be, there would always remain holes through which the fugitives might escape. Or, he frowned, they could have decided to lie low in some cottage . . . though he had instructed his men to make checks wherever possible. Full descriptions of Russell and Vogt had been circulated by teleprinter to all neighbouring forces, while Scotland Yard were doing the same service in the south and commencing a watch on Russell's London haunts. One trump card held by the police was that Russell didn't know Wilson, and more especially McBride, had survived the cottage fire. His plans were known, his guilt proven beyond all doubt; Vogt's identity was firmly established; and the hunt was no longer a weak-kneed "detain for questioning" affair, but a full-blooded pursuit.

Wilson's thoughts were at least partly professional. He still marvelled at the narrowness of the escape they had had in that cottage cellar. He still felt a cold shiver at the brutal, callous disregard for life shown by Jonathan Russell. But something—or somebody—else kept cropping up in his mind, no matter how firmly he tried to shove the matter into the background. He risked a sidelong glance at Paula, marvelling at the sheen in her hair, the smooth clean beauty of her face, the soft curve of her figure . . . and gave an almost blushing grin as he found the girl's eyes returning his glance, softly mocking, yet with a glow in them which made him feel like gulping.

To cover his confusion, he made a noisy show of summoning the barman and ordering another round of drinks. Before they arrived, however, the hotel proprietor came into the lounge, heading straight for Superintendent Melvin. "It's the phone," he explained. "The police station is wanting you."

"Dunoon?" queried Melvin.

The hotelier shook his head. "It's big Andy Drummond, the sergeant at Ardvare," he replied. A puzzled look on his face, Melvin followed the man from the room to the hotel's solitary phone, situated in a draughty box beside the office. He returned a few minutes later, looking more puzzled than ever. "We'll need to get over to Ardvare," he told the expectant group. "There's something funny going on at the local power station. They've been on the phone to Ardvare police, and from what I can gather we'd better take a look ourselves. We'll need about half an hour to get there. I'll take my own car . . . you follow on."

Ardvare power station stood on the outskirts of the village, a big red-brick box of a building. A police-car was already parked outside it, and the sergeant and constable crew were waiting in the main switch-room with the two duty engineers.

Melvin returned their salutes with a nod, acknowledged the introductions to the two electricity men, then got down to business. "You say there's something wrong with Vonnach meter station . . . what's it got to do with us?"

"Quite a lot, I think, sir," said the sergeant. "But I think I'd better let the power station men tell you themselves."

The smaller of the two engineers waved his hands excitedly. "There's something wrong all right . . . and it's police we're needing. The men at Vonnach are sending SOS messages . . . someone's taken over the power station."

"Taken it over?" exclaimed Wilson. "How can you be so sure?"

"Because of the messages . . . look, why are you waiting here? You're wasting time."

"Easy, easy," soothed Melvin. "Tell us what's happened, then we'll have a better idea what to do."

The little man simmered down a trifle. "All right. First, we can't raise them, either on the outside phone or on our own carrier telephone system." He frowned impatiently at the blank looks which met his statement. "We can superimpose a carrier telephone band on the high frequency voltage cables," he explained. The looks grew blanker. "I'll make it as simple as I can. We can use the power wires as telephone lines without stopping the normal electricity going through them. We made a routine check call to Ben Vonnach at eight-thirty, and spoke to the duty engineer. Everything seemed in order. But immediately after the call the power was cut twice, just for a second or so each time."

"We noticed that," nodded Melvin.

"That was only the start. We tried the two phone systems, and found them dead. Then just afterwards this morse message began. Someone was feeding an oscillation into the current and using the control key to make and break the signal."

"An oscillation?"

"A test signal note. There's a special apparatus for doing it. You see, we'd switched on to check the line after the twin fades. The oscillation's a high-pitched sound. From the way it comes over we can tell if the power lines are in good condition. Whoever was sending this probably had the apparatus working so that no sound would be heard at his end. And the message . . . that's what really shook us." He picked up the message pad lying before him. "Here it is, Superintendent. We didn't realize what it was at the beginning, and missed the first word. But the rest was 'men here guns'."

Melvin swore softly. "Russell," he declared.

"That's not all. We kept the apparatus on, and about half an hour later there was another message. It was the oscillating signal again. 'Held guns SOS.' The outside phone's dead, the carrier phone's dead, and whoever is sending from Vonnach is switching off the oscillating apparatus as soon as he finishes his message."

"How long since the last message?"

"About fifteen minutes. And the power flickered twice just before it began. They're trying to get help, Superintendent."

Melvin spun on his heel. "How far to Ben Vonnach? Eight miles?" he asked one of the waiting police. The man nodded agreement. "Right," snapped Melvin.

"We'll get weaving right away. I'd like you to come along too," he told the engineer. "Your mate can look after things and see if any other messages come through . . . and there's a chance we may need your help."

The three cars set off minutes later, Melvin, the engineer and one of the local police in the first; Wilson, Paula, Kearns and Lachie MacLeod in the second, and more local police in the third. It was a slow, nerve-wracking journey over the roads, where slush and churned-up snow had been frozen into slippery, glass-like sheets by the cold night air. Rounding one sharp bend, Melvin's car slid helplessly across the road and scraped along the hedge, smashing a headlamp glass, bending a wing. But it was otherwise intact, and continued in the lead. In the cold, clear night, with a bright moon shining, the wild landscape took on an even more savage aspect, great white-clad mountains rearing ghost-like upwards, their spear-like peaks for once plainly visible against the velvet blue, almost cloudless sky.

Then the lights of the leading car winked out, leaving only sidelights visible. The others followed suit . . . and a slow, crawling mile later, Melvin waved the procession to a halt and stepped out of his vehicle.

"It's just over the rise," he said as the others gathered round, walking warily on the glassy surface of the road. In a body, they trudged the hundred yards to the hump, and looked down the long slope on the other side to the bright pool of light that was Ben Vonnach meter station.

Melvin raised a pair of binoculars to his eyes, carefully focused them, and gave a faint grunt of satisfaction. Without a word he handed the glasses to Bill Wilson. The detective trained them on the same target, the low station building, swept along it to the first large window, then whistled. The powerful lenses pulled their image across the distance as if only a few feet separated the watcher from the bright interior of the room. One man—probably Harry, guessed Wilson, from the figure's build—was standing with his back to the uncurtained glass. Farther back was a stranger, sitting quietly in a chair—probably the meter station attendant. And at the desk, lolling back, just visible, was another figure. The distance was too great to pick out finer detail, but of the men's identity there was little doubt. Wilson lowered the glasses, his blood quickening.

"That's them," he agreed. "But the station looks a pretty tough nut to crack. We'll need to get darned close up, then surprise them. Otherwise they might try to force their way out, using these electricity characters as hostages."

Melvin nodded. "The same thought's been running through my head. Seems to me a wee reconnaisance is called for.

"Hey, Lachie," he called. "Over here a minute." The young constable hurried over, eager for action. "Lachie, I want you and one of the Ardvare men to take a sniff around down there. Don't try anything daft . . . just go right round the outside of the fence, see if that main gate's locked, and whether there's any other way of getting in. Leave your caps up here . . . that moonlight reflects off the badges like nobody's business. Remember, come straight back, and keep your eyes open and your big feet quiet."

Lachie beamed his pleasure. "Chust as quiet as mice we'll be, sir," he assured Melvin. "But would you not want us to be taking a wee look inside if we can?"

"No. Straight back, lad. I want you to act as guide when we really go in . . . so let your mind soak that layout up like a sponge soaks water."

Bareheaded, overcoats tight to the neck, Lachie and the Ardvare man struck off down the slope, dark figures against the snow then quickly indistinguishable to the watchers as they used every shadowed ripple of ground, every whin-bush clump to cloak their movements.

"They'll need a clear half-hour," growled Melvin. "We'll leave a couple of men to watch, and the rest of us might as well get back to the cars for a heat and a smoke. Don't worry about Lachie . . . this is like old times to him. He was in the Juvenile Court for poaching more times than anyone else before he joined the Force . . . he knows what he's doing. And my feet are getting hellish cold."

14

IT was almost an hour before Lachie and his companion, caked snow clinging to their clothing, returned to the waiting cars.

"We crawled round effery inch of that fence," said the young policeman. "But there iss no way in whateffer, except the main gate . . . and it is locked tight. We will not be getting in so easily, unless we can be finding wire-cutters and snipping through the mesh of the fence."

"What kind of lock is it, Lachie?" asked Wilson.

"A big, heavy affair, sir," replied MacLeod. "We managed to get right up and try it. The whole building is lit up too, except for one wee window at the back . . . and there's a car parked round the side. It will be the one that wass stolen, I'm thinking."

Wilson gazed quizzically at Rab Kearns. "What do you think?" he asked.

The sergeant gave a faint smile. "We'll manage," he nodded.

Superintendent Melvin saw them off. "The cars will come down the road to help as fast as they can whenever you sound a whistle or we see things happening," he promised. "On you go—and good luck. You'll need it." Wilson and Kearns slid down the path at Lachie's heels, the young policeman tracing an easy path that still took advantage of every scrap of cover. He set a killing pace, and both men were thankful when at last they found themselves lying behind a large, snow-draped whin clump, some twenty feet from the main gate. Bill Wilson gave Kearns a soft jab with his elbow and the sergeant, crossing his fingers, wriggled clumsily forward on hands and knees into the rim of the harsh pool of light and on until he was crouched in shadow at the base of the gate pillar beside the lock. For a couple of minutes he peered up at the oblong lock cover, then slid a twisted piece of thick wire from his coat pocket. Hugging the dark side of the slim pillar, he rose to his feet and quietly probed the lock with the wire. The faint clicks made as metal scraped metal carried faintly to the ears of his two companions and Wilson, biting his lip with the strain of waiting, was beginning to despair when the noises stopped and Kearns waved a beckoning paw. One at a time, Wilson and MacLeod crawled across through the light and into the sheltering shadow. Then, gently, an inch at a time, Kearns pushed the iron gate open, wincing at its creaking hinges.

His lips inches from Lachie's ear, Wilson whispered, "Give me a minute's start, then follow me to the far side of the station building—away from that window." Rising, he slipped through the narrow gap of the opened gate. The snow muffled his footsteps as he sprinted across the brightly lit yard and crouched against the rough, cold stonework. Lachie came next, and Kearns last, the sergeant taking time to push the gate shut again. They hugged the wall, breathing heavily, watching the office window, praying that their dash had not been noticed. Long minutes ticked past before Wilson was satisfied. "Round the back," he gestured. "Take us to that window, Lachie."

They stole round the corner, and reached the back of the building, where the maze of switch equipment, cable towers and insulator erections began. One window—and one alone—was in darkness. Wilson gazed at the tightly snibbed metal frame inches above his head and pulled out his pocket knife. He ordered, "Give me a lift up . . . you first, Lachie." Bending, the young policeman heaved as Wilson climbed on his back then, feet braced apart, strained to bear the weight while the Canadian began to slice long, swift strips of putty from one of the dozen panels of the frame. At last he gasped, "You'll need to come down, sir. I canna hold you any more."

Wilson dropped lightly to the ground, and, as Lachie groaned with relief, Rab Kearns took his place as a stepping-stool. Once again the knife's flashing blade sank into the soft substance, hacking, gouging, scraping. Then it was Kearns's turn to mutter, "break . . ." and to swop places with Wilson while the latter gave his back as a platform. Only two small retaining strips remained when Wilson got up again, using Lachie as his ladder. Swiftly he sliced them clear, forced the narrow blade of his knife into the tiny gap between glass and metal, and began working the heavy pane free.

Now came the last stage. Muttering encouragement to Lachie, standing stoic-like beneath, he used one hand to press firmly on the bottom of the pane while the other hand used the knife as a lever at the top edge. Slowly the pane stirred, then came away from its metal seating. Dropping the knife, Wilson caught the glass in both hands and carefully handed it down to Kearns before dropping to the ground himself. Lachie was still grunting with relief at being freed from the weight and flexing his cramped muscles when Wilson went up again, this time on Kearns's back. He slid his hand through the space where the pane had been, opened the window from the inside, then clambered through, to land cat-like on the floor below. He snapped his cigarette lighter and, by the flame and the light streaming through the window from the outside, saw he was in a large store-room, its walls lined with a variety of crates, boxes, drums and coils of wire. Cautiously, Wilson moved to the door, listened, and gently turned the handle. The door opened a slit, and he peered out into the main meter-room of the station. There was no one in sight. Gently, he closed the door again and returned to the window. At his "all clear" signal, Sergeant Kearns clambered up, being given a "boost" by Lachie. Then Wilson leaned out to grip the youngster's hand and pull as he scrambled up in turn.

Speaking in little more than a whisper, he explained, "That door leads into the main building . . . the meter-room. If I remember what the Ardvare engineer said about the layout of the station, the office where Russell and Harry Vogt seem to be staying runs off a corridor that comes into the meter-room at the far end from here. Get your baton out, Lachie, and watch how you tread."

Rab Kearns had already produced a short wooden club and was handling it lovingly. "No heroics," whispered Wilson. "We'll sneak through, see how the land lies, and try to jump them by surprise if we can."

He opened the store-room door, and, the others at his heels, tip-toed out.

Squeak . . . squeak . . . squeak . . . he turned, staring angrily at his sergeant. "For God's sake, Rab, get your ruddy shoes off," he muttered hoarsely. "You can hear them a mile away." Blushing, Kearns pulled off the offending footwear and stuffed them behind the nearest meter panel. They crept on towards the arched opening at the far end of the huge room . . . and suddenly heard a door being flung open, and the swelling sound of voices.

"Watch it," hissed Wilson urgently, and they squeezed into the narrow gap between the nearest bank of head-high meter panels and the wall, crouching close to the dusty tangle of wires. Scarcely breathing, they strained their ears while the sound of foot-steps came near. As the mumbled voices grew louder, Wilson risked a quick glance round the edge of the bank of panels . . . and pulled back as two men walked into the room from the corridor. The engineer was in the lead, Harry strolling a couple of paces behind, Luger held carelessly in his right hand. He grumbled as he walked, "Get a move on with whatever you have to do, twiddling those knobs. After we're through, I'm going over to that cottage of yours again, to see if there's another bottle of whisky around."

"There isn't," said the engineer. "You've gone through all we had." He stopped in front of a switchboard panel. "This is the first one," he explained.

"Agh, get on with the damn thing," growled Harry, fumbling in his pockets for his cigarettes. Wilson risked another quick glance . . . the men were at the panels almost diagonally across the room, a good thirty feet away. The footsteps began again . . . coming nearer. The three men behind the meter board crouched lower still, and Bill Wilson discovered that his right arm was starting a faint, involuntary tremble. He silently cursed his jangled nerves. The two men were close now . . . only the breadth of the meter panels separated them from the hidden police. They could hear the restless scuffing of Harry's feet, the steady click of switches as the engineer set to work . . . was this the panel he was sending those messages from, wondered the detective, marvelling at the man's tenacity of purpose in the face of such danger.

The footsteps began again . . . moving

farther up the hall. Then Harry's voice rang out, "Hey . . . that door! It wasn't open the last time we were in!"

It was the store-room door. The engineer said, "It's got a loose catch. It often swings open."

"I'm having a look," growled Harry. Wilson sucked in his breath. If Harry noticed that missing window pane . . . But the fat man seemed to content himself with a quick glance into the darkened room. The door slammed shut, and a moment later they heard the fat man cursing again. "How much ruddy longer are you fiddling with those knobs?"

The engineer muttered a reply. And the footsteps began to return. Wilson gestured to the two at his side. He mouthed, "when they pass."

The footsteps grew nearer . . . level with the panel, passing. Wilson sprang out, one hand going for Harry's gun arm, the other clamping firmly across his mouth. Lachie was by his side, grappling the man . . . and Rab Kearns had slapped a hand tight across the startled engineer's mouth, whispering a warning in his ear.

Struggling to free himself, Harry

pressed the Luger's trigger . . . his eyes rolled despairingly as the gun clicked on the safety catch. He slid the catch off with his thumb and triggered again . . . but Wilson had a finger between trigger and guard, blocking the action. Lachie brought his baton down in a vicious side-of-the-neck blow and the fat man slumped. They caught him as he fell, and Bill Wilson stooped to free the gun.

Kearns had released the engineer, and was about to turn to Wilson . . . instead, he shouted a sudden warning. Brief as the scuffle had been, its sound had reached Russell. He was coming down the corridor —and as he caught sight of them, the gun in his hand levelled and barked. The sergeant gave a coughing grunt and spun to the floor. Russell fired again, but missed, and the bullet smashed into a meter panel bringing a sudden mad crackle of electricity and a cloud of thick blue smoke.

Crouching at almost floor level beside Harry Vogt's unconscious figure, Wilson scooped up the man's gun and snapped a quick shot back towards Russell. The bullet tore through the slack of the man's jacket . . . and the sudden, constant blare of car horns came from outside.

Melvin's men were moving in, spurred on by the sound of the shots.

Russell fired a third time, blindly, then dived back towards the office door and disappeared into the room. There was a sudden smashing of glass, then silence, broken only by involuntary gasps of pain from Kearns as he clutched his side, a rapid staining of blood seeping through his fingers.

Lachie at his heels, Wilson sprinted down the corridor and barked recklessly into the office, gun at the ready. A figure was hunched in one corner. Wilson's gun swung up, then dropped again. It was the other engineer.

"Where'd he go?" demanded the detective, and the man, wrestling with his bonds, nodded towards the smashed window. "Grabbed his case, threw a chair through the window, and jumped out," he gasped. "Cut me loose, Mac . . ." But he was speaking to empty air. Wilson dived through the jagged hole in the glass, and even as he landed in the snow Lachie was at his side.

They glanced around the brightly-lit compound, with its sparking insulators and buzzing cables. And the sound of a car's engine starting up reached their ears, even above the constant scream of the police car horns as, headlamps blazing, they came rocketing down the road.

"The car he stole from the crofter," shouted Lachie. "It was round the side!" They spun round . . . just as the old Austin, engine bellowing, spun round the corner, spraying snow in its skidding turn, Russell crouched low at the wheel. Bill Wilson snapped off a shot as it passed, a side window starred and splintered . . . but the car quickened pace, streaking across the open space in front of the building, straight for the gate. Then, as Jonathan Russell saw, perhaps for the first time, how near the approaching lights were and that the gate was still shut, the car seemed to spin almost in its own length, streaking through a savage U-turn towards a far section of the wire mesh fencing.

"He's trying to crash out," yelled Wilson, breaking into a run. The car struck. There was a sound like a hundred violin strings being snapped. The fencing bulged outwards, wires twanged . . . but it held, and the car stalled.

Russell jumped out, satchel still in one hand, groping for his gun with the other, and sprinted back into the depths of the compound, dodging in between the towering transformer shells and the grey-painted oil-bath switches, fantasy structures in the unreal light. Wilson hammered after him . . . and suddenly felt his feet plucked from under him. As he fell, three shots drummed out in quick succession, and he kept on rolling, rolling until he was behind the shelter of a tall metal girder tower.

"Sorry, Inspector," gasped Lachie MacLeod, lying beside him and spitting out a mouthful of snow. "But I saw him turn, and you were like a sitting duck." The youngster had made a fast, sliding tackle . . . the long marks of his path were gouged in the snow.

The police-cars had reached the gate now. Their engines idled while a man from the leading car threw the gate open. One of the Vonnach engineers was shouting and waving to them from the door of the meter building. Deaf to the noise, Wilson rose to his feet again, and dived across the open ground to the next cover . . . the nearest oil-bath switch. Feet pounded ahead of him. Russell, gun reloaded, was running still farther back into the metal maze. Then suddenly he stopped running and dived for the metal tower beside him. He jumped, and his feet began to clatter up the narrow iron ladder built into the tower. Wilson fired . . . the bullet spanged and whined off the metal, and Russell's Luger flared a blind, answering shot that bored through the cylinder, releasing a fast, narrow spout of coolant oil.

It was Wilson's turn to run forward. He headed for the ladder, half-conscious of Lachie's frantic shout of "watch the wires". As he reached the foot of the tower, the detective heard Russell clattering above him along one of the network of metal catwalks that laced between the towers. Jumping for the rungs, and starting to climb, Wilson realized the fugitive's game. The network of catwalks led close to the side of the fence . . . a wild jump might clear the fence and land Russell in the soft snow beneath, outside the prison in which he found himself. Faster than ever Wilson sped up the ladder. As his head reached the top, he saw Russell ahead, outlined in the glare of a flood lamp only a few feet behind him. He was at the junction of two catwalks, looking frantically along one then the other. He chose the right, began to run . . . then realized it led to a dead end. But, even as he turned and clattered back over the metal plates, Wilson was sprinting towards him. Russell swung the Luger . . . and the detective dived at the man's knees, the bullet screaming over his head.

Down they went on the narrow catwalk, the breath smashed from their bodies by the force of impact. Russell's knee came up, and caught Wilson on the cheek. Dazed with pain, the whole gantry seeming to swing in a hazy red nightmare before his eyes, the detective made a clawing, frantic swing, and thudded down on top of his quarry. Crazy with hate and fear, Russell jabbed his elbow upwards, digging a groove along the detective's ribs, his other arm chopping with the Luger. The barrel raked down Wilson's scalp, even as the Canadian's fingers, seeking a grip on Russell's oiled hair, slipped down and swept Russell's glasses from his face.

Gasping, grunting, the man rolled clear, and went off in a staggering run, still gripping the satchel. But the bag caught on a projecting spar . . . and as he wrenched frantically, the leather tore, its contents falling in a sudden sparkling flood to the snow beneath. Sick, groggy, Wilson pulled himself to his knees and felt towards his gun, lying on the catwalk edge where it had dropped in the struggle. He grabbed it, and instinctively rolled clear of the expected bullet.

But Russell, short-sighted eyes straining in the sudden, hazy world into which he had been plunged, was running, running wildly . . . and down the wrong catwalk. Suddenly, he tried to stop, arms flailing wildly as he realized his mistake. His foot skidded on the ice-flecked metal, his body crashed against the low guard-rail . . . and he plunged over with a shriek that was cut short by a blinding, roaring flash of released power. There was a sudden, sickly smell of burning flesh, that horrible, sweet smell that no one ever forgets.

Wilson looked over the edge of the

catwalk, and quickly drew back, face pressed close against the cold metal, faint with horror.

Jonathan Russell lay folded across one of the power wires, his body a strange, burned and twisted wreckage, charred stumps of arms still caught round a metal stanchion pole. Even as Melvin and Lachie ran over, the limp carcase swayed gently and slid off the wire. The blackened corpse thudded at their feet.

It was three in the morning at the Ross Arms. Every light in the hotel burned bright as the staff bustled about, tending to the needs of the returned party.

Face painful and swollen, eyes red and bleared, Bill Wilson was back on the couch where, what seemed days ago, he had relaxed after dinner. Gently, Paula Terry placed a lighted cigarette between his lips then sat beside him, clasping his right hand in both of hers.

Melvin bustled into the room. "That's that," the superintendent declared. "The local doctor's hauled that bullet out of Sergeant Kearns. He'll need some time in bed, but he'll be all right. Harry Vogt's in the village's only cell . . . and young Lachie MacLeod's probably got a swollen head it'll take me months to deflate. Hmm . . . your own head isn't such a pretty sight. Still . . . hmm . . . aye . . ." Eyes twinkling, he left the room.

"What was that in aid of?" puzzled Bill.

"This," said Paula. And Wilson found her explanation completely satisfactory.

THE END

GUIDE
TO THE COLOUR CODING
OF
ULVERSCROFT BOOKS

Many of our readers have written to us expressing their appreciation for the way in which our colour coding has assisted them in selecting the Ulverscroft books of their choice. To remind everyone of our colour coding—this is as follows:

BLACK COVERS
Mysteries

★

BLUE COVERS
Romances

★

RED COVERS
Adventure Suspense and General Fiction

★

ORANGE COVERS
Westerns

★

GREEN COVERS
Non-Fiction

MYSTERY TITLES
in the
Ulverscroft Large Print Series

Henrietta Who?	*Catherine Aird*
Slight Mourning	*Catherine Aird*
The China Governess	*Margery Allingham*
Coroner's Pidgin	*Margery Allingham*
Crime at Black Dudley	*Margery Allingham*
Look to the Lady	*Margery Allingham*
More Work for the Undertaker	
	Margery Allingham
Death in the Channel	*J. R. L. Anderson*
Death in the City	*J. R. L. Anderson*
Death on the Rocks	*J. R. L. Anderson*
A Sprig of Sea Lavender	*J. R. L. Anderson*
Death of a Poison-Tongue	*Josephine Bell*
Murder Adrift	*George Bellairs*
Strangers Among the Dead	*George Bellairs*
The Case of the Abominable Snowman	
	Nicholas Blake
The Widow's Cruise	*Nicholas Blake*
The Brides of Friedberg	*Gwendoline Butler*
Murder By Proxy	*Harry Carmichael*
Post Mortem	*Harry Carmichael*
Suicide Clause	*Harry Carmichael*
After the Funeral	*Agatha Christie*
The Body in the Library	*Agatha Christie*

FICTION TITLES
in the
Ulverscroft Large Print Series

WESTERN TITLES
in the
Ulverscroft Large Print Series

Gone To Texas	*Forrest Carter*
Dakota Boomtown	*Frank Castle*
Hard Texas Trail	*Matt Chisholm*
Bigger Than Texas	*William R. Cox*
From Hide and Horn	*J. T. Edson*
Gunsmoke Thunder	*J. T. Edson*
The Peacemakers	*J. T. Edson*
Wagons to Backsight	*J. T. Edson*
Arizona Ames	*Zane Grey*
The Lost Wagon Train	*Zane Grey*
Nevada	*Zane Grey*
Rim of the Desert	*Ernest Haycox*
Borden Chantry	*Louis L'Amour*
Conagher	*Louis L'Amour*
The First Fast Draw *and*	
The Key-Lock Man	*Louis L'Amour*
Kiowa Trail *and* Killoe	*Louis L'Amour*
The Mountain Valley War	*Louis L'Amour*
The Sackett Brand *and*	
The Lonely Men	*Louis L'Amour*
Taggart	*Louis L'Amour*
Tucker	*Louis L'Amour*
Destination Danger	*Wm. Colt MacDonald*

NON-FICTION TITLES
in the
Ulverscroft Large Print Series

THE SHADOWS
OF THE CROWN TITLES
in the
Ulverscroft Large Print Series